Trance
Logic

Trance

Logic

Richard Rowland
Billingsley

NEW PULP PRESS

Published by New Pulp Press, LLC, 926 Truman Avenue, Key West, Florida 33040, USA.

For information contact:
Publisher@NewPulpPress.com

ISBN-13: 978-0692672952 (New Pulp Press)
ISBN-10: 0692672958

Printed in the United States of America
Visit us on the web at www.newpulppress.com

"To my mother of blessed memory, Dorsey Lee.
And to my dad also of blessed memory, M. J."

Trance
Logic

Prologue

It was a Tuesday afternoon when the long cars turned off Maryland Route 175 and approached the gate to the military base Fort George G. Meade. At the gate were a long line of cars stopped by MPs and searched. But to the dismay of the waiting traffic the long cars were immediately waved through the main gate. They drove the paved street to the back of the base. The long cars parked in front of a row of plain white and beige one story buildings. The sign in front said **THE DEFENSE INTELLIGENCE BUREAU**. Men in neat Brooks Brothers suits exited each of the three cars. They were met at the front door by Major Roswell Hane. His uniform was crisp and sharp looking but he wore it with some distain as though he thought the rank was beneath him.

He escorted the three men inside one of the small squat buildings. There he shook their hands. They all smiled at each other but the smiles were short lived. One of the men said to Hane, "The Program is cancelled unless you can put something out of your ass."

Hane said, "I have someone I want you to meet."

Another said, "I read your report about her. What makes this woman any different from the rest?"

Hane still smiled broadly, "I promised you our best. Most Remote Viewers have a rating of seventy-five percent, she is nearer ninety-five."

One of the other men answered, "I don't have to tell you how important this is. We have a new administration and they aren't convinced psychic spying really works."

Hane's smile was becoming forced, "We have dealt with skeptics before. We can handle it."

"What's her name?"

They approached a large metal door. Hane said, "Rainbeaux Le Blanc."

Hane opened the door for them and they entered a small observation room. Here there was a two way mirror. Through the mirror they saw a young woman with long blonde hair wearing colorful clothes lying on a leather couch. There were wires running from under the couch and into the wall. On a console in front of the two way mirror, her vital signs were displayed and recorded.

"What's her target?" one of the men asked.

Hane said, "We are going after the Man in the Mountains."

"Then the ninety-five percent will really be put to the test, won't it?"

Hane's smile was genuine again. "I don't see why that won't ..."

His gloat over the three men was interrupted by an alarm and flashing red light. A glance at the screen told him her vitals were cratering. Immediately he was on the intercom. "Get a crash cart in here stat." Then he let out a barely audible, "No."

He ran into the room. Squatting by her side, he gently lifted her head, "Rainbeaux."

Her eyes fluttered half open. "Roswell." She shut them again.

Hane checked her pulse and turned his head toward the door. "Hurry up with that blasted cart!"

Within seconds two medics raced in with their medic bags and a stretcher. They assessed her and said that she could be moved. One of them told Hane to try to bring her around.

"The word is, Ghosts of New Orleans."

Her eyes opened again. One eye was deep green and the other was of such a light blue it was almost grey; she had heterochromia iridum and this was her most remarkable and memorable physical feature. She tried to speak but Hane told her to be quiet. It wasn't just for her comfort, the three men were behind them listening to every word.

A few hours later the men had left. Hane did his investigation into what happened and he didn't like what he found. She was recovering in the infirmary when Hane strode in. She looked up and smiled at him. He didn't smile back but threw a thick manila folder down instead. The label on the file read **THE MABUSE FILE.** Rainbeaux made an *oh shit* face.

"What do you think you are doing?"

She was defensive, "After what happened with Margot …"

"I told you that was classified."

"What happened to Margot wasn't classified to me. I was there. I held her while she thrashed around in her seizure. I wanted to look into it because we have RV's crashing on us every other day. These are my friends. Now it's happened to me!"

"You know this is what may have caused you to … What brought the Entity to you."

She glared at him. "What, specifically, are you not telling me?"

Hane breathed a sigh. "I know you want to help. I appreciate that. But this file is beyond top secret. Just know I am looking out for you."

Rainbeaux said, "You don't want to know what I saw?"

He shook his head in affirmation, of course he would have to know.

"Because you know, it was the devil, Roswell. I saw the devil."

"We don't know what this is. We are studying it."

"That face, we make jokes about evil and stuff. But that was pure evil. Just looking at it, I felt pure terror. It was like I had an acid nightmare."

Hane jangled his keys and pocket change. A nervous tick of his. "This non-local consciousness is a mystery but remember that how we perceive it is how it will interact with us."

"You have got to be kidding me. Because I found out that you are trying to reach out to this non-local consciousness as you call it. You are trying to make a deal with it. Or Him."

"Goddmanit, this was labeled Ultra for a reason."

Rainbeaux couldn't look at him anymore. "The reason is you want us to become psychic assassins. And you want this being's help."

"That is enough."

"Are you insane? Killing people remotely! I won't do it."

Hane was becoming impatient with her. He didn't like that because he was losing control. "I said that's enough. You don't know how much trouble you are in right now."

"I won't reach out and kill people." Rainbeaux continued, "I can't believe I got myself into this mal pris."

He smiled at her bitterly, "You know I don't speak Cajun dialect."

"I'm stuck in a bad situation. I feel like it anyway. So I tell you what, I'm out."

"What?!?!"

"I'm quitting. I'm outta here. How many ways do you want me to say it?"

"Don't. Don't leave. We are so close on a number of things."

She covered herself up with the blanket on her bed. "I know you need me. But this is over. And you aren't going to talk me out of it."

Hane tried though. He reminded her of how she was rescued off the street. How this job has given her so much;

financial stability, an education, friends, meaning, purpose. When that didn't work, he bullied her. She laughed at him. She was having none of it.

There was a process to letting her go from the service. The Mabuse File was Ultra Top Secret so they couldn't let her waltz out the door. She had to sign endless nondisclosure agreements. There was a hypnosis protocol to suppress the memory of the File and what she saw, experienced in her last session into the Zone. She had saved up and invested her money during her time at the Defense Intelligence Bureau. That along with her six months' severance gave her money so she could support herself while she found herself and got her head together. Hane was sad to see her go. But she was happy. She felt free as she left Fort Meade. Free of the fear doing secret work engenders. Free of the danger of the malevolent spirit that was attacking the Remote Viewers. She was free and never intended to come back.

Chapter 1

Daisy Yellow Yancy loved to sit and watch the witch's house. She sat under a canopy of trees across the street and studied every line and curve of the old home. The heavy timbers, the brick walls, and the vines climbing up to the top of a rough stone chimney. There was a gable at each end and best of all, a turret with a room at the top jutting off the side of the gable on the left. That made it look like a witch's house to the neighborhood children. Something out of a picture book.

Daisy giggled about that. Her job was to uncover the identity of the woman who lived here and report to the coven. She knew what the occupant looked like, but she didn't know her.

The thing is, people didn't know Rainbeaux Le Blanc. So talking to neighbors only resulted in a physical description which she knew well. A tall blonde woman with weird colored almond shaped eyes who wore "hippie" clothes. Daisy wouldn't have said hippie it was more urban chic. Rainbeaux worked about thirty hours a week at a small bookstore. How this woman who lived on her own could afford a house in an older upscale neighborhood on a part time retail paycheck was beyond anyone's guess.

Daisy knew one thing; Rainbeaux was an artist, a painter. Daisy hadn't been inside the house but she had slipped into the barn shaped workshop out back. Here she discovered Rainbeaux's studio. She walked through a few times. She took time to examine all the pictures Rainbeaux had rendered. Daisy would have kept creeping in there but Rainbeaux took to leaving her notes. The notes said she knew that Daisy was poking around and it was okay. Rainbeaux wanted to meet her. Daisy wanted to meet Rainbeaux too but she knew the one she worked for wouldn't like it. She was just supposed to snoop around and find out what she could then report to the coven and then to him.

Ordinarily one couldn't hope to keep anything from him. But Daisy had. She kept what she knew of Rainbeaux locked in those places she cultivated in her heart that even he couldn't break into. And then he and the rest wouldn't know anymore about her than they already knew. Which wasn't much.

She hoped they didn't know.

Now in the darkening gloom at the end of the day, a light came on in the turret off to the left of the front door. Soon the electric light was replaced by the flickering light of candles. Then even those were put out and another light shone from that closely watched upper room. A light that penetrated Daisy's heart in the places he couldn't go. So she sat there in the dark and loved watching the house. And the Light.

Chapter 2

From inside her house Rainbeaux watched Daisy watch her. She didn't know Daisy by that name yet. Rainbeaux was casually dressed in an ankle length flower print skirt, sandals, and a silk blouse. She looked out the window into the night and wondered how much longer Daisy would sit out there. She wondered what Daisy wanted. She hadn't responded to her invitation.

As if she didn't have enough to worry about. Her stocks were trending down and she faced the likelihood that her funds would run out. She couldn't live off her retail clerk wages for very long. She wondered how much longer before her past came back to torment her. There was so much in her past, the fearful face she saw when she was in a trance during a Remote Viewing session. All the secrets she had uncovered as a psychic spy. And her missing memories. Her old boss would be looking for her too. She thought about going out and talking to Daisy.

Instead she went upstairs to find answers using the surest method she knew. Up she walked into the turret room Rainbeaux called the Psychotorium. There the dancing glow of burning candles illuminated a long leather couch that sat on a dais in front of a large white screen.

She walked around the dimly lit Psychotorium and slipped her sandals off. She extinguished the black candles on the candelabra. She placed an envelope marked TARGET on the floor beside the couch and laid down. She started to breathe deeply and appeared dreamy as she stared up at the screen. She went into her Zone, what she called her Spook Zone; a deep meditative state where everything is NOW.

She experiences the screen began to shine with ethereal light that reflects off her face. Thus she penetrates a membrane that allows her to travel a world beyond flesh. During her altered state she enters that world, which is also called the Imaginal Plane, through the light from the screen.

Now she glides through the filthy air over a dark decayed city landscape. She is in control as in a lucid dream, but not dreaming; not searching for anything specifically, open to what she finds there.

Now she dives in a spiral under a grimy city street, down into a kind of mall in an underground grotto; a postmodern image of Dante's vision of Hell.

She spirals downward to labyrinthine structures piled on top of and beside one another like an elaborate puzzle. Here there are hundreds of doors and passages in each maze that lead from one labyrinth to another. In each labyrinth distinct entities or shapes wait for the energy of attention to activate them. They represent everything from dirty neglected children to haunted adults to fantastical monsters.

Off to one side a strange light comes from a figure that catches her attention. A serene sepia colored woman surrounded by a fiery red glow. Rainbeaux recognizes that this is a living presence. She starts to move toward her.

Just then she is drawn down in a spiral to a bone yard at the bottom of the grotto. Human remains lie on the cold Floor of Hell with flesh half decayed off the bone. The stench almost overcomes her so that she might pass out. One corpse draws her attention because it is in color in contrast to the dingy gray here. The corpse is a woman, split open like a fresh kill. The woman's mouth moves. Rainbeaux cannot understand what she says. She looks back up to the stacks of labyrinths which pile upwards to the dark smoggy sky.

Then.

In one of the labyrinths she sees someone moving on his own. This is no static picture, no image or potential; she encounters him as he moves on his own volition. The male figure is a handsome preppie rich kid, wandering toward ...

Someone she recognizes. Another sentient being in this place of vision. She is immediately afraid of this being, a demonic figure with an apish face draped in trench coat, large hat and glasses. She doesn't know his name but she knows him. This one moves between labyrinths. The demonic apish figure is amused by the young male. He makes a welcome motion to the young male. She understands it is to lure him off the edge and fall into the grotto with the decayed corpses. To fall on the technicolor corpse of the murdered woman down there.

Rainbeaux knows better than to panic out here in the Spook Zone. She panics anyway. She calls to the young man and reaches out to him. But he is impossibly far away. She calls out to him again even though no sound comes from her mouth.

Yet, the young man looks at her. She knows that he wonders if she is real, or just a dream after all. The blasphemous demonic presence turns his attention to Rainbeaux lying on the couch. His face fills the screen and his eyes glow like red coals as he faces her prone form.

Back in her Psychotorium Rainbeaux stares back at him on the screen, each alarmed at the other. Rainbeaux in a state of shock as though her heart will burst.

She came out of her trance and shot up off the couch. The screen went white sealing off whatever was in the Imaginal Plane from this world.

Groggy and disoriented she rose with difficulty as she stumbled from the room. She was so scared she had to remember to breathe. She wondered what the vision meant. She sat at her kitchen table until the early morning hours, drinking tea and contemplating what she saw. All she knew for sure was that the Entity that had driven her from her high security Federal job in Maryland had found her.

As if she didn't have enough to worry about.

Chapter 3

After a sleepless night she got to work at Reading Nation, the tiny shop crammed with books where she worked as a clerk. It started when Rainbeaux stood at the small table where they kept the coffee maker. She busied herself brewing coffee.

Theodonia, the owner, entered. "Good morning."

Rainbeaux managed a half-hearted, "Hey."

She gazed at Rainbeaux's haggard appearance. "Don't you look chipper this morning."

"Not so much."

"More dreams?"

"You could say."

"Stress causes dreams. At least for me."

The coffee finished brewing. Theodonia poured some. Rainbeaux didn't want to get into anything personal at the store. Plus she could tell Theodonia was up to something.

Rainbeaux said, "I was thinking of moving these two shelves to a discount table to make room for the new releases."

Theodonia was thinking of Nancy Yancy's party. "Did you decide about doing any fortune telling? Tarot cards and the like?"

Rainbeaux really hoped that wouldn't come up again. "I don't think ..."

"It's extra money. Relieve some stress."

Rainbeaux stumbled around. She really wanted Theodonia to stop hassling her about the goddamn rich bitch's party. "I don't need ... money really isn't the issue with me."

Theodonia turned and walked away. Rainbeaux had met Nancy Yancy once in the store. She had a feeling that something was not right there but didn't know what it was.

Rainbeaux couldn't decide if she was tired or sleepy but the dragged down feeling made the day go by more slowly than usual. By mid-afternoon Rainbeaux felt the tug of hours and hated it. She had been so happy here. It had taken a while to acclimate and settle in. Now she had that hinky feeling that things were going to change again. Her unease was unwelcome. She didn't want a repeat of Maryland and the Defense Department mess she left behind months ago.

Theodonia stuck her head from between two stacks of books. "I heard something out back. It could be that delivery."

Rainbeaux said absentmindedly, "I don't mind if I do."

She walked out of the back door with heavy leaden feet. She gasped at the stench from the alley. Someone was living out here and the rank human smell gave it away. She looked one way down the empty alley. Then she looked the other direction toward a cluster of cardboard boxes. The first thought in her mind; it looked like a child's fort built with the boxes his Christmas presents came in.

Rainbeaux checked over her shoulder. No truck. She approached the box fort slowly. Half bending down she squinted her eyes, afraid of what she'd see, and said, "Hello?" Then a moment later. "You there? Want a sandwich? Some water or coffee?"

The boxes moved as a dirty little man crawled out: Aziz. He gripped his leather medicine bag, startled to see her.

"You," was all he managed to get out.

"Me. Rainbeaux. You?"

Aziz squinted as he looked her up and down. "Don't matter. You see don't you?"

She knew what he meant, there was a cold feeling in her center. She sensed fear in him but power too.

She played it cool. "I'm here to see if you need anything."

A change came over Aziz; he looked like a five year old child. "What do you want from me?"

"I'm doing this because we're neighbors. I work in that shop."

He looked up, there was another change in him that was barely perceptible. "Reading Nation." Said evenly, the way a clinician would it at the Austin State Hospital.

She was feeling more and more afraid. "So you want anything come on in and we'll fix you up."

Aziz looked her up and down. Heavy on the judgmental. Like she was a thing to be used. "I'll fix you up."

Rainbeaux backed away. "Okay, dude, just tryin' to help. No harm, right?"

She backed down the alley toward the back door to the shop. She kept her eye on him. He shook all over. She knew that something inside him switched. She could tell Aziz didn't want her to go. "There's different parts," he said hopefully. "You can talk to another."

Rainbeaux waved as much to put him off as to indicate she was leaving. This was going to be too heavy. She reached behind to open the door when her hand fell on something. Something that wasn't there seconds ago. She held it up. A doll made of rag and bone; it's arms, head and legs spread out like a five pointed star.

She wrinkled her nose not liking it one bit.

Aziz said, "You don't want it? It's not from me to you for me. I work the magics. Magics I work. For you. Not on you."

"I get it. Thanks. Sometimes a gal needs a little help." She rattled the door. Make that the locked door.

Aziz smiled again hopefully but not believing it either, "We're friends?"

She slipped a key from a ring on her belt and coolly inserted it into the lock. Click, the door opened.

9

"Absolutely. Like I said, come in if you need anything."

After she got home Rainbeaux remembered to destroy that doll. She looked for it in her garage where she left it. It wasn't there. She searched for and found the rag and bone doll outside on her covered back porch. It worried her how it moved out there. In the backyard she started up the grill to use for an unconventional purpose. She used prayer and a simple ritual burning to take the power out of the doll. Now it was destroyed and no longer a threat. Whatever, she had been found even without the doll but she felt better that it was gone.

Chapter 4

ater that evening clouds filled the sky. The rain started a few hours after dark. The Blasphemer; dressed in trench coat, thick glasses and wide brimmed hat that hid his eyes; entered the rain-splattered alley off Sixth Street. He walked in measured steps to Aziz huddled in his crumbling cardboard box. He called softly, "Aziz."

Aziz crawled out of the box. "What do you want?" He sniffed, something smelled rotten, even to him. When he looked up and saw the Blasphemer's face he clawed at the ground to get away.

The Blasphemer clamped his hand on Aziz's neck. "Come with me and I will show you a mystery."

Aziz had no choice but to follow, the Blasphemer was his Master.

Within moments they came to the place Aziz hated. Through the drizzling rain the Red River Motel looked like a crack whore's nightmare. The Red River Motel was a two story building. The office was in the center of the property with a manager's apartment on the second floor. There was also a breakfast room for the guests free morning meal. Not that the guests of the Motel stuck around for cereal.

Aziz felt his stomach drop when he saw the riotous white hot lights from inside the room on the second floor. Aziz reflexively mumbled his prayers for protection. Then stopped because it was his master to whom he prayed. He knew he wouldn't gain anything by prayer tonight.

The Blasphemer held Aziz tight on the neck and pushed him toward a room with 462 painted in white letters on the door. When Aziz was roughly shoved inside he was assaulted by the stench of baking chemicals, mold, shit and blood. The room was a horror. The glare from the lights accentuated the bright red gore splattered on the walls. Weird symbols of some heinous devil cult decorated the walls along with sexually explicit graffiti. Loud music blared with a pounding hypnotic rhythm.

There were other people in the small room, but Aziz focused on Marilyn LezElvis squatting in the corner. She had been pretty once. Now she was covered in tattoos, tough leathery skin and looked fifty-six instead of twenty-six. Her facial piercings looked infected and her short spiked hair was unkempt. She grinned through green teeth.

"I'm the Protector."

Instantly Aziz forgot the smell and the fear of the room.

Marilyn laughed like she was the wicked witch of the west. "You're so fuckin' cool, man. I really dig you, right?"

Aziz felt a shift inside himself. He was someone else now. Someone important and in charge. Someone with a raging hard on. "Right."

Marilyn's mood changed super fast in a flash from friendly to angrier than hell. "Can you fuckin' deal with this shit!"

Marilyn yanked a curtain back to reveal a woman's mutilated corpse hanging from a meat hook anchored in the ceiling. Her face slashed and ruined, her torso split open from chin to clit, her internal organs hung around her neck. Her blood pooling under her bare feet just inches above the floor.

Marilyn began to scream, turning her head side to side. "You fucking know who did this right? Right?"

Aziz was paralyzed with fear. At once the room went dark then a soft yellow glow filled the space. Marilyn's scream pierced through Aziz's defenses. He felt like he was falling. Marilyn's scream went on and on.

Finally Aziz stumbled out of the room. He vomited over the side of the railing. Then he stood in the drizzle and yelled, "Joe Bear!"

Inside the apartment Marilyn's throat was raw from the smell of rancid rotting meat and her own shouting. She stopped and howled. Then she listened to Aziz calling out in the pouring rain.

He stood in the downpour of acrid oily rain as though to wash away what he just saw. Lightning flashed with each word, "Joe Bear! Joe Bear! Joe Bear!"

He lost time. The next thing he knew Aziz fell over trash cans and garbage as though pushed. Back in the alley. His alley. He heard someone. To an observer he carried on a one sided conversation. "I don't want anything you can give me."

His answer was an unearthly laugh like a howl from the Land of Phantoms. Aziz tried to threaten the Blasphemer. "She's here. A woman who sees beyond the walls of illusion. She sees into souls. She sees into the very eyes of God." Aziz listened to indistinct voices buzzing inside his head. "She runs from secrets into mystery."

Something hit him. He landed down on his knees in garbage and filth. He cried and clung to a talisman like the one he gave Rainbeaux. The thunder rang in his ears, it was directly over his head.

Chapter 5

Samuel Elliot "Sam" Chessman was handsome in a preppie rich kid twenty-seven year old sort of way. He had a head full of thick blonde hair. He was tall, built like a football player. He slept on an old army cot, his possessions in boxes piled around the bare white walls of his apartment.

Sunlight streaked through the dirty window and hit Sam in the face. He sat up. "What?"

He looked around confused by the memory that flooded his waking mind. He used to be wealthy. He used to have all he wanted and more than he needed. "How did I get here?"

He rolled over and covered his head with a blanket.

Then the scene mildly out of focus as in dream or memory. He stood in front of a vine covered building at Yale University, his cell phone tight against his ear. "I don't care, Daddy. I'm coming home to be with Angelique."

Then he remembered the outdoor mall in Houston Texas. The love of his life, the woman for whom he defied his all powerful father, Angelique Lauren laughed at him. "If your daddy cut off your trust fund, and you have no money, how will you take care of me?"

She didn't wait for an answer. She bent over seductively and picked a flower. Sam wanted to believe that he stood tall as she waved the flower at him and walked away. He knew that he hung his head and sat down hard on a bench. He knew he cried like a baby.

There was a large florist in the middle of Austin. Sam had driven past it many times. It always stuck in his head as a place he would go to buy flowers. He didn't know why that was. But he knew he was going there now. He was going to send flowers to Angelique. He was going to get her back. Things were different now. He had a job. Could (mostly) take care of himself. He had a plan for approaching his father and repairing that relationship. Maybe get his trust fund back. So he quickly dressed and went out in the wind and the misting rain and the thunder to get those flowers for the woman he still loved.

In the parking lot of his apartment building dark storm clouds blew up and promised more than the drizzle of rain that he felt on his face.

He drove faster than he should have to beat the downpour that was coming. Once at the florist's he quickly got out of his car and entered the large green house. Looking behind him as he wandered a wilderness of flowers he almost bumped into a clerk standing in the aisle. "Do you know what to get for someone you haven't seen in a while?" he asked. The clerk absentmindedly pointed toward roses. "I'm looking for something different."

There was a loud ring. The clerk answered the phone instead of Sam's inquiry. Sam frustrated, walked down another aisle.

The rumble of thunder shook the windows. Sam startled, caught his breath, then ambled onward. Thunder so loud now it's like it struck the building.

Sam startled again. He shook it off until the lights went out. Perfect.

Then Sam saw the silhouette of the woman in the dim shadows. Next thing, wild lightning illuminated Rainbeaux Le Blanc. She was characteristically dressed in long skirt, boots, colorful blouse, and a variety of beads and rings. Her hair hung straight with red ribbons twisted through the strands. She was surrounded by gardenia flowers that provided a frame around her. She stood so very still it was hard for Sam to tell what he saw.

16

He stared through the early morning gloom, puzzled: is she real or a statue? He moved a little closer.

Lightning simultaneous with Rainbeaux's movement. Sam jumped back wide eyed.

The lights blinked back on with the sound of an electrical hum. Rainbeaux held a potted flower in the crook of one arm, she touched Sam's arm with her free hand. "Are you going to be okay?" Something about her. As though he knew what she was thinking. She wondered if it was he: Are you the one?

Sam blinked. "I think so. Now."

"What are you doing here?"

"Just looking.

"Did you find what you were looking for?"

Sam was smitten. And something about her mismatched almond shaped eyes. "I found something different." Sam picked up some gardenias.

"Right on." Rainbeaux looked back at Sam as she left. "Later."

Sam offered Rainbeaux the flowers as a gift. "Do you like, uh, you want some flowers?" He immediately felt dumb for stumbling over himself like a twelve year old.

Rainbeaux held her flower up. "Got 'em already."

Sam helpless as Rainbeaux turned to go. Then, mercifully, she stopped, looked off in the distance as though she considered something. "Why don't you come by Reading Nation?"

Sam was all a-jabber, "Reading Nation."

Which Rainbeaux, again mercifully, recognized. She helped him out. "It's a book shop. I work there."

"You couldn't keep me away." He was surprised he could get that out.

Rainbeaux smiled and the world lit up for Sam. She quickly exited the store.

Sam stared after her dumfounded. "Wait, your name?"

But she was long gone.

Sam woke to the sound of his cell phone alarm. He looked around the shitty little apartment. He allowed a moment of nostalgia for the nice home he grew up in on a quiet street of an exclusive Houston suburb.

He placed the cell on a dock and pushed a button on the player. Morning music, good old George Harrison.

It was another day at APD as Sam strode through the locker room, bagel in his mouth, coffee in his hand. Sam opened his locker and reached inside to grab his police uniform. His bud, Rip Rivera already in uniform, came up from behind. "Gotta lead on a job."

"A case or on the job?"

"A nice piece of change working security for some rich white folks. You know, like you used to be."

Sam chuckled. "Text me."

Rip and Sam weren't tight, they hadn't known each other that long. But they have gone out and gotten tight together. Such were the bonds between men that alcohol made.

Later that day, Sam got the text. Lucky he was off this weekend. The party was up in Round Rock, at the Yancy place. Derrick Yancy was the scion of a huge computer fortune. He was looking forward to going. Somehow he knew he would see her there. Then he thought that was silly wishful thinking. Still if it is to be ...

Chapter 6

Saturday afternoon at Rainbeaux's witch house. Theodonia parked her SUV at the curb and honked. Theodonia had insisted that Rainbeaux ride with her since Rainbeaux hadn't been to the Yancy house. Rainbeaux reluctantly agreed to the ride. At the second blast of her boss's impatient horn she hoisted her heavy shoulder bag filled with the stuff to make her Tarot Card Reading Booth. She carried it out to Theodonia's SUV. Theodonia didn't bother to get out, she remotely opened the rear hatch.

After loading her stuff, Rainbeaux climbed in and slumped in the front seat. The ride up to the mansion was long and Theodonia kept up a long monologue about who would be there. Elected officials from Travis county. The head of Travis County MHMR. A local singer Rainbeaux had heard of but not seen yet. Marilyn LezElvis, an Elvis impersonator. At least seeing her wouldn't make the party a total waste. And seeing someone else, the cute guy from the florists. She hoped to ride home with him. She didn't dare tell Theodonia. She would never hear the end of it if she did.

When they finally rounded a curve she saw the Yancy Mansion imposingly perched up on a hill. And couldn't have been more yawn inducing for her.

They parked around back to unload. She moved slowly through the hired help hustling to and fro before the guests arrived.

Inside the place was huge like a grand hotel. Just inside the front door was a main hall where the party was to be held. In the richly furnished great room the caterers and hired people prepared for the party.

Rainbeaux was shown to her table. She set her bag on

the floor, opened it and began to set her booth up. She was about half way through when she saw Sam enter the room dressed like a million bucks. Sam saw her and she knew he was nervous. But he walked over to her keeping totally cool.

Rainbeaux continued to set up her booth like she hadn't seen him. She set her sign up. She laid the Tarot cards out.

Sam was midway across the vast space of the grand hall when he stopped. He watched Theodonia and Nancy circle the Tarot Card Booth. Nancy said something to Rainbeaux. He waited until she and Theodonia walked away before he stepped forward. Sam made eye contact with Rainbeaux. They smiled happy to see each other again.

Sam said lamely, "Tell my fortune?"

Rainbeaux thought it cute so she went with it. She pushed the tarot card deck toward him. He cut the deck. She grinned, "Hmm, let's see." She flipped some cards. "I knew that Austin musicians without a day job or a girl-friend were homeless. I didn't know it was true of police-men too."

Sam couldn't believe she nailed it. "Is one foot in the street homeless? I work security part time to get a better place. What about you?"

"I'm just goin' with the flow. I knew I'd see your mug again."

Sam pointed to the Fortune Teller sign over her booth. "That's right, you would, wouldn't you?" As she reacted to that, Sam thought Rainbeaux had the sweetest laugh. And her eyes. He saw what it was about her eyes. One was green and the other blue, almost grey.

"So you don't need the money. Say, you aren't secretly wealthy are you?"

Rainbeaux flipped a card. "No, but you are."

Sam blushed and fumbled nervously, "Guests are arriving. Duty calls. Gotta shred." And he walked off.

Rainbeaux sighed. "Shred" indicated that he was a biker at some point. Probably dirt bikes.

As she placed some more things out she sensed someone was watching her. This was real Presence, not just an idle stare. How to handle it. She looked up suddenly to confront the person and saw the singer Marilyn, dressed as young Elvis in jeans, tie and satin jacket. She wore a wig combed up in a pompadour with long strands of hair for sideburns. Marilyn stood close enough to be noticed but not for contact. Their eyes locked. Rainbeaux followed that sense of something deep there. Something with weight and strong vibrations. Not sexual but there was a strong sexuality there too.

Marilyn seemed to notice Rainbeaux reading her. She moved away and out of sight.

Still scanning the room Rainbeaux saw Daisy Yellow Yancy lean against a wall like a sad little girl. Daisy looked up full of anxious dread. Something about to happen. Rainbeaux knew at once that she was the one spying on her. That she had been in the studio. How to handle that too?

Across the room William Happurstadt, the Travis County District Attorney and Doctor Shneed, executive director of Travis County Mental Health and Mental Retardation, watched Sam.

Sam watched them watch him. He saw them engaged in earnest conversation. They nodded in his direction from time to time. Sam didn't like people talking about him. He didn't know what they were talking about and he hoped his old man didn't have anything to do with this. He decided to walk over and see what would happen. As Sam moved closer ...

Shneed shrugged.

Happurstadt buttoned his jacket. He walked toward Sam with a greasy smile.

Back at the Fortune Teller booth, Rainbeaux was a terrible fortune teller. A brunette junior league wannabe in a little black dress, already drunk, walked up. She giggled as she asked, "How are things gonna work out in my love life?"

Rainbeaux handed her the deck. "Cut the deck and flip four cards, please."

The drunken woman sloppily flipped four cards.

Rainbeaux studied them and looked at her. "First, you are way too bitchy for the guy you are with." She couldn't help but tell the truth.

This woman wasn't impressed however. "What the hell?"

"My advice," Rainbeaux continued, "ease up on your old man or the red headed bartender will steal him."

They both looked at a hot looking red headed bartender who hung all over her really handsome guy.

The woman got up knocking her chair over as she did and stormed off.

Rainbeaux looked at her with mock sadness, "You don't have to leave in a huff, you can leave in a minute and a huff."

She saw Theodonia glare at her from across the room. She mouthed the words, "Hey, Groucho Marx," at her. When Theodonia didn't respond, she decided not to care so much. She looked around the room to see what Sam was up to or to make eye contact with another potential customer.

After a moment she found Sam walking the floor, mingling with guests. Near the bar she saw two men watching Sam like a pair of hawks. Suddenly she remembered her vision and got a hinky feeling. She knew they were linked to her vision even if she hadn't seen them in it.

They seemed to talk intently about Sam. She didn't know what they said, but could read their body language. Shneed looked at Sam like he can hardly stand to touch him. Happurstadt seemed interested in Sam the way a man will examine a tool at a garage sale. But overall, there was a blackness over them so thick it could absorb any light that came close to them. Now she wished she could read minds, something her instructors at Fort Meade Maryland had promised they could teach her.

She carefully left her booth and started walking around the room and introducing herself to the guests. And so doing, working her way slowly toward the two men and Sam.

As she got close to the bar she heard Happurstadt and Shneed. They talked about Derrick Yancy. Or seemed to. Happurstadt said, "He has graced us with his presence."

Shneed said, "Not here!"

Rainbeaux heard in her head the word in Shneed's voice, "Asshole." Maybe she could read minds a little after all. She knew he wouldn't say that to Happurstadt.

"He's late. We need him here now." Shneed's voice was cold and sounded like broken glass.

Happurstadt replied, "He was in charge of the initiation. Why didn't he make sure she cleaned that up?"

"I don't know. He's been acting strange lately."

"He's scared. But he would be. Now that he's here."

The red headed bartender moved closer to them. She was listening to their conversation too. "Get you gentlemen anything?"

Happurstadt waved her off. Shneed said, "Another Rum Collins. Next time pour some liquor in that would you."

The red head became angry, "I don't pour light." She went to pour that drink.

Shneed wanted to know what Happurstadt meant,

23

"Okay, scared of what?" There was a loud piercing scream.

Rainbeaux looked up and saw Sam watching her. Then he ran over to a group of guests who gathered around a drape.

Sam pulled his badge out and held it up. "Austin Police Department, stand aside please."

Looking behind the drape he saw Derek Yancy, the host and the scion of the computer fortune, lying in a pool of blood with some of his internal organs, including the spleen, removed and placed around his body. Above his head random blood smears made by a human hand on the wall.

Everyone was jazzed about the corpse. There was an air of unreality in the room. The bored party guests treated it like they were on a TV show. They made jokes even as Sam contemplated the damaged exposed heart. He thought he saw it move. It freaked him out.

He knelt and did an initial examination. There was no pulse and he wasn't breathing. Sam wouldn't have known how to start CPR because of the heart exposed through the chest wall; this was beyond his training.

Rainbeaux saw Marilyn appear from a door across the room. She wiped something off her hands with a hand towel. She and Rainbeaux locked eyes again. Marilyn seemed to say something without moving her lips. Then she breezed out of sight.

Across the room, Daisy began to scream. Everyone turned to her as she paced in circles. "When I was walking up the stairs, I met a man who wasn't there, he wasn't there again today, I wish, I wish he would go away."

She chanted the old poem over and over.

Sam's attention was drawn momentarily to Daisy. Poor kid, seeing her father like this. He looked back to Derek Yancy. He wondered where his wife, Nancy, was. Finally he pointed to a short guy who looked like a jock gone to seed. "You! Go call 9-1-1. Tell them we need police back up and EMS now."

He bent to examine Derek Yancy again making mental notes of the murder scene. He noticed the clotting blood. Yancy hadn't been here that long.

Behind Sam, Happurstadt appeared horrified and pale.

Shneed walked up and his jaded sarcastic veneer dropped like a curtain. "He's dead?"

Sam didn't look at him, "I'd say so. Aren't you a doctor?"

Shneed said, "Of psychology. I can't render assistance here." Shneed looked to Happurstadt.

Happurstadt was grim with a strange satisfaction about him, "Relax. Life is about directing accidents."

"This wasn't an accident." Shneed was still freaked out by what he saw.

Sam looked over at Rainbeaux. He was disappointed to see her look at the ceiling. She appeared to talk to herself.

One of the older woman staggered up to the scene. "Isn't this exciting? A murder!" She bent over to examine the corpse too.

Sam returned his attention to the corpse. "Please everyone stand back. Don't touch anything."

When the growing crowd started to push Sam into the area he tried to cordon off Happurstadt cut in, "Yes, give our officer some room. Don't spoil the crime scene."

Like guilty children at the site of a playmate's accident some guests started to move toward the front door.

Happurstadt addressed them too, "Need I remind you that you are all witnesses? No one can leave."

Rainbeaux took the momentary distraction to kneel by Sam. "Don't wanna bother you while you work but did you read something on the wall?"

Sam looked at her quizzically. "There was nothing written here." He didn't know what she meant. So why did he feel like he had done something wrong?

Happurstadt and Shneed noticed Rainbeaux and Sam talking. Shneed made eye contact with Daisy. She nodded her head in return. Then she walked to them as Sam asked Rainbeaux, "What are you talking about?"

"I can't explain it now, but ..."

Daisy appeared next to Sam. She said evenly with a grown woman's voice, "Come with me and I will show you a mystery."

Sam was stunned by this girl. To him she appeared out of nowhere. Rainbeaux was less happy of course. There was more to it than sexual competition. She started to intervene. But wisdom took hold of her, and she decided to allow things to happen to see where these events would go.

Meanwhile Happurstadt looked at Shneed, who nodded his head as sirens blared from outside the front door.

Happurstadt put his hand on Sam's shoulder, "I think reinforcements have arrived. Chessman, why don't you go look? I'll handle everything here."

Sam was confused and unsure but he moved toward the stairs. "Yes sir." Sam was ever polite.

Daisy followed Sam to the stairs. "There's a key in a chest of drawers in the second bedroom on the left on the second floor."

Sam trotted to the top of the stairs. At the second story landing he gave himself time to scope the area before climbing the rest of the way up. It looked safe enough. Sam went to the room Daisy described.

Inside he found a room that looked like the typical abode of a rather immature adolescent. Keeping in mind that all adolescents are immature, this was clinging to childhood. Sam felt sorry for her. Somehow he sensed the tremendous pain that the decor scabbed over. He wondered when that pain would pop up and spill out. The key was where Daisy said it would be. The key to Room 462 at the Red River Motel.

Back in the Great Room Rainbeaux hung back observing everything carefully. She watched Happurstadt and Shneed shitting themselves. She watched bored hausfraus play Jessica Fletcher or Nancy Drew. She watched nervous brown skinned serving staff walk discreetly toward the kitchen. She watched Sam walk back down the stairs as if in a trance.

Sam held up the evidence bag with the key to Happurstadt. He smiled and asked, "What will you do now?"

"That's up to you Mr. Happurstadt."

"Obey orders. Good boy. Why don't you go to the motel? It's in Austin so you have that jurisdiction. See what you can find out. Report to me in the morning."

Sam walked to Rainbeaux. She saw that didn't escape Happurstadt's and Shneed's notice either. Sam said, "I'm sorry I didn't catch your name."

She mimicked Sean Connery, "Le Blanc. Rainbeaux Le Blanc."

"Gotcha. I'm Sam Chessman. But you knew that right?" They smiled at each other. Sam dashed out.

Rainbeaux wasn't looking forward to the long night ahead. She heard a loud woman's scream. She looked around and it appeared that no one else heard it. She walked toward a door that led to the library.

Inside the library she found a naked hollowed eyed Marilyn cowering in a corner, her knees drawn up to her chest. Her pompadour wig was on the floor. Her short spiky hair was flat against her head. Her translucent skin appeared old, covered in violent occult tattoos, and her piercings looked like they were swollen with infection. As Rainbeaux approached slowly, gently she wondered how the infection set in so fast.

"Are you hurt?" Marilyn shook her head no. "Anyone in here with you?"

"They all are."

Within the minutes the medics arrived. Rainbeaux alerted them and Marilyn was taken away on a stretcher. Rainbeaux saw the Round Rock police detectives shake their heads. She overheard that Marilyn was going to get nailed for this for sure. Most interesting to Rainbeaux was the reaction of Happurstadt, Shneed and Daisy. They were all worried about her. How did they know her? Why would they be concerned?

Chapter 7

Night at the Red River Motel. The lights in Room 462 have gone out. The room dark like all the rest. No light, no signs of life in the building made it look more like an empty factory than a motel. Rain fell in a perpetual soft drizzle as Sam arrived. He had called Rip in on this. Rip was jazzed to get in on a major case.

Rip and Sam stopped in the lot in front of the motel; the lights on top of the vehicle still flashing. They were uneasy. It was too dark. Too quiet.

Sam stepped out of the patrol car. Rip continued a convo from the car, "Don Draper is the best. Try telling him no ladies."

"You still have blue balls for that bitch?"

Rip pointed to a group of rooms including room 462. "Let's go check it out."

As they walked up the crumbling concrete steps Sam said, "So beat off to her and forget about it."

"Why don't you beat me off? You can use the OT."

They took a few minutes walking up the stairs. Listening for noise from the room between their banter. Sam stopped at room 462 and studied the door.

Rip walked up, "Something wrong?"

"You're not Don Draper."

"Congratulations for putting your philosophy degree to work. Let's go inside."

As Sam started to speak, Rip reached around him and knocked on the door. There was a loud bump from inside.

They looked at each other. Sam said, "Sounds like someone in trouble to me."

"I heard 'em yell for help."

The cheap plywood splintered as Sam and Rip crashed through the door. The pad was dark. The stench was horrible. Sam strained his eyes to see. Rip started to reach up to flip the light switch. "Gloves?" Sam said.

"Thanks for reminding me."

The cheap low wattage lights revealed a dirty, blood splattered room. There was dried gore on the bed where the work must have been done. Too much evidence that could be spoiled by stepping in the wrong place. It took a few minutes to take in the scene. To catalog what they were finding there.

Then, just like in a horror movie, the closet door slowly swung open with an aching CREAK.

Sam and Rip turned and saw the woman's butchered corpse. Sam was too stunned to speak. All Rip could manage was a quiet, "Fuck me."

Sam just stared at her while Rip called it in. Rip nudged him as he hung up, "What do you make of that?" Something written on the wall. Rip squinted at the words, "Can't read it." Sam shone his flashlight on it. "Still can't."

Sam approached the wall. He could see it. But the sirens announced the ambulance and other police on the way. He would read it silently. He didn't realize he was in a trance until Rip tried to shake him and it took Sam over a minute to become conscious of it.

Later, after securing the crime scene, collecting a mountain of evidence, answering questions from detectives Sam and Rip watched while the room was locked up and taped.

Sam looked at Rip who was disappointed. "Guess that's it for us." They walked back to the patrol car.

Sam said, "You need a girlfriend."

"Look who's talkin", Rip said in response.

CHAPTER 8

When he heard that Marilyn was found naked at a murder scene, Sebastian Brenner knew he had to go see her right away. He had to sneak out of the clinic to go to the hospital. The MHMR bosses wouldn't like him going to check on her, they had incompetent social workers for that. No, he was supposed to maintain his "good working relationship with her" by sitting at his desk and grinning like an idiot once every three months for a whole fifteen minutes. He loved working with the people assigned to his case load. He despised his bosses.

He walked up to a nurse's station. He quietly asked for her room.

The nurse checked her chart. He wasn't on the list. He watched her look him up and down. He was a mature man, age forty-two if she had asked, in a very sharp three piece suit. She asked him for a card. He produced one. He was slightly amused at her reaction. He worked for MHMR, *Well you can't win them all*, the nurse must have thought.

He explained that Marilyn was on his case load. She took a chance and pointed further down the hall. Brenner nodded and continued walking.

Marilyn stared at the ceiling. The dope dripping into her arm couldn't take the pain away. She knew what would but was scared. She wanted to tell Doctor Brenner. She almost had a bunch of times. The door clicked open and she closed her eyes.

Brenner entered. He stopped and watched Marilyn lying still in her bed. He assumed she was asleep. Slowly he crossed the room and looked down at her with a gentle smile. Then he quietly walked to the end of the bed. He read her chart. There was no information on the crime. He expected that. He was anxious to know what happened.

Then she opened her eyes. "Hi, Doc."

"Hi, Marilyn. How are you feeling?"

"Awful."

"I guess I'm curious how you ended up here."

"Bad things, I don't know. I don't know what, but bad things, Doc."

Marilyn was becoming agitated. He had dealt with this many times in session with her in the office. There he felt he had some control. He worried what happened to her out on the street, on the stage when she performed. He worried what would happen to her here. Or in prison. He came around to the side of the bed and soothed her.

"I want to hear but let's go slow."

"I'll tell you okay? But I ain't talkin' to no cops."

"Is this Reburta?"

"She's talking too. But it's me. You don't know who me is do you?"

"You know you have to tell me who you are."

"Well, I will. Soon. But no cops."

"May I make a suggestion?"

"No cops!"

"Please cooperate with the police."

"No! You don't fuckin' understand! You don't get it. Well, I'm not. Not ..."

"I'm afraid you're in trouble I can't help with."

"You gotta. I can't go down for this." She grabbed his hand.

"I'll do what I can. I won't abandon you. But you're going to have to get yourself out of this."

"How? How can I? What did I do to get myself here?"

CHAPTER 9

It was later Monday afternoon when Sam came in for his shift. Rip met him at his locker. "They wanna talk to you."

Sam said, "About."

"About Saturday night. They nailed a singer."

"If they want to talk. Let's go talk. Their lead is a singer?"

"She was supposed to perform at the party." They walked for a minute. Rip looked at Sam. "You look like shit."

"I couldn't sleep."

"Those of us on the night shift offer no sympathy."

Sam had changed by now and as they walked off. "Okay Officer Whiner, next week you rotate back to days ..."

Rip led the way to the District Attorneys' suite of offices. Sam expected to talk to Happurstadt again but Rip led him to a smaller office.

The first thing he saw when she opened the door was that Virginia Van Horn was thirty- nine years old and too rapidly approaching middle age. Her hair a mess, her stomach pudgy, her professional clothes wrinkled. She was distracted by her job. Her office was small to the point of cozy, with a personal touch in the decor that informed Sam it was a woman's office. The most remarkable thing about the office were the conspiracy posters up on the wall. Also a movie poster for JFK by Oliver Stone. Another one announced that she wanted to believe. Sam was a little surprised that she was so open about her paranoia. The Truth was Out in here in any case.

He and Rip stood in the doorway. She motioned them

in. They all sat.

Sam was congenial, "I'm Sam Chessman and this is Rip ..."

But Virginia cut him off, "I sent for you, I know who you are." She didn't even realize it was rude.

Sam and Rip looked at each other. Rip nodded his head slightly. He was expecting this.

Virginia spoke from her diaphragm, "Let's get down to business. You've both answered calls at the Red River Motel before?"

Rip said, "Sure, all the time."

Sam added, "It's a hot spot."

Virginia was digging for something specific, "But nothing like this?"

Sam noted that she wanted something specific and started digging into his memory. He couldn't think of anything she would want. "Nothing as ... I mean, we bust hookers and dealers, but this was the Jack the Ripper show."

"Find any crazy religious symbols? Or something that could pass for a gang tag but wasn't?"

Sam and Rip looked at each other as if to challenge each other to think of something.

Rip said, "We kept seeing gang tags that were unfamiliar to us. We inquired but the Gang Task Force didn't recognize them either."

Sam added, "I checked the room out pretty thoroughly and I know I've seen those symbols around. I can't think of where."

Virginia stared at the paper in front of her. She had been writing or doodling on it. She said, "They are going to try to pin it on a local singer with this crime. Marilyn something or other. I haven't seen the warrant yet. Her show is impersonations of famous singers."

Sam glanced down. She touched up a drawing of a

pentagram with razor wire halo. It looked like a crown. "You sound like you have a different opinion."

"She didn't. Her prints don't match the scene at the Yancy house. There are no prints at the Red River Motel even though she admits to going to that room many times." Virginia looked up and saw Sam watch her. "Let me emphasize how much we don't talk about this to anyone else. Do you think Marilyn did it?"

Rip shrugged. Sam jumped in, "No. Whoever did it had real physical strength. There were signs of a struggle. Then the act of tearing the victim up like that. Then lifting her up alive and struggling onto the hook. Then finishing her off." His voice trailed away, it was difficult for him to finish.

Virginia nodded and looked kindly at Sam. "Thank you gentlemen. I'll call you in again."

Sam and Rip stood and started to go out the door. "Officer Chessman." Sam half turned toward her.

"I like the way you described the victim as 'her'".

"I was raised in the South. Born and bred to be polite."

Virginia very careful what she said next. "I would like you to go look around the room again."

Sam was happy to. "Sure. Am I looking for anything in particular?"

"I'm concerned, that, er, some of the evidence wasn't picked up."

Sam puzzled, "I'll go back during my rounds."

"I'd prefer if you didn't go during business hours."

Sam cocked his head. "I'll go tonight." Sam turned and headed out the door.

"By the way. Aren't you one of the Houston Chessman's?"

Sam didn't bother to turn around for this one. "Used to be."

Virginia said, "I'll be watching you."

That night at the Red River Motel; rain water splashed out of a puddle as a car tire rolled through it. Sam had just arrived in his old beater sedan and was dressed in his civilian clothes. He stepped out of his heap. Immediately he stepped in an ankle deep puddle. The water felt cold and nasty. He didn't appreciate the baptism. The light rain seemed to burn his face. He thought of acid rain. Couldn't be, not here in Austin.

Then he saw Aziz hanging around by the front walk. Sam approached him, "Hey there, Aziz. You aren't gonna catch pneumonia again are you?"

"I didn't see anything in the room, room four sixty-two."

Sam liked Aziz even though most didn't. He felt some compassion for him. He didn't want to believe Aziz said that. "Stay there."

Sam jimmied the door to 462 open. He gave it a moment before entering the room again. He felt like he was entering a carnal house where something alien butchered people for pleasure.

Sam walked over to the bed. He saw the blood stains and cut rope where the Jane Doe was tied to the bed. How could anything human do something like this? She was someone's daughter, granddaughter, someone loved her once. Someone had held her close and delighted in her.

Then she ended up like this.

Sam walked around the room to re-familiarize himself with the crime scene. It looked for all the world like a ritual murder. Weird runic and cuneiform symbols clashed with the generic motel decor. Yet, Sam had a gut feeling that whatever did this, did it for shits and grins.

One picture stood out. An upright figure with a lion's head and snaky body that split at the tail so that two curling tendrils support the impossible body. Sam knew the picture from Greek mythology class back at Yale; Abraxas.

Now the buzzing flies drew Sam's attention around to the bed. There was a small night stand. And sure enough, like DA Van Horn had said, evidence in the form of pill bottles left on the night stand. Sam picked up a pill bottle with a gloved hand. The label read **MONICA FLETCH-ER**. Now Sam could understood why Van Horn was concerned but he didn't know why something like this was left behind.

Damn sloppy, he thought. He slipped the bottle in a plastic bag.

He continued to look around the room. He was unnerved as his gaze settled on the words written in blood on the wall over the bed. This time Sam read the words aloud, "I walk the shadows of night, I walk without the light, I walk places far and near, I walk the places that you fear, I walk a World Beyond Flesh."

The change in Sam was almost imperceptible. A shift in his balance. A slight doubt in how he had viewed the world. A small change, a seed planted, that will lead to something bigger over time.

Just then outside the room the drizzle turned to a downpour. Aziz leaned against a wall. Shaking as he turned his face to the sky. Rain pouring down his face gave him tears he couldn't make for himself. Lightning flashed and he screamed, "Joe Bear. Joe Bear. Joe Bear."

After a long night dealing with arresting Aziz and collecting evidence, Sam sat in front of the Van Horn's desk. He reported what he found. Van Horn opened a packet. She smiled, "I made a request for additional staff to assist on this case. Happurstadt approved you."

Sam without irony, "From what I've seen you could use it."

Virginia placed a badge and a nine millimeter automatic pistol on the desk in front of Sam. His response, "Wow."

She explained, "A temporary assignment to the prose-cutor's office. If you do well on this case, I'll see to it that you are promoted to detective with us full time. Interest-ed?"

Sam found the impulse to snatch the pistol and badge up impossible to resist, "Absolutely. This is a great honor."

He slipped the items into his coat pocket.

Virginia laughed a little, more out of relief than any thing else, "That's okay, 'Detective' Chessman. I know how ambitious you are. Now, don't you have some leads to fol-low?"

It didn't take Sam long to go to his apartment. He dressed in a much nicer suit than anyone would have thought he owned. A couple of hours later he walked into the DA's detective bureau for the first time. His mood lighter and his confidence up, he grinned like a Cheshire Cat.

He walked to an empty desk. There was a name plate with his name on it and a card that read, **Welcome to the team Sam**. This day was turning out to be the best day in a long while. Sam started arranging his desk when Rip strolled in. Sam waved him over.

Rip smiled, "Yeah, buddy, I was coming by to check on you."

Sam couldn't stop grinning, "I don't believe it. It hap-pened just like that," and snapped his fingers.

Rip pulled up a chair. Lowered his voice when he spoke. "Don't get too comfortable here."

"What's up?"

"You heard of the X-Files?"

Sam said, "I own the complete series on DVD. Back home. In my old room. So?"

Rip looked around, "This is just like that." He snapped his fingers. "Nobody trusts Van Horn."

"Come on, can't you be happy for me. Rising tides float

all boats, Buddy."

"She's into some spooky shit, my friend. Word around the campfire is there's a lot of resistance to this investigation at the top."

Sam didn't mention Happurstadt wanting him on the case. He and Yancy had been friends so Sam had his concerns about why he, a relative newby was here. But he buried them. "Okay, whatever, I'm going to make the best of the situation."

"Fine. I'd be disappointed if you didn't."

Sam was disappointed that Rip wasn't happier for him. "Thanks for the situational awareness Bro." Sam began to plot which bar he would take Rip to and get enough beer in him to open up. When he looked up toward the door that opened to the hall. He saw Aziz in manacles and county orange jump suit led by a jailer. Sam jumped up and ran out to catch them.

As he got close he said, "Sorry about the bracelets."

Aziz laughed a little and said, "That's okay. They go with the outfit."

Sam said to the jailer, "Hang back. I'll talk to the witness alone."

The jailer said, "Hey you get promoted or something?"

Sam said, "Something like that."

He led Aziz back to his desk while Rip chatted up a female officer and the jailer hung back.

Sam and Aziz sat. Before Sam could ask him anything, Aziz's face went into a spasm. Sam looked at him trying to snap to what was going on. At first he thought Aziz was playing him. "How many times have I run you in? Three, four in the last six months?" Aziz stared at Sam with an odd smile. His face twitched again. "You gonna answer me? Last night you wanted to talk."

Aziz's answer was a laugh that had an odd tinge to it. "What's with the twitch? You didn't have that last night."

That triggered Aziz facial tic to get worse. Then he spoke in a strange voice. "I'm Quziz."

"Quziz?"

"That's my name now."

Sam picked up pen and paper, "How do you spell that?"

Aziz had a manic quality to his voice now, "Q-U-Z-I-Z. Quziz, Quziz."

"What other names do you go by?"

"Many. Many parts but only Quziz now."

"What do you know about the Red River Motel?"

"I saw them with the girl. Then I went blank."

"What do you mean you went blank?"

"I lost time and time changed." Aziz smiled wickedly at Sam, "You met a woman who runs from secrets into mystery."

Rip walked over to the desk. "That's all you'll get out of him. He requires a special touch."

Just then Sam saw Happurstadt grimace at him from the hallway door. Rip must have seen it first and was watching Sam's back. Aziz couldn't see Happurstadt but sensed it. His whole body went into a spasm again and he laughed like a gorilla. The sound of that laugh hurt Sam's ears. Rip took Aziz away.

Sam watched this feeling deeply troubled. He noticed a pill bottle on his desk. Sam picked it up and read the label, **DOUG JAMISON**. Below that, just like Monica Fletcher's bottle, there was the imprint for Travis County MHMR. Sam knew where he wanted to go after his next stop: a small book store.

Within minutes Sam entered Reading Nation. He was nervous and tried to concealed it by snatching a book off a shelf. He slyly looked around for Rainbeaux.

Theodonia got a good look at him and she grinned. "May I help you?" She was obvious.

"Is there a blonde woman about so high here?" Sam held his hand up to display Rainbeaux's height.

"I'd be happy to assist you."

Small shop, Rainbeaux heard everything. She remembered the cute guy from the flower shop, from the vision and from the murder scene at the Yancy's. She noted that he seemed to be three different people. She didn't think anything of it, she didn't know him that well yet. Still his showing up was the best thing anyone had done for her in weeks. She appeared from the stacks behind them.

He said, "I'm not here for a book. It's personal."

Rainbeaux made a shoo hand sign at Theodonia from behind Sam's back. "How personal?"

Sam suddenly felt like a sneeze coming on from the dust of the old books. He stifled it and smiled at her, "I'd like to see this young woman socially."

She was cool, "I'm not sure; you aren't her type."

Sam moved closer to Rainbeaux so only she could hear. Which didn't work in such a small space. Theodonia slithered away still able to hear.

"Fair enough. But I ask for one date, a try one date."

"A date?" Rainbeaux didn't bite on the 'try one' thing. "As in a block of romantic time together? I seem to remember those."

"I want to give you flowers, a teddy bear and a box of chocolate candy. I'll take you out and hold your hand. We can watch the bats fly out from under the Congress Street bridge. Then I will take you home where we will have one sweet innocent good-night kiss."

Corny as it was, it worked. She was enchanted. "Yes, that will be okay. We can do that."

She wrote her address on a piece of paper in a neat precise hand. Sam glanced at it as he put it in his coat pocket. She had a beautiful hand. An artist's handwriting.

"Friday night at seven PM." Sam quickly exited the store. He knew from hard experience to breeze while you can.

Rainbeaux looked at the front door. "Seven. Friday. Perfect."

41

Chapter 10

Travis County MHMR was located in an aging neo modernist building; a design from a previous attempt to gentrify East Austin back in the eighties. It was way out of place in this neighborhood back then, it was way out of place in any attempt to make Austin the modern city it wanted to be now.

Sam sat in his car and studied the building. He tried to picture who would come here for service. Not the diagnosis, but the personality of the individual. What would coming here do to someone who was too confused to pull their life together?

He pulled the two pill bottles from his coat pocket. He looked from the bottles to the drab county building.

Inside the building Sam walked to the information desk in the lobby. The male receptionist was so short his head barely cleared the countertop.

Sam smiled politely, "I would like to speak to Monica Fletcher or Doug Jamison's case worker."

The receptionist appeared both bored and turned on by Sam at once. "I can neither confirm nor deny that we have a have a consumer by that name."

"Sure." Sam pulled his shiny new detective badge out. "This is a police matter."

The receptionist started to shake his head no when a voice came out of the corridor, "That's okay. He can talk to me."

Sam turned around to meet Sebastian Brenner, dressed like an old fashion gentlemen in his three piece suit.

The Receptionist was ironic, "Okay Dr. Brenner."

Sam smiled at Brenner and said, "You're his psychiatrist?"

Brenner grinned, "Not quite. But you can talk to me anyway."

Brenner talked as they walked down the short hall to a cramped office. Sam noted the bleach smell over the scent of mold and mildew. Just like the Red River Motel. The dull paint on the walls. The tacky floors. How would all this impact someone coming here for service?

Inside Brenner's office Sam handed Brenner one of the bottles.

Brenner looked it over. He looked familiar and sad at the same time. "Oh boy. In the slam again?"

"He wasn't picked for vagrancy this time. This is a murder investigation."

Sam could tell Brenner expected this. He shot Sam a look but kept his cool. "Do you think he did it?"

"Maybe, I don't know. I've seen some weird shit today."

"Tell me about it. I see it everyday."

Both men laughed. Sam handed Brenner the other bottle. Brenner read the label. Sadly he said, "She's a patient here."

Sam decided to break the news. "She was the victim we found in the Red River Motel."

Brenner was speechless. Shaken up. Sam continued, "Are you a psychiatrist?"

"I'm a clinical psychologist. I have a PhD. Psychiatrists are medical doctors."

Sam liked this guy. "I got ya. That means you work for a living."

They chuckled this time but the news of death hung over them.

"Ms. Fletcher was on my case load. I've been treating

Aziz for years. His birth name is Doug Jamison."

"That brings up something I wanted to ask you about. I've only ever know him as Aziz. But he went by different names today."

"You know you're the only APD officer to comment on that."

"I want to know what that's about."

"How much time do you have?"

"Not much. Can we meet for lunch tomorrow?"

"No good. I've got a conference. How about next Tuesday?"

Sam whipped his cell out. "I'll put it on my calendar."

Brenner smiled weakly, "I'll look forward to it."

The rest of the week sped by in blur for Sam. New job, new responsibilities. There was a lot of evidence to sift through. He tried to go to see Marilyn at hospital. Staff informed him that she was unable to receive visitors. Her primary care doctor promised to call Sam when he could see her.

Back at the DA's office he studied the reports on Doug Jamison, Monica Fletcher and Daisy Yancy when he finally got them on Thursday. Rip wasn't lying about resistance to the investigation. Most of the records clerks and secretaries took way too much time when it came time to look anything up for him. One even refused. She appeared afraid.

When he got records he saw that all of them; Aziz or Doug, Daisy and Monica; had records. All had multiple hospitalizations at psychiatric facilities. Many suicide attempts. He noticed that the suicide attempts and hospitalizations almost stopped when they started going to the clinic where they were treated by Dr. Brenner. Sam thought he must be a great doc. Marilyn LezElvis was absent from the records. Except that she came to group therapy sessions led by Brenner with the others.

Finally Marilyn's doctor called. He could see her now.

When Sam tried to follow up on Marilyn, he was informed that she had been released. But hospital staff didn't where she was. Sam thought that was bullshit.

He called Van Horn. She informed Sam that Marilyn had gone home for now. There was no arrest. Sam went back to records. The clerk told him there was no forwarding address. He chalked it up to more resistance. Sam completed his first week at the new position. He felt like celebrating. By Friday night he knew he had to go see a girl.

Chapter 11

Night time, the right time at Rainbeaux's house. Or maybe not. She stood in front of a mirror while she rehearsed her speech to Sam stumbling over her words. "You know, Sam? Dude. Sam. Shit." Ok, that was no good. She started over. "This isn't working out. I mean, you are nice and all, but ..." She looked at her image in the mirror. "What am I doing?"

At the same time Sam was on the way over to Rainbeaux's place. On top of everything else, he had forgotten to take his dirty clothes to the cleaners. Then he forgot to take them back into the apartment before their date. Now when he braked hard at a traffic light, he caused some of his dirty clothes to fly from the back seat and hit him.

"How are you? I didn't do my laundry yet. You look nice. You smell nice. Unlike my laundry. Lovely evening isn't it?" He picked up a dirty shirt and threw it in the back seat. "For laundry." Sam shoved some more dirty clothes aside. "Don't be nervous. Why be nervous?"

Because there was something about this girl. He didn't know what it was. He just knew that he was more anxious about dating her than he was about dating Angelique. Or any girl for that matter. Maybe she wasn't his type. Maybe for once it didn't matter.

Then he was at Rainbeaux's house.

Sudden.

Quick.

Too fast.

Sam was sweating. His hands white knuckle vise grip on the wheel. He tried to control his breathing. He looked up at the two story English Tudor style with a round turret off to one side of the left gable. He saw the light flicker from a second floor window- the Psychotorium. Though he didn't know to call it that yet.

As if in a dream, moving through molasses Sam walked to the door. He knew it wasn't a dream because the ground felt solid under his feet. He waited impatiently until he remembered to knock. Then he didn't do it. Instead he glanced down at a small note pad. Moved his lips as he rehearsed what he would say.

Rainbeaux opened the door to her house slowly, allowing the image to sink in. A hall light shone behind her head creating a halo effect. She looked like a sweet beautiful angel.

Sam stuck the note pad in a back pocket. "Hi." He handed Rainbeaux a dozen gardenias, Frankenstein and Bride of Frankenstein stuffed toys and a box of chocolates.

Rainbeaux took them gratefully. "Hey you," she smiled.

Shortly after that and a short car ride downtown, Rainbeaux and Sam walked hand in hand along Congress Avenue. Sam started to relax now. He even remembered to talk. "So tell me about yourself."

Rainbeaux seemed to glow in the lights of downtown Austin. "What do you want to know?"

"The usual. Where do you come from, what's your family like, favorite colors. The usual."

Rainbeaux replied, "Green. I grew up in New Orleans. My family is old French. At home I pronounce my name Lay-Blaw."

"Is everyone in the family French then? Or do you call it Creole?"

"Not at all, we're mutts. We have a Native American branch of the family and a Cajun, not Creole, branch. I have Irish cousins who will drink you under the table and wake you up for shots."

They laughed at Rainbeaux's joke.

"What about you? Yourself, personally that is."

"I don't how to describe myself. I mean, I don't feel comfortable talking about me."

Now Sam was uncomfortable. He looked around for a remark. Or something to remark upon.

Rainbeaux came to the rescue. She pointed to the street; a woman drove by in a 1967 Camaro SS convertible with the top down. It was red with white leather interior. The engine rumbled and there was a deep burble from the exhaust. Rainbeaux smiled wickedly, "That girl has style."

Sam smiled at her, "She isn't the only one."

Which Rainbeaux caught, "I predict you will meet a woman running from secrets into mystery."

Sam shocked to hear Aziz's words repeated by her. When she looked at him puzzled he said, "I heard someone else say that."

Rainbeaux lightened up, "I am psychic about some things."

Sam too, "So I noticed. What will happen with us?"

Playfully she waved her hands in the air like a side-show magician, "One innocent kiss."

Sam feigned disappointment. "That's all?"

Was she smirking at him? "Next time ask for more." Playfully Sam slapped his head. "At least you get some lip lovin'." She grabbed Sam and kissed him quickly on the mouth. Another smile from her, "Now I predict we're going to the Continental Club. Bonne temp rolle, bay-bee."

Inside the Continental Club the joint was jumpin'. An off the wall band of hillbillies played rock-a-billy on the stage.

Rainbeaux grabbed a table and Sam fetched drinks. She ordered an Old Speckled Hen, an English ale she had come to love while overseas.

Marilyn rounded a corner, stopped and stared at Rainbeaux.

Sam set the drinks on the table. Rainbeaux hoisted her glass, "Can you deal with an ale drinkin' woman?"

Sam said, "If you can deal with a scotch drinkin' man."

"Scotch? Let me have a sip." Rainbeaux took a sip. "This is the good stuff."

"I'm a Chessman. We drink Macallen eighteen years old." She drank the rest of it. Sam taken by surprise again, "Hey!"

Rainbeaux said, "Get another one. And one for me." Sam looked at his empty glass with mock disappointment. She was coy, "I'll wake you up for shots."

They smiled at each other.

Just then the crowd erupted in applause as Marilyn mounted the stage in full 50's era Elvis costume. She was joined by four hellbilly female musicians tricked out in slit up clothes, body piercing and tattoos.

Marilyn leaned into the microphone and whispered seductively, "Come with me and I will show you a mystery."

Sam's head snapped around and he stared at Marilyn while everyone else was preoccupied with partying.

Rainbeaux saw Sam stare with alarm. She moved her hand up and down over his eyes. It took Sam a second to respond. "Was I zoned out?"

Rainbeaux was concerned, "Something like that."

Marilyn screamed, "I'm Marilyn LezElvis and this is The All Out Lezbo Band. Four tough chickie-babies who are belted, booted and buckled and we're after your girlfriends!"

The crowd erupted in laughter, shouting and applause.

The music came from the stage in a wave. Marilyn was an excellent dancer, singer and actor. Her moves, her voice, she left the audience all shook up like Elvis. The crowd loved her. Most of the songs were covers of Elvis songs or songs from the Sun Records era in the fifties like

"My Bucket's Got A Hole In It".

Rainbeaux took Sam by the hand. "Let's bust a moby."

Sam "What?"

"Dance, mon amie."

Sam was game, "Bonne temp rolle."

As they danced, Marilyn's gaze locked onto Rainbeaux. Her lust rolled off the stage while Rainbeaux danced her ass off with Sam.

Over in a dark corner of the club, Aziz huddled over a drink. His dirty clothes, greasy hair, his brown leather medicine bag full of black magic clutched to his chest. He stared at Sam as the music stopped. Then Aziz averted his eyes to the table top. He didn't want to risk eye contact with him. Not yet.

It didn't work though. Between sets when Sam went to the bar he saw Aziz sit in the corner nursing a drink. Sam started to go say something to him. But Aziz suddenly ducked out and vanished out the door. When Sam followed he saw it was into the alley. He didn't see Aziz, just a trash dumpster. He wondered if Aziz was behind it. He decided not to follow.

Inside the club he saw Marilyn talking to Rainbeaux. He went back to the bar, paid for their drinks and took them back to his table. As he moved close enough to hear, Marilyn twirled the curl of hair over her eye, "Hey, hippie chick."

Rainbeaux smiled at her, "Awesome set."

"Do you follow the flesh?" Marilyn asked. Only now she sounded like a fifteen year old.

"I was out on a date. Just now."

Marilyn said, "There is wisdom in flesh. Follow your flesh and I will make you very wise." Then she shook her body and grimaced. She opened her eyes as though waking up after a long time. "The world was different wasn't it?"

Rainbeaux was stumped and that doesn't happen often. "How do you mean?"

Marilyn looked around like she didn't recognize where she was, "I mean, it's different now."

"Things are always changing."

Marilyn was suddenly very fragile, "No, you don't understand. It wasn't supposed to be this way." Then she broke down into sobs.

Rainbeaux tried to be supportive, "Can you help me understand what you mean?"

Sam decided this had gone on long enough. As he moved closer Marilyn glared at him hatefully. She appeared to change again and left quickly.

"That was interesting."

Rainbeaux took her glass, "Was it?"

"What did you talk about?"

"Nothing. She wanted to say hi. Being polite. You know how some singers like to work the crowd."

Someone off to the side screamed so loud it pierced the club's wounded soul.

Marilyn jumped up on the stage and screamed, "I'm metal as fuck!"

Sam looked at Rainbeaux. She said dryly, "Very polite."

A woman screamed again. Sam glanced around until Rainbeaux tugged his sleeve. They both looked across the club. A college age woman was sobbing hysterically in a corner with a drape pulled back. She was crying as she stared at the floor.

They pushed their way through the crowd to get to her. Sam was surprised and a little turned off by how masculine Rainbeaux was in this situation. She was able to plow through a gaggle of linebacker or biker types with little effort.

Marilyn shook her body again and a change came over her. She gyrated her hips, pushed her breasts together and pursed her lips. Thunderous music cascaded through the erupting dancing crowd. That was when Rainbeaux and Sam reached the sobbing woman. And the head. A desiccated human head laid on the floor. Someone had wanted Rainbeaux and Sam to see it. Sam thought of Aziz. He didn't know why.

Rainbeaux said, "That's an oldy moldy for sure."

Sam said, "It's from someone who's been in the ground a while."

Sam held up his badge and made a cutting motion to get the manager to stop the music. When that didn't work Rainbeaux said she would do it. She knocked some guys aside. They looked like they wanted to start trouble until they saw Rainbeaux. Then they smiled at her but she was gone. She cut her way through the crowd.

Within a minute the music stopped. Sam had HQ on the line. They told him to stay with the body. He told them there wasn't a body. Just the head. He figured that was it for tonight.

Meanwhile Aziz crept out into the ally. He looked carefully over the brick wall for an old poster that read **GhostFace Killah**. It featured a human head covered by leather face mask with a zipper mouth. Aziz giggled then removed a couple of bricks from the wall. He reached inside and pulled out an object wrapped in cloth. He unwrapped it and looked it over. It was the a gnarly looking knife used in the ritual murder. There was dried blood along the edge of the blade.

After rewrapping the knife he walked over to a dumpster. He lifted some of the garbage and hid the knife there.

Softly he whispered, "A woman running from secrets into mystery," as though it were a prayer.

Then he hugged the wall as he made his way to the entrance of the alley. He jumped back when he saw Sam exit the club and report to a small group of officers. With a delirious grin Aziz watched the way Rainbeaux and Sam looked at each other and knew they were already in love. He creeped on Rainbeaux until he sensed a change behind him. He turned around to the Red River Motel in the back ground, lit up like the red and blue neon Gate to Hell. He stopped grinning. Whatever relief from misery he felt turned to terror.

At the club Sam had told the detectives what he knew fifty times. He was tired and wanted to tell them to shove off. But he was on the job now and it was required of him. When the suits got bored of asking him the same thing over and over they let him go. He figured she was long gone.

But as he walked out he saw Rainbeaux sitting in a folding canvas chair. She got it somewhere, who knew how. If figured that she would find it. He smiled. She looked up at him with a studious expression on her face. He didn't know what to make of it. She seemed to understand something he didn't.

"Want to finish that date?" He took her hands and guided her to her feet. As he kissed her, he felt her press against him. He was going to apologize for the late hour. It was early morning by now. Sam pulled back. Sam smiled and kissed her again. More firmly. She sank into his passion. All was well.

They walked to his car. The sky was about to start to lighten. Sam could smell dawn about to break.

Back at Rainbeaux's house Sam walked her to the door. She looked at him with anticipation. But Sam was thrown in more ways than one. He wasn't sure what to expect so he took a stab at it. "I guess this is it." And leaned forward to kiss her.

"Have a good time?" She interrupted him.

"Sure. I heard a strange hipster language that I don't understand. Oh, and I got to dance with you and watch you drink my scotch. Plus the dead bodies which I hope aren't going to be common place on our dates." He was easing into it now.

Until she threw him off again. "I had a good time too."

Her looks seemed to give him permission so he kissed her lightly then passionately.

Suddenly Rainbeaux broke away. "That's your kiss." Abruptly she turned and opened the door. She watched Sam stare at her open mouthed as she entered her house.

Sam stood there, unsure of what to do.

Rainbeaux was delighted. "You want to come in?" She wanted to be more than delighted.

"Does this involve more lip lovin'?"

"Only one way to find out," she teased.

Sam grinned. He figured it out.

Rainbeaux took Sam on a tour of her house. She made a point to ignore the turret staircase. Sam was used to luxury. He had grown up with all kinds of fancy home interiors. But the spiral stairs up the turret impressed him. He looked up those stairs like a small child eager to explore, "What's up there?

"Hey, right down this way is my art studio."

In a moment they walked to the studio. Sam behind her as Rainbeaux unlocked the door.

"So I get to see your etchings?" He was trying to be funny when he wanted to see what was up those stairs.

"Yep." The door clicked open. She made a sweeping motion with her hands. Sam's mind was taken off the stairs for a moment. The studio filled with her paintings, all of them excellent. Sam quickly rehearsed what to say about the artwork. "But not that room," he blurted out. Ouch.

Rainbeaux appeared dour. She might as well jump in and lead him to the room. Wait for him to laugh at her and then ... watch him leave. Been there and done that to death.

Reluctantly she led him back out the door and into the house.

The Psychotorium was a round room done in black. Sam didn't know what to make of it. What was a large white screen doing on a small raised stage at one end of the room? Those unlit half- melted candles on black candelabra stood by the couch he could understand. But the couch on a raised platform like a dais?

"This is my Psychotorium."

"Your what?"

"A space where I can be creative."

"Cool, the Psychotorium of Rainbeaux Le Blanc. Can I watch?" Sam beamed at her. She was caught by surprise. He was genuinely thrilled to find out something so unique about her he hadn't known.

"What I do in here is private." She caught herself trying not to stammer.

"Now I really want to watch." The seduction in that statement caused her to take a moment to snap to what was happening. Understandable, most of the guys left by now. Or were on the floor in a laughing fit. But not Sam. Sam was here with her all the way.

Rainbeaux took him by the hand. "Watch this."

In another moment they walked slowly, dreamily into the living room. Really cool sexy music came on. Sam also grew up on jazz. He knew "You Only Live Twice" written by John Berry sung by Nancy Sinatra when he heard it. Rainbeaux turned with the smooth practiced grace of a dancer. With one hand she pushed Sam gently onto the couch. As the music swelled she danced for Sam while she pantomimed the song.

This is where you usually read that he felt the throbbing of his sex. Or he knew his manhood was stirring in his jeans. Actually to be straightforward, Sam got a huge brutal hard on. He was running hot as he tried to make small talk. "You listen to Nancy Sinatra a lot?"

The slow movement had become a long slow lap dance. "Actually, I dig on anything good."

Trying to think of something hip and cool he said, "I groove on George Harrison."

"Right on. Anyone into George Harrison can't be all bad. You get an extra lip lovin' for that."

She was on him and kissing him while her hot snatch wiggled and throbbed over his hard aching cock.

Soon they were in her bedroom. Sam didn't notice the king sized bed. Or how she decorated the room in a sentimental homey style. He was focused on her. On making her happy. Rainbeaux and Sam moved and writhed and made passionate love. As they finished, again, Sam rolled over, "That girl has style."

She propped herself up on one elbow and smiled down at him, "I am a goddess."

"I thought you didn't like talking about yourself?"

"Your turn."

"For what?"

"Tell me about you." Rainbeaux kissed him between words. "Sweet. Wonderful. You."

"I came from a very wealthy family. I always did what I was told. Then one day, in law school, I decided it was time to be independent."

"Which law school?"

"Yale."

She heard him spit it out. He wasn't ashamed, he was angry about something though. She decided she didn't want to know what it was. Not yet. "A Yalie. I'm impressed."

"My father wasn't when I left; he cut off my trust fund. I ran up a large credit card debt trying to live. Now my credit's bad, and I live in a shitty apartment. I bought the old bomb to get around until I straighten things out with the folks."

"Know what? That's brave of you to trust me with all that. Most guys would lie but you got guts. I like guts." Rainbeaux dug a finger into Sam's side. It tickled him. Sam laughed and squirmed.

"I don't know why I told you. I'm not proud of it that's for sure." She knew that wasn't it. He was mad at his father. And something else. Probably a woman. It was always about a woman. She didn't have to be psychic to understand that.

"Maybe it's better for you to be on your own. Be your own man. I dig that too."

"I know who you are, Rainbeaux Le Blanc. You're a good woman. A real woman."

"And you are one groovy right on dude." They looked into each other's eyes and kissed again. "I worry about you, you know."

"Why?"

"You're being set up."

"Hey hippie chick, are you psychic?"

He looked deep into her green and blue eyes.

Rainbeaux got a far away look in her eyes. She was authentically attracted to Sam. But she had been dodging something else. She knew she could help. She just wanted him to be safe. Still jump right into this too. "Ask me about something else."

Sam looked at her unsure what she meant.

"About the case." Rainbeaux reached over to her night stand and grabbed a paper and pen. "Write your question on this and don't let me see it."

Sam took these from her while Rainbeaux got up from bed and slid into a long sleeve pajama top. He wrote, folded the paper and handed it back to her.

"I'll be right back."

Sam laid back. He closed his eyes, a smile on his face. A deeper satisfaction than he had ever felt. Even with Angelique.

He jerked awake as Rainbeaux slid into bed beside him, drawings in her hand. Rainbeaux turned a light on. "What's this?" As he rolled over he saw old scars from cuts up and down Rainbeaux's arms. Which shocked him. Rainbeaux saw Sam look at her arms. She pulled her sleeves down over the scars.

Sam sat up. He shuffled through the drawings.

"I went to the Psychotorium."

Sam pointed to a sketch of a large box. "What's this?"

She furrowed her brow as she looked at it again, "It's a juke box?"

Sam laughed gently, "Looks like a large dumpster."

A flash of recognition for Sam. He remembered that dumpster behind the club when he looked for Aziz.

She pointed to the picture again. "There you will find what you need. And there were some old books. They were falling apart. Something there not holding together very well."

Looking at the picture Sam could tell they were files. He didn't correct her.

Sam shuffled through the pictures again. "Is that what you and Marilyn talked about?"

Rainbeaux put her fingers to Sam's lips the same way he did to hers. She shook her head *No*. He stared into her eyes again. They fell into a kiss.

Chapter 12

They were exhausted on Sunday so they hung out. They alternated between small talk and slow love making.

It was early Monday morning when Sam arrived at the dumpster. At the same time a garbage truck turned down the alley. Information overload. Sam was aware of movement all around the dumpster. Like phantoms in peripheral vision, only somehow seen full on. Sam tried to make sure of the phantoms until the truck honked its horn. Sam flashed his badge, "Yo, fellas, need a few minutes here."

Two city workers shrugged their shoulders and leaned back against their truck for a cigarette break.

Sam shook off the vision and climbed into the dumpster. "Only about fourteen things I need to be doing right now. Still nothing like a little dumpster diving to start the week off right. Not that I'm gonna find ..." As he rummaged around he found a heap of rag. He slipped on a pair of rubber gloves and unwrapped the cloth. Inside was the single edge knife covered in blood. "... Anything." He thought, *you just did.* He climbed out and put the knife in a plastic evidence bag. "Okay fellas."

The diesel engine revved, then amid the crash scrape bang of the lift hauling the dumpster into the air, Sam turned toward another noise. On the other side of the truck Aziz stared at him.

"Quziz?" Aziz ran, the medicine shoulder bag hanging around his neck flapped behind him.

Sam chased him down the alley and out onto the empty city street. Aziz was a pigeon toed flat footed runner and Sam easily caught him out on Mary Street. "Saw you at the club night before last. What are you doing out of jail?"

Aziz appeared scared all out of proportion to the situation, "I need to see Marilyn. I knew Marilyn when she was Reburta, a protector. Spell that R-E-B-U-R-T-A. There you go, crazy spelling and all."

"Quziz, what is going on?

"I'm not Quziz now.

Great, Sam thought. What is his deal? "Okay, who are you then?"

Aziz stood up straight and said, "The game is over and I refuse to answer any more questions."

Sam reached over to take control of him and said, "Okay, let's go."

Aziz ducked under Sam's arm and took off. He zig-zagged between and around clumps of students walking down the street to school. Sam did his best to keep up. He was big and athletic but Aziz was small and fast when he didn't have to run in a straight line. It didn't help that as Sam got near Aziz three homeless people grabbed him. "Wot chew doin', man?" "Got any change?", they asked. Sam could still see Aziz as he ran straight down West Oak. He took a gulp of air and took off in a sprint.

As another homeless man grabbed him and asked for money, Sam felt his body being lifted up and thrown to the ground. He looked up to see a pair of uniform policemen putting cuffs on the homeless man. Sam knew it wasn't the homeless guy who threw him down. As Sam scrambled to get up, one of the officers made a motion for him to stay down.

Sam whipped out his shiny new detective badge. "Officer in pursuit."

To his surprise the officer said, "My kid got one like it from a cereal box." As Sam stood up, the officer started to pull his weapon.

Sam didn't want to get down on his knees. He continued to hold the badge up. "I got my badge the same place you did. But at the end of the day I'll still have mine."

That seemed to give the officer pause. Just then Rip came driving up in a squad car.

"Hold it, that's my partner, Sam Chessman."

Sam nodded, he recognized the officer in front of him now. "I walked a beat out here with you."

The other officer backed down. "I didn't recognize you without your uniform." His smile was insincere. Sam didn't just know something was very wrong, he felt down deep in his stomach. He looked around. Aziz was gone. Nowhere in sight. For some reason, it occurred to him that the uniform pair were out looking for Aziz too.

Sam moved away from them as Rip yelled, "Thank you, Rip!"

Sam tried to work out where Aziz might have gone. But there were too many places he could hide downtown. And if the two uniforms were looking for him too, Sam didn't want to ask them to search.

He smiled at Rip. "Thank you, Rip." Then he handed him the knife wrapped in a rag.

"He remembers," said Rip.

They talked for a minute. Then Sam walked down Colorado Street. He had that uncomfortable feeling he was being watched. He didn't look around though. Soon he walked toward Fifth. He turned down Fifth and walked west back toward Congress Avenue. Off to his right, a cough and the sound of a trash can being kicked, accidentally on purpose, caused Sam to check his peripheral vision. It was Aziz. Standing in the middle of the alley as if he wanted to be found. "You want to talk?" Sam asked looking ahead.

"Why would I talk?"

"Those officers were looking for you too. I would like to help."

"I can take care of myself. By myself."

"Fair enough. But I have a job to do too. I have a responsibility ...”

Aziz sprinted away.

“Shit!” Sam took off after him. As he turned the corner of an alley all he saw were scraps of paper blowing in the breeze. Sam ran on.

Aziz pulled his body out of an impossibly small space. He went to look for Sam. Which didn't take long. Sam was searching fruitlessly in the street. Aziz giggled. He loved to play hide and seek. Survival skills learned as a kid. Aziz watched Sam look for him helplessly. He smiled to himself then he ran down the street.

Within a moments he ran to the corner and stopped. He let himself breath heavy while he rested. Then he started to laugh. The sound of footsteps caught him off guard. With a look of disbelief he looked around the corner.

What Aziz didn't see was Sam holding his shoes in one hand while goading a freaked out looking civilian male to walk nosily toward the corner. Sam slipped past the man so that he and Aziz could touch each other except for the corner.

Aziz moved toward the corner afraid to look around it.

Sam motioned for the civilian to keep walking. Then he when he was almost to the corner he signaled the man to stop.

It worked because the lack of noise now worried Aziz. He was too curious not to look around that corner and ...

Find Sam waiting for him.

Aziz started to run, but Sam grabbed the medicine bag. It slid off Aziz into Sam's hands.

Aziz stopped. He came back to Sam looking beaten down. While Sam put his shoes back on Aziz tried to snatch the bag away from Sam. Sam easily held the bad out of Aziz's reach, “Oh no you don't.”

Sam shooed the civilian away who left gratefully.

Aziz whined, “It's mine.”

"What's in here? Any contraband?"

"Stuff."

Sam opened the bag while Aziz looked helplessly on. Sam rummaged around in the bag saw it was filled with stuff he didn't recognize. He would learn that these were the accouterments of magical practice.

Sam held a pentacle up. That is, a five pointed star with a circle around it. "Afraid of werewolves are we?"

Aziz said glumly, "More than you know."

Sam held up the rag and bone, "Like to play with dolls?"

Aziz sniffed, "As if you don't!" Sam glowered at him. "Yours is alive."

After Sam collared Aziz, he was up to his ass, as he would say it, in the investigation. Crime lab was looking at the knife. Aziz had poured out a serving a nonsense on the ride back. Sam wasn't sure what he understood of it could be verified. The head found at the club was in the coroner's office for identification. Sam put in a request for cold case files. He tried an APD intranet request for murders similar to the Yancy snuff.

Nothing came back and he wondered if he knew how to access the database properly. It seemed needlessly tricky. Odd, too, that no matter how many times the clerk told him, Sam couldn't operate the machine. He couldn't dwell on it too long, or he could become confused again. He left his desk. Time to question Aziz. Again.

The interrogation room was just like on those TV cop shows. Except it was smaller, dirtier and smelled like week old piss.

There was a dual pane window that made a one way mirror where Virginia Van Horn stood next to District Attorney William Happurstadt. Together they watched Sam work on his interview techniques as he questioned Aziz. Sam was painfully amateur. Something that didn't bother

Happurstadt the least. "Where were you the night of ...
What did you see?" Sam asked too many questions together.

Aziz broke in finally. "Rainbeaux knows. She knows
everything if you would just listen."

"She hasn't got anything to do with this."

Virginia and Happurstadt saw that Sam was too defensive. Virginia turned the intercom volume off. "He's not
getting anywhere with him."

The other stroked his chin. "The subject mentioned
someone named Rainbow several times. Detective Chessman keeps redirecting him."

"They both know her."

"What is she? A prostitute?"

"I'll find out."

"Let's talk to her. Don't tell our Detective."

"That would be best." Virginia usually agreed with
Happurstadt though it wasn't her favorite thing in the
world.

He nodded to her, reached over and twisted the intercom back on.

"I love it there, because the magics are strong there.
With the powerful magics I can do things. The things I
need to do because they need done."

"I wish he wouldn't say that." Happurstadt was suddenly glum. Virginia Van Horn had a reflexive gasp of
fright.

Meanwhile Aziz looked Sam up and down with pity.
"You havin' some mighty big problems."

Sam nodded. "It doesn't help you that you talk around
my questions."

"You want help in the case? I help you in the case."

"How will you do that?"

Aziz smiled.

Chapter 13

After Sam left Monday morning Rainbeaux was too tired to go to work. She called in sick and tried to work in her studio. She was unfocused. She got online and checked out car ads. She was looking for something specific and she found it. Soon she was in South Austin scoping out a 1969 Pontiac Firebird convertible. It wasn't the '67 Camaro she saw on Congress when she was with Sam but it was close. The owner allowed that the car was in non-working condition. He agreed to let her have it towed to a garage she knew about; a shop where they restored old performance cars.

At the shop the head mechanic there took a look at the Firebird and let out a low whistle. "She's a beaut."

"Oh yeah, I have a good feeling about this." She went shopping for a couple of hours while he and his crew looked the car over. When she got back, she got good news.

"The reason it doesn't run is very easy to fix. I could have it up and running in thirty minutes. But it needs more work if you want it to run properly."

"Right on." Rainbeaux handed him a list of modifications. "How long and how much?"

He looked the mods over. They went to his office where he played with figures. Or so he said. Rainbeaux knew he knew everything he needed to know already. He gave her a piece of paper with a time line and a price. "Ordinarily, it would be two years and about two hundred fifty thousand. But the body and top are in good shape due to an overhaul he must have done about fifteen years ago."

"That's still a lot," Rainbeaux's eyes watered.

"Well, there are the mods to the chassis. You want independent rear suspension. Modern brakes and of all things, unassisted rack and pinion steering!"

"That's why I asked for a large steering wheel. I know it'll be tough parking and slow speeds," she held her hands at the three o'clock and nine o'clock position, "but I want that communication with the road."

"You certainly know what you want. Okay, but if you find it too hard to steer, and I'm not being condescending here, because it would be hard for me, we'll fix you up with low power hydraulic assist."

They soon came to a price and shook hands. She gave him a down payment on the work. The head mechanic said, "We can start on it right away." She looked around the almost empty shop. He said, "The not so great recession."

"Then I'm glad I can send a little sunshine your way."

He held her check up, "Oh yeah, this is sunshine, Sunshine. You aren't seeing someone are you?"

"I am."

"You think about seeing two fellas?" he laughed.

"You're nice, but we are close. This is for him as much for me."

They parted on good terms, this is laid back Austin after all. She went straight home. She had a hard time working in the studio. By early afternoon something drew her to her Psychotorium. Nothing came of it. So she went to her bedroom to take a nap. When she got there first thing she punched a button on her cell. When he didn't answer, she left a message, "Hey Sam. It's my day off so call me anytime when you get this."

She dejectedly put the cell down. She frowned as she laid down on her bed. Slowly she drifted off to sleep.

Then she dreams that she sleeps in her bed. Beside her a single blue rose on a yellow coverlet. She becomes aware within the dream. It is a message from someone she left behind months ago. He found her here. He always knew where she was.

Now awake Rainbeaux shot up on bed and cried, "No!"

Tuesday morning she woke early. She hadn't heard from Sam yet. Rainbeaux was curious about the blue rose dream. She wasn't excited about who sent it. But she wanted to know why.

Rainbeaux picked up her cell phone and breathlessly pressed a button on the keypad.

On the LED screen the name *Roswell Hane* lit up. Rainbeaux's thumb hovered over the green call button. Her eyes teared and she closed her phone. It was supposed to be in the past, damn it. No more. She wanted no more. But they wouldn't leave her alone. She wanted to talk to Sam. She had to talk to him. He was in trouble, her vision was coming true. Then she hoped she wasn't using him to escape the past that was reaching out for her again. She tried to not judge herself. But what was happening was a shock.

So, time to reassess and plan. Talk to Sam as soon as possible. Warn him and while she's at it, tell him everything. He seems to have accepted a certain amount of information without walking away so far.

Then, as a back up, start to get ready to pull out and change her identity. Sam would have to know about that too. If he is understanding about the first thing she wanted to tell him, he will understand about leaving too.

Finally Sam called. He sounded ... official. "How did you know about the dumpster?"

She blurted out, "I wanted to tell you about it. Can we meet over dinner?"

He asked for a moment. He put her on hold. Then came back on the line. "Sorry, busy day. I'll call tomorrow."

He rang off.

She said, "Okay", and put her phone down. Now she was worried. She reminded herself that he was busy with a new job. She had helped find some evidence from the sound of it. Well duh. That is what she did. This is why Roswell Hane sent her the message. Maybe she could talk to Sam tomorrow. She liked the idea of that.

Meanwhile Sam rang off just as staff unlocked the door to the cold case files room. Sam walked in and began to work. She had told him something was here. What he found was a wall of boxes. This would take a while. Good thing he told her he couldn't talk tonight. He poured through box after box. He read about a snuff in Deep East Texas. Everything about it just like the Red River Motel. That was worrying enough. Then he found something in the file that caused him to call Brenner.

The next day at Reading Nation as Rainbeaux squatted down to lift a stack of books onto an almost empty shelf Theodonia entered with the police: two uniforms. Rainbeaux's past gave her the reaction to run. She controlled that impulse. There was no need even though she knew they were there to pick her up. She wondered what for. No matter, it was just some time in county until she would be free again. Unless these two were going to kill her on the way to the courthouse, which she doubted, it was a matter of some inconvenience.

Trouble is, she had never had the chance to test the system and see if it would work. One of the uniforms asked her to stand up and turn around. As he put the cuffs on her, she thought that she was about to find out how well it worked.

The ride down to booking was brief, Reading Nation was just three blocks from the county courthouse complex.

Everything seemed routine until the uniforms handed her over to two plain clothes detectives. They took her into the same room where Sam had interviewed Aziz though

Rainbeaux wouldn't know that. Specifically she sensed that Sam had been there. She wondered who he had interviewed in here.

The detectives started off by telling her not to worry. That they just wanted some questions answered.

That is when she started to worry. "Questions about what?" she asked.

They told her it was in reference to the Red River Motel and the Yancy murders.

"I don't know anything," she said evenly. She hid her anxiety and her thoughts of Sam from them.

"Detective Chessman told us he got his information from you. Information that only the perps could have known."

This was the problem with abilities; in the movies and TV you were treated like a super hero. In real life you were a suspect. She only hoped that the system worked. Worse than all of that, Sam had betrayed her. She should have known. Good thing she didn't spill to him after all.

The questioning didn't go on much longer. But she could see how this would go. They were trying to wear her down. She wasn't going to break; her federal training gave her the inner strength and discipline to wait them out. Then there was anger: They didn't care about truth, or justice. They wanted a conviction so they would all get a feather for their caps; the persecutor would get a judgeship.

The proceeding was interrupted by a knock at the door. She was quickly escorted out. She was led to a holding area. She felt exposed, everyone could see her and her hands were still cuffed behind her back. She was helpless and in their not so tender mercy. But she knew what the removing her from the room meant. She hated the person she was going to see in a matter of time. He would want to come and retrieve her himself. But she could tolerate him more easily than the two monkeys putting on the show back in the interview room.

71

Chapter 14

At the Detective Bureau, Sam quickly and efficiently put papers away in his desk. He glanced at his watch for the time and saw Rip's reflection on the glass face. "Have an appointment, detective?"

"Sure do."

Rip walked up to the desk. "It's not a hot blonde with a hippy name is it?"

"No, it's with a middle aged man in a spiffy suit."

"And yet I don't have a chance."

"I have a liberal bone in my body, just not that liberal."

Rip said, "I just came by to see if you knew anything."

"About what?" Sam was mystified.

Rip smiled cryptically and split. Sam thought nothing more about it. He walked down to the lobby and left the building for his lunch appointment with Brenner.

At the steak house Sam saw Brenner at a table, his eyes glazed over at the menu. Sam strolled up quickly. Brenner smiled, "There you are."

"Sorry I'm late."

Brenner stood and the men shook hands and sat down. "I have a bad habit of being on time. It tends to put busy people off."

"And you aren't? Busy that is."

"Swamped."

"I won't keep you long."

"No, it's good to get away. And I want to help Marilyn and Aziz. Doug."

Sam realized he haven't given much thought about what he was going to do about Daisy Yancy. She knew something and that had to be addressed. "About those names. How do they change? I mean, I see them react or tremble or something and then they insist they are different people."

"They aren't really different people. Although, I'll give them that that is their experience."

They decided to cool it when wait staff walked up. The wait staff took their drink order and left. Brenner grinned and said, "The county mental health deputies are never far away if civilians overhear our crazy talk. Let's figure out what we want to order. I was thinking of the lunch special."

Sam was horrified. He was raised on the finer cuts of beef. "Don't worry, this is department business, I have a card."

"Hey thanks but I'll still have the special," said Brenner cheerily. Sam was sure he could see his distaste for what must surely be some gag-worthy piece of crap cheap steak.

"Back to the names. I am treating a number of clients for Dissociative Identity Disorder."

Sam's distaste moved to other issues. "I'll bet that's very controversial."

"You have no idea. But the treatment works. These folks are, for the most part, more stable than they have been in a long time."

"And this involves recovering memories?"

"Yes. It is part of the treatment. I suppose you want me to tell you about any memories that relate to the case?"

"Sure. But I have to admit that I don't believe in it myself." Sam choose to be forthright.

"A lot of people don't. All I ask is that I be allowed to continue my treatment."

"I can respect your position but this is still a lot of bunk to me. A way to evade responsibility."

"Well, since we are going to cooperate with each other I can either help you understand or we agree to disagree."

Sam asked, "How do you know you have a case of multiple personalities?"

"First we look for people who have had been in and out of hospital. Have had multiple diagnosis and been unresponsive to medication. Then we do DSM interviews. Finally follow up with our treatment. If that works in stabilizing the person's symptoms, then you can say they have DID."

To Sam's blessed relief wait staff came back with the tea. "If you're ready I'll take your order."

While Sam and Brenner ordered lunch National Guard helicopters swung around the airspace of Austin Bergstrom International Airport. Not the most clandestine entry but he was in a hurry. As the FBI jet landed, the typical black car was on the tarmac to take him downtown.

Hane hadn't seen her in months. He knew she was mad as a hellcat by now. He knew her very well. His plan was to get her released, take her back to Fort Meade where she belonged and let bygones be bygones. There was a lot of work to be done. For one, the main target wasn't located in Afghanistan. She was the only one who ever got them close to nabbing him.

He glanced at his watch. They were bound to be a bunch of inbred hicks in Austin, Texas. This shouldn't take too long.

Back at the steak house wait staff brought plates of food. Both men smiled as their waiter disappeared. Now they could dig in. Sam had let slip that it was Rainbeaux who led him to evidence in the case. Brenner didn't laugh but was curious in a clinical way.

"So this new friend of yours, how did she know to send you out to the dumpster?"

"She just seems to know things. Maybe Marilyn told her at the club. That's what I think."

Brenner doubted that Marilyn told Rainbeaux anything. He was thoughtful, "That's interesting, if true. Marilyn isn't that trusting of people she doesn't know well. Maybe they knew each other before."

Sam felt protective of Rainbeaux, but he was at ease with Brenner. "Okay, this is kind of wild, but she claims to be a psychic."

Brenner stopped his fork midway to his mouth. He almost laughed. Sam was a little disappointed. Brenner said, "Sorry, I've heard of psychics trying to attach themselves to the police."

"You don't think they could help?"

Brenner said, "No. Sorry to break this to you but these things lead to a dead end usually."

In a way Sam was relieved that he could have his doubts and still care for Rainbeaux. "No kidding. How could such a thing work?"

"It can't. Nature doesn't allow it." He continued to think about why Marilyn would tell this Rainbeaux anything. "So she and Marilyn know each other?"

"Just going by appearances I would say that they just met."

Brenner chewed on that while he chewed his food. "Now I wonder why Marilyn would tell your friend about the knife."

"Rainbeaux is very approachable. I can see where people trust her instantly."

"Like you."

"Well yeah. Oh, and Aziz was there. Doug I mean."

Brenner frowned. "I was worried that Doug and Marilyn were associated outside the clinic. Did he talk to her?"

"No. He saw me and ran."

"Then you saw him the next morning at the dumpster."

"That was Saturday night. I saw him Monday morning at the dumpster. What's with the medicine bag?"

"One or I suspect several of his personalities think he is a magician; a sorcerer. He keeps his ..."

"There you go with multiple personalities again. Sorcery. It's all mysticism to me."

"You said yourself that it works in getting Doug to talk."

Before Sam could retort his cell phone rang. He pulled it out of his vest pocket. "Detective Chessman, talk to me."

He listened as Rip filled him in on what happened to Rainbeaux. His face turned gray. "No, no, no. Why didn't ... okay. Thanks for telling me." Sam hung up as he stood and put on his suit coat.

Brenner asked, "What's up?"

"Rainbeaux is in trouble."

"Sam, what happened?"

It took Sam a moment. "I have to go."

"Is everything okay?"

As Sam and Brenner exited the building Sam told Brenner what had happened. Brenner asked, "Why would they arrest your friend?"

"That's what I'm going to find out. And I want to know why she didn't call me."

Sam got in his car and took off leaving Brenner behind. He was at the jail in minutes.

Chapter 15

Inside the jail, a humbled Happurstadt accompanied a dapper officious prick; Roswell Hane as Director of the Defense Intelligence Directorate was dressed in civilian clothes. Happurstadt led him into the jail well ahead of Sam.

Happurstadt led Hane up to a row of benches where Rainbeaux sat in grumpy silence. Her hair was done in a under flip with a swath of blonde bang across her right eye. The sun to her back cast a halo around her. She looked like a Veronica Lake inspired angel. She didn't feel like a happy angel; she was put out.

Sam still well behind Happurstadt and Hane saw her too. His first response was to want to reach out and protect her. Then a heaviness in his chest preceded a negative voice that rumbled inside him. Something deep inside blamed her for this. It said she asked for it. Sam almost started to hate her for being arrested. His legs went rubbery and he slowed his pace. This allowed Happurstadt and Hane to reach her first.

This time her hands were cuffed in front of her. As they approached Hane said, "I thought I'd asked ..."

Happurstadt anticipated his request, "Yes, of course." He made a motion with his hands.

The jailer standing by Rainbeaux quickly unlocked the cuffs. Rainbeaux saw the men approach and frowned.

Happurstadt took her hand and said, "Ms. La Blanc, I'm so sorry for the misunderstanding."

Sam saw this as he walked rapidly up the little group. He fought the awful voice inside him and regained his tender feelings for her.

Hane spoke to Rainbeaux, "I'm happy to see you are

well."

Now Sam joined them. Sam saw that Rainbeaux wasn't comfortable with Hane so close. She started to tell Hane about it, "Well, I'm not ..."

Sam almost breathless from the fear and shock of seeing her under arrest. "Rainbeaux, what happened? Are you okay?"

She looked at him hatefully, "You don't know!" Sam was shocked by this. His surprise was interrupted by Happurstadt who pointed him, "Where have you been?"

Sam was still trying to recover, "Oh, I was discussing the case with ..."

Happurstadt crossed his arms, "With who?"

Sam stammered, "A consultant. A consultant on the, the ..." Sam watched Rainbeaux interact with Hane, "Case."

Happurstadt was not amused, "I see."

While this was going on Hane pulled Rainbeaux off the side. "I sent you a dream. Did you get it?"

Rainbeaux tried not to glare at him, but failed, "Yes, the blue rose. Very David lynch. I hope he doesn't sue you."

"We need you back on this one."

"I'm not working for you again." She stepped back to rejoin the others.

Sam was there waiting for her. "Why didn't you tell me you were arrested?"

"Didn't you have something to do with that?"

"What? No! I would never. Are you okay?"

"What a question! No, I'm not fucking okay."

"I'm sorry ..."

"First, I lost my job over this shit. Not cool! Now your thugs are going to come into my home and toss it like I'm the criminal in a pulp novel."

Sam wanted to help but he was stumped. He refused

to give up, "Let me check into that."

"Can you? Can you stop that?"

"I don't know. I can't promise anything."

"I didn't think so. And what about reading me my rights?" Rainbeaux said loud enough for Happurstadt to hear, "Which didn't happen by the way."

He said dryly, "It's not like it is on television."

Hane jumped in, "I'll vouch for that. It's not." Rainbeaux and Sam shot him a look. Hane raised his hands and stepped back.

Sam asked, "What is her status now? Is she under arrest?"

Happurstadt shook his head, "No, she is being released. She was picked up on some faulty intelligence we obtained. It was all a misunderstanding."

Now Sam was angry. It was slow in building but it was there. "Wait a minute, she hasn't been in custody long enough to determine anything."

Rainbeaux shot back, "What? You want them to keep me here longer?"

"NO! It just seems too ... too." Sam looked around but there was no one to support him on this.

Hane stepped in, "It is a matter of national security that Ms. La Blanc not be in incarcerated."

Sam was incredulous, "She had a get out of jail free card?"

Happurstadt made a slight nod of his head.

Hane put his hand on Rainbeaux's shoulder. Which made both Sam and Rainbeaux uncomfortable. "Ms. La Blanc did some excellent investigative work for us at the Department of Defense."

That got Happurstadt's interest, "What kind of work?"

Hane couldn't help but brag, "She used creative investigative skills to gather difficult to obtain intelligence."

Rainbeaux glared at Hane again. He was not going to

be her favorite person.

Happurstadt put on a show stroking his chin, "I see. Detective Chessman, was she working with you?"

Rainbeaux thought fast, "No. I didn't tell him anything!"

Sam started to say, "Rainbeaux, I ..."

Now Rainbeaux pulled Sam off to the side. Sam let himself get pulled away. He said, "It's not that bad. Let them think what they want."

She spoke extremely fast, "It's a terrible idea. What if I'm called to testify? What if the DA's office wants my help? Plus, I was just arrested as a suspect in not one but a series of murders. What the hell are you thinking?"

"I didn't know they were going after you."

"You're on their *team*. Tell me another one."

"I don't know what to say. I don't want to see you hurt. I'm sorry this happened."

She wanted to believe him. She needed some time, "I need to get out of here and think."

"I'll see if you can leave."

"I can take care of myself." Rainbeaux was still furious with him. She turned to the others and smiled sweetly. "I'm leaving now. If you don't have anything else."

Happurstadt was still studying her, "We learned what we needed to know. This confirms your connection to the case."

Rainbeaux, Sam and Hane detected the hint of threat in that statement. Rainbeaux said, "I'll be going." Everyone nodded except Sam as she went to gather her things and go home.

Sam followed her, "We okay?"

Rainbeaux didn't look at him, "We need to talk."

As Rainbeaux wheeled on her heels and strode out, Sam said, "We will."

Chapter 16

At the Yancy Mansion later that evening three rebels held a meeting in the library. Aziz was bent over going through his medicine bag. While Daisy paced in a circle, Marilyn stood in the center of the room just in front of the fireplace and two easy chairs.

Daisy said, "Bread crumbs, pebbles, pieces of string, go round and round just like a thing."

Marilyn said, "Agreed, it isn't safe here."

Aziz snapped into a British persona, "It isn't safe anywhere is it?"

Daisy replied, "We knew what would happen if we tried. Thoughts in our heads tell us."

Marilyn put her hand on Daisy's shoulder. "How do you feel about it?"

"Too late to ask that now. I'm glad he's dead."

Aziz said, "Dead to this world yes. But I think it means that he's more powerful now."

Daisy hated that idea, "No, no, no. He's going into the ground."

Aziz asked nonchalantly, "Is there a hell?"

Marilyn said, "There is for him. Speaking of that, why turn on her?"

Aziz shrugged his shoulders, "I did what I had to do."

Marilyn shook her head, "Every shitty apologist for the Power says the same sad thing. At least killing Derek is a start. So tell me, Mr. Jamison, how do you propose to dispose of the other two."

"That will happen. But they aren't the ones to be worried about. We still have the Big Fella."

Daisy stopped pacing. She said evenly, "Yes, the Left Hand. Don't let the Left Hand know what the Right Hand is doing."

To which Marilyn and Aziz said, "Amen."

Happurstadt and Shneed met in the ritual spot not far from McKinney Falls off William Cannon Road. They approached the stone circle and dried blood covered altar with the noise of new housing construction and the highway whine of cars providing a soundtrack.

"Getting too built up out here," said Happurstadt.

"We're doing something right," Shneed was smug. He thought about what he said. He corrected himself, "He is doing right by us."

"Up till now."

"Don't complain with your bank account full."

Shneed was finally getting on Happurstadt's nerves. "We've lost a valuable member of the group. And he wasn't just a lynch pin for us, the larger community lost his power."

"We'll acquire someone else. We always do."

Happurstadt said, "He was a friend."

Now Happurstadt got on Shneed's nerves. "We don't have friends. We have allies or enemies. That is all."

Happurstadt appeared disgusted. Shneed barked out a laugh, "Don't tell me you had warm and fuzzy feelings for a child molester."

Happurstadt walked into the stone circle and removed some debris. He put some dead twigs in the oven part of the altar. "He, and we, had a purpose to that. It served Him and it wasn't a compulsion the way it is for most of those slimy sick bastards."

Shneed said in a cold dead voice, "Shit can those human feelings. They just get in the way. What about the new recruit?"

"That one is tougher than we realized. But he will break."

"I'll believe it when I see it. He's too weak for what we

have to do."

"When he kills that girlfriend of his you will believe it. I wonder if she can foresee that?"

In her studio Rainbeaux worked on a new painting. She was inspired, working from an emotional center, the piece spoke to her at the deepest level of her passion. She gave her whole heart to it. But she was heavily conflicted about what she was rendering. She knew she was operating from disappointment, from pain, from hate. She wasn't comfortable with these emotions and she wanted to let them out.

She made quick strokes over the canvas. She was in too much of a hurry and messed up. Just as quickly she wiped and smeared paint then started over.

She heard the knock at the front door all the way out here. She was expecting it anyway. He was hitting the door pretty hard. Probably not aware of it either. Impatient too. She let him knock. She wasn't the only one operating from hurt and anger.

In front out the house Sam stood at the door and pounded. He stopped and rubbed his knuckles. He knocked some more. Then- he was rewarded as the front door opened slowly. The hall light created the same halo effect as when he first saw her.

Only this time, she wasn't smiling.

"I know I shouldn't ..." He started.

Rainbeaux finished, "Then don't."

She started to close the door.

Sam held it open, "I don't want to leave it like this."

"I do."

"Okay, I get you. I feel we can talk this out."

"It's out already."

"Talk through it. I mean."

Rainbeaux stood with the door in her hand. Ready to slam it.

"This takes two. Don't make me do all the work. Please."

She opened the door wider. Then stepped away. "Goddamn stop whining. Close it behind you."

"Thanks," he said without meaning it. Sam entered. He followed and watched her walk down the hall. He almost laughed as she slapped her bare feet against the hard wood floor.

"If you'll give me a chance to explain ..." A forehead slapping moment. He has the chance.

They walked through the house, out the back door and arrived at her Art Studio. She leaned against the door daring him to follow her inside as she turned the knob. "Come on in." She swung inside with the door.

Sam admired the dancer-like movement. "I'm glad you're okay."

Inside the studio Rainbeaux led him up to a covered canvas. "You're glad. I'm glad. We're all glad." She yanked the tarp off as he began to speak.

Sam came face to face with an unflattering caricature of himself. "Guess I learned not to piss off my art major friends." He stood there a moment. "I was surprised when they brought you in. Last thing I expected, since I didn't say anything about you."

"Who would have then?"

"I don't know. No, wait. Aziz."

"Oh. That explains it," she said without enthusiasm.

"Does this hurt us?" Sam studied Rainbeaux's pained expression. Then looked at his portrait again. Even he knew some things were too much. Defeated, Sam started to leave.

Rainbeaux put her hand on his shoulder. "I'm feeling very protective of myself right now."

Sam glanced at his portrait. Rainbeaux was sardonic, "It's not done."

Sam wasn't letting go, "No, we aren't."

Rainbeaux picked up her easel and brush. "I'm busy."

Sam took her shoulders turned her around to face him. He looked into her eyes. He softened. "We're busy. We're busy making sure you understand that I had nothing to do with that clusterfuck."

Rainbeaux appeared to soften. "Okay, Clark Gable, I believe you. It was a clusterfuck."

"And if I had known I'd have warned you."

She put her paints and brush down. She faced him, serious about this. "What would I have done if I had known?"

"Gotten a lawyer."

The logic of that took her by surprise and pleased her too, "Oh. Good point."

Sam continued, "You could have prepared mentally. Not been so shocked."

Rainbeaux put her arms around Sam. She held on to him, "I just don't need. More."

"What?" He liked that she trusted him and held him so close now.

"Pressure."

Sam thought for a second. Then he realized what she meant. "We are still new aren't we?"

"The ship has hardly sailed. We hit rough water right off the first point out of harbor."

"Well, you have an experienced captain."

Rainbeaux slapped his ass. "How experienced are we talking here?"

"Not that experienced. But enough. Oh, come on, I'm no angel."

Rainbeaux stood on her tip toes. "Neither am I." They fell blissfully into a kiss.

Daisy was alone in her bedroom. Marilyn and Aziz left an hour earlier. She paced the floor and muttered to herself. She stopped at her chest of drawers. She opened a drawer, took out a knife and lightly cut her finger. She walked to a wall with drawings and designs all over it. She sang in a sing song childish voice, "Now he's gone. No more. Went away."

She began to draw on this wall in her blood. She stopped and shuttered; a jerky movement over her whole body. Her voice changed to that of an older man. "You'll be looking. For more kills. It's the only thing that makes sense to you."

Her body jerked and her voice changed again, "If only you knew there were other ways to solve problems."

She continued to draw a graveyard scene in a childish scrawl. When her finger stopped bleeding, she looked at it confused that there was no more blood. She shuttered again and spoke with an old person's voice. "They were killers. Roam and roam. Looking for someone."

She had a flashback to the Red River Motel murder. She remembered it like an old movie reel; shaky and blurred. The front door opening in front of her. There were bright lights here too. And screams in the room. A naked woman covered in blood ran to her "No. No, please."

Daisy's voice wasn't her own, "And you found them." Her voice changed, angry. "Stupid Bitch! She should have known better." Her voice became a sing song, "No she didn't. But you taught her."

Daisy was present with herself in her bedroom. She remembered the technique Doctor Brenner taught her. She allowed awareness of the carpet under her bare feet. She felt the cool air blowing out of the vents. She observed the sunlight shining on her bed's comforter. She felt the prick of the blade as she carefully cut her finger again. She continued to draw the gristly scene from the graveyard. Her voice changed again this time to something that sounds like her voice. "And after all the men. Everything you did to break me. You couldn't. I still outsmarted you."

Daisy flashed back to the Texas State Hospital Lobotomy Graveyard. She saw the four teens, three boys and a girl, running through a hole in the fence. Their flashlights on, the beams of light bouncing as they ran. They shine them at each other and goof around.

"They found the trick to bring you here. Found the bitsy bits that tie you here."

The teens were now standing over a grave marker. There was a thud as a shovel dug into the ground. "They brought you up."

The four removed a small box from the grave. As the flashlights shone around, one of the teens was a very young Aziz; Doug Jamison. "Open it," he said.

The teen girl's name was Cindi, "What's inside?"

Aziz, that is, Doug, smiled weirdly, "The lobotomy of Quelle Cade."

"What now?" she asked.

Daisy said it with Aziz/Doug, "Magic happens."

Sitting in her room, Daisy admired the crude picture of the graveyard drawn in her blood. She sucked her finger. She stood and walked in slow bouncy steps toward her bookcase. As she stood in front of the tall case, she shuttered again. She hunched over as though she were very old. She moved a book on a lower shelf. She withdrew a coffin shaped box.

"They thought they were so smart. But I was smarter. They found the means to bring you into this world. I have it now." Daisy closed her fist around the tiny coffin. Blood spurted out of her finger tips and dripped off the coffin onto the floor. "And no one else knows. But I have the means to send you back."

Sam stood at his beat up metal desk in the Detective Bureau. He trembled and shook. Unbelievable. He stomped down to Virginia Van Horn's office. She looked at the text he received. She wasn't that surprised.

"They used a text message to tell me the evidence has been lost."

"Welcome to my world. Jack booted thugs."

"Then why trust the lab if they are in cahoots with whoever is opposing your work?"

"I have protocols to follow. This isn't television."

"No, of course not." Sam had a television quality idea.

A few blocks away in the Federal Building there was another energetic meeting taking place. "You spied on me." Rainbeaux was standing over Hane's desk in his office on the third floor.

He blinked. He wasn't used to her being this forthright. "That was blunt and direct. You know this how?"

"How did you know I was arrested so quickly? I didn't call the man at the desk."

"Well, when the arrest record went into the national database ..."

"Cut the shit, Roswell. The system doesn't work that fast even in post nine-eleven America. Even in two thousand and ..."

She had him there. He said evenly, "You were a valuable asset and we were obliged to keep tabs on you."

"Were?" she shot back. "If I WAS an asset how could you justify spending the dough on me."

It wasn't a question and Hane knew it.

"You were our most valuable asset, now you 'are' our most valuable potential asset. You know, we have that guy to locate." She smiled and he saw it. "So you're going to come back?"

She stopped smiling, "I told you where he is, that house in Pakistan. Not that you acted on it. Or will."

She pulled a document out of her purse. "I will come back to the Company under these conditions."

She dropped a three page proposal in front of him.

He cleared his throat and read over the document. "I, we, can't agree to this. The Office of Personal Manage ..."

"Then I'm walkin'." She headed for the door.

"May I explain something before you storm out of here?"

She turned and crossed her arms.

He picked up her proposal and read it. "We can provide protection for you. But this, Entity as you call it, has worshipers spread out over a wide network."

"Do you know Its name?"

Hane was exasperated. He didn't like giving up this much information. Plus not knowing the answer griped him. "We have no idea who or what it is. Except that it is very powerful. Not just in the Other Place, the Spook Zone as you called it, but here as well. We're talking captains of industry, politicians and religious leaders."

"So the truth is," she began slowly, "I don't need you as much as you need me. Is that it?"

He was defeated and he knew it. "I'll agree to your conditions." She smiled. He held up one finger, "But if we take over the case from Travis County DA we alert this Entity and it's human network and lose stealth."

Rainbeaux said, "I have some renderings for you to see."

Hane smiled weakly. It wasn't the best but it was something. "I'll have the papers drawn up. Your salary and benefits re-start immediately."

Rainbeaux wouldn't tell him but buying her house, furnishing it and now the Firebird and its restoration had drained her accounts.

"If you were spying on me then I was 'on call'. So pay me for status too."

Hane took his rubber stamp with his signature and slammed it down on Rainbeaux's proposal. "Done." He handed it to her. "Say, you didn't remark that I'm in civilian clothes now."

"Does it matter? One uniform is as good as another isn't it?"

"Just so you know, Defense Intelligence ..."

"Bureau wasn't it?" She smiled mischievously.

"Is now Defense Intelligence Directorate."

She shrugged her shoulders and started to leave. Hane said, "Excuse me." She turned at the door. He held out an envelope. "Target. For the next time you go into the Spook Zone."

Chapter 17

Sebastian Brenner was about to be fired. He hadn't expected that but when the director of the East Side Clinic wanted to see him, he felt a sickening twist in his gut. He approached the office with butterflies in his stomach, rubber in his legs. As he thought about it later, he remembered entering the office and the director speaking a low voice. He knew about Dissociative states so he understood why he didn't remember the words the director said. He remembered the emotion behind them. The restrained violence. The hatred for Brenner's theories and methods. The victims of childhood sexual abuse weren't deserving of compassion or mercy. The director honestly believed that they were to blame for what happened to them. Now they were messing with his clinic. He wanted them out and Brenner out. Brenner tried to remain calm. He tried to be rational. It didn't matter. He was told to go home. The director would review Brenner's performance and decide whether he could continue to work there in three day's time.

Brenner already knew the answer. He knew that the director would search his office. He knew that the director would shred his files on DID. It was illegal and he feared that records of his clients would not be available when they needed them. Like in another clinic or hospital or at a murder trial. And that is what made Brenner dangerous. He was writing in records that were hard to alter once he put something in. These idiots were willing to break Federal law and try to cover it up.

He wanted to walk briskly back to his office. He wanted to clear it out himself but the director had the assistant director go with him. He was allowed only take a few "personal items".

So Brenner walked slowly with the assistant director by his side. Furious. Ringing in his ears. He wondered what he would do now. He got his things and got out.

At home he broke down and slept on the couch for hours. Finally he got up. He called his family and broke the news to them. After talking to them, he wished he hadn't. His parents were elderly. His mother took it hard, his father was stoic. His sister asked if he needed any money. He said no, he had saved some up. After he hung up, he thought about selling his car, a nineteen eighties Porsche 944. He had kept it in mint condition. But it was expensive to run and insure.

Then he thought of calling Sam. This might have something to do with the investigation. He hated feeling paranoid, but he couldn't come up with any other reason why they let him go.

At her home Rainbeaux took the box from the delivery man. Inside were all her things from Reading Nation. Up until now it was as though she heard she was fired. This and her meeting earlier with Director Hane made it concrete. The box was something she could hold in her hands. She put the box on the kitchen table. She started to open it. Might as well put it away now and be done with it.

She looked up and saw Sam through the window walking around to her kitchen door. She opened the door and he marched in. She looked at him with some bemusement. Sam didn't break stride but marched in circles around the kitchen. Then he stopped and addressed her, "You didn't wait for me to knock."

"You had a certain look of purpose when I saw you through my kitchen window."

"Who was that man who came and got you out of jail?"

"Yes, well, there is a story there." Rainbeaux was nervous. It was a long difficult story and she no longer had a complete memory of it all. She made a snap judgment to try and find the short version. "I had a high security clearance job with the Federal Government. The man, Roswell Hane, was my recruiter and boss. After I left, he still watched out for me."

"So you can't spend any time in jail? I thought the CIA get out of jail free card was a myth."

"No, it's real. By the way, myths are stories that explain why things are the way they are. It doesn't mean the myth story isn't real. The myth story can be fiction ..." She was watching him while she talked. "Or true." He was deeply disturbed by something. "What brings you here?"

"I don't understand what is going on. You hear about it, then you see it and it stumps you." Sam looked at Rainbeaux for the first time since he arrived. "I don't mean the thing with you and that man."

"If I had to guess, and I guess I'm going to have to guess, someone above you is interfering with your investigation."

Sam touched his nose.

"And you are wondering if I could use my connections with certain agencies of the Federal government to help you?"

"I know it's a lot to ask."

"It is."

"And I shouldn't. I'm sorry. I'm feeling desperate."

"And frustrated. Don't forget frustrated."

"That too."

"What about your father? Isn't he a rich guy with political connections?"

Sam suddenly didn't know if he had told her all that. "I don't think we can depend on him."

"I see." She put her hands on the kitchen counter. She made another decision. "I was a Remote Viewer. Translate that as psychic spy. I worked for a number of different departments in the defense and intelligence side of the government."

"So that's the real story."

"While I was there, I encountered ... something. It scared me. I tried to run away from it. But I think, scratch that, it <u>did</u> find me."

Sam stopped pacing. He was interested. She saw that and kept going. "Roswell Hane, that guy you are so jealous of, wants me to work for him again."

He started to tell her he wasn't jealous except he was. He waited until he was sure she wasn't going to follow that up. "Is it possible that what he wants you to investigate has something to do with my case?"

"The easy answer is that 'everything is connected', but yes. It is exactly the same thing."

Sam thought for a moment. "What was it that scared you?"

Rainbeaux took her turn to think. What should she say? "I met pure evil as we know it. It wants me under its control or dead." She paused for a moment. "It was a demon."

Sam didn't know whether to laugh or hug her. "A demon?"

"A demon as we understand it," she said with certainty.

"Does it have ..." Sam stopped.

Rainbeaux could tell he didn't know how to take this. "If you were going to say 'horns', cut the funny. If you were going to ask for a name, I don't have one."

She watched him a moment. He was pushing down a reaction. A scarier reaction than to laugh at her. "I just call it the Entity."

There it was, she was laying the cards out on the table. She knew Hane and the Company wouldn't be able to provide real help for Sam or much protection for her. She just hoped the resources would help her learn how to exorcise this thing back to where ever it came from. Whatever she could learn would be useful.

Sam said, "Brenner was fired today."

"Who?"

"Sebastian Brenner, a psychologist. He knows the suspects in the Red River case. I think you two should meet."

She smiled, "If you're trying to set me up, I have a boyfriend."

Sam was preoccupied, he looked at the door. "I have some places to be. Talk later?"

Rainbeaux said yes. He left without saying anything else. He left without a kiss.

Rainbeaux didn't know what to make of that. She wasn't sure how she felt about it. He had most certainly read the words on the wall. Although she didn't know what that meant. It had come to her at the Yancy Mansion in one of those rare flashes she received when she wasn't in the Spook Zone. Roswell said they would train her to receive more flashes of vision or insight or whatever too. But now she was stumped. Was Sam suffering from what he read on the wall? Or was he simply preoccupied?

Now she couldn't put off going up to the Psychotorium any longer. She wasn't up to it, especially after that brief if tense meeting with Sam. But she went up anyway.

In the room it took a moment to prepare. Then she laid back on the leather couch and went into her Spook Zone, the Imaginal World.

She felt her soul leave her body and enter the bright glow of the white screen. Before her is an old decrepit house. She can see through the walls of that house. A curious fat little man dancing around from room to room in his underwear and a sleeveless tee shirt. The house is almost bare except for some scattered pieces of old furniture. There are heavy wooden blinds over the windows.

The man is bald on top of his head. He dances to Tony Bennett's In the Middle of an Island.

He dances by a window, the blind opens and revels a rotting corpse half buried in the dirt. He winks at Rainbeaux as he turns on old fashioned box TV.

He dances by another window, the blinds open and there lies another rotting corpse.

He dances over to the wardrobe. He opens the doors where another corpse lies with her face cut away.

He opens the door to a closet. A woman hangs butchered like a piece of meat, her bloodied skeleton still drips with fresh blood; her beautiful face, left untouched by the knife, a blank stare.

Rainbeaux knows the woman still can't believe what happened to her. The blood drips into a sewer that feeds something monstrous living there. She cannot see the monster but feels the creature in icy waves of terror. She bends to look beneath. She tries to examine this place under the curious man's house.

Instead she-

-Enters a suburban living room. She sees a family; father, mother and three children; sit on a couch. The wall they face is covered in digital video images. The images move and run across the multiple small screens very fast. On some of the screens the individual words for the message "I walk a world beyond flesh" appear, winking on and off.

Images of the White House and Capitol Hill appear.

Ads for pharmaceutical companies wink on and off. The father's mouth is covered with pages from a document covered in blood. A DVD sticks to his forehead. The family are suddenly covered in their blood and gore. They sit there murdered and try to talk to her. But they appear as though they gulp air like fish out of water.

Before she can see anymore it is as though she is ejected out and back on her leather couch.

She gulped air while she recovered.

After she got up, she got a call from Hane. He was cryptic but seemed to want to know if she had done something different.

"No," she said.

"Can you come in today and bring your results?" he asked.

"No, I want to complete my renderings. I'll be in at 9 AM sharp tomorrow. Promise. Oh and Sam said that the evidence was missing in his case."

"Okay, I need to check something out anyway. I'll look into that too. See you then."

He was angry. She didn't know what it was about. She got to work on the pictures she had started during the session.

Chapter 18

The next day Sam drove at full speed to meet Brenner. He had considered going to Rip. Rip was a good guy but he was more of a drinking buddy. Because of that Sam didn't think Rip would be sympathetic or believing. They did plot to get the evidence out of the various labs and agencies that had them. Sam didn't know Brenner's character, he had a good feeling about him instead. Not much to go on, but then he had just met Rainbeaux too. He trusted her no matter how skeptical he was of the Remote Viewer story.

Brenner wanted to meet at a coffee shop away from his office. Sam saw him when he pulled in off Burnet Road. It was a new place; The Monkey's Nest. The interior style was urban contemporary.

Inside they sat at a table, the place only had a few scattered customers that time of day. Sam explained what had been going on, what he had done and what he suggested to Rainbeaux. When he got to the part that Rainbeaux had been a Remote Viewer Sam saw Brenner react with interest.

"I've heard of the program," he said.

Sam smiled, "But what?"

"I always thought they cooked their books on their success rate."

"It sounds like a lot of baloney to me."

"Join the club. No one was really sold on it. That's why the program would move from one agency to another."

"But they must have been coming up with something useful or they wouldn't have kept getting funding."

"I'm sure from time to time they did. The human mind, notice I didn't say brain, is very complex. And very powerful. There is a great deal about ourselves and our universe we don't know yet. They could have come up with something interesting. I doubt it was due to psychic ability. There has to be another explanation."

Sam thought for a minute while he drank some coffee. Finally he said, "Damn good coffee."

"It is a damn fine cup of coffee." Brenner and Sam shared a smile.

Sam continued, "She said she would help. We agreed that we would work together on this. She's going back to work for her former boss at the Remote Viewer project, Roswell Hane. She wants to see if he can get the evidence back and analyze it for us."

Brenner nodded, "You said us?"

"Will you work with me too?"

Brenner had to pretend to think about it so he wouldn't come off too eager. "I was hoping you would ask." This was the first good news since he had been let go. It had come pretty fast, so this was a good sign that things weren't so awful after all.

The good signs wouldn't last. The next day Rainbeaux arrived promptly at the Federal Building at nine as she promised. She took a deep breath and processed that she was back to work at the Defense Intelligence Bureau, scratch that, Directorate. She quipped, "We're directed to be defended against intelligence."

Hane was not in a joking mood, "Let me see your results."

She opened her messenger bag and took the small stack of drawings out. He looked her renderings over. He sighed as he said, "I have to ask you about this."

He showed her a photo that exactly like that of the family she had seen in her vision. She was weirded out by the fact that it was a photo of her vision. Her breath left her. "They were found like this?"

"As far as that goes we haven't found a case like this in the data base. From what I can tell <u>this crime hasn't happened</u> yet."

"Wow. Where did this come from?" She meant the photo of the family.

"The AG's office in Virginia. Came right off the printer."

"Fuck me," she said.

"Oh, fuck us all. If this is a message. We are being followed and the adversary wants us to know."

Rainbeaux closed her eyes and tried to gather her thoughts. "I like that you said adversary."

Hane was restless, unusual for him. "Officially this is Project Nemesis."

Rainbeaux appeared confused. He saw that. He wondered if she would recover her memories of the Mabuse File or the Velvet Morning Project. "This is all new. Other than the reports of RV's seeing demons over the years, we don't have much experience with something like this Entity. Also we found that missing evidence Detective Chessman told you about. It wasn't missing so much as hidden. I have to wonder if that triggered this."

His finger tapped the photo.

Rainbeaux gathered her inner strength. "Okay, things are going downhill. I say we work with that and get things moving. Let's have your people look at my results. In the meantime, how can we get the evidence back?"

"I requested a summary of evidence from the county. They are giving me static already."

She asked, "Is that a problem?" She knew it wasn't.

"I'll get it. If the suspected Federal component doesn't start to run interference for them." Suddenly Hane was thoughtful.

"What?" she asked.

"Nothing, just thinking that they haven't. Since the locals attempted to arrest you I'm going out on a limb and say the Entity knew where you are and that you are involved in the case."

"Yes, if It had any doubts, assuming you can say this thing doubts. Yes, It knew for certain who I am and that I am involved."

"And that's through Chessman." Hane not so much asking a question as making an accusation.

Rainbeaux said, "Sam is not so much a problem, the problem is how to extract him from this."

Hane was seeing new sides to her all the time. She had been the Queen of Dispassion back in Maryland. He didn't know if he liked her sense of compassion now. Or the fact that she was in love with someone from the Other Side.

At the Detective Bureau Sam worked his case even though he now realized that most of what he was asked to do was for show. The higher ups didn't want results. Indeed they feared results. Sam asked for a search warrant for the Yancy home and the Red River Motel. Happurstadt told Sam that the crime scenes were searched already. Happurstadt promised reports that Sam knew would not come.

After he got home he called Brenner. Brenner said he was boning up on forensic psychology. He said he would meet Sam and Rainbeaux. Next Sam called Rainbeaux. She also agreed to meet him the next day.

The Monkey's Nest had a small room that offered some privacy. They met there to review and debrief the results of what they had uncovered so far. And so Rainbeaux could meet Brenner.

Rainbeaux was there waiting when Sam entered the room. "Hey you," he said.

Her smile was pretty as she said, "Hey you back."

"Brenner not here?"

"Met him already. He's getting some coffee. How are

you?"

"I feel fine. This is exciting, like I'm a spy or something. How are you?"

"I'm pretty damn skippy for someone who lost her boring inadequate job and had to crawl back to her old employer and ask for favors."

Now her smile wasn't so pretty. She left out the creepy message the Entity sent Roswell. She wanted to show Sam, but Roswell didn't think it a good idea for anyone outside the Company to see it.

Sam saw the stack of documents Rainbeaux had on the table next to her. "I'm impressed he got all this. Hane coming?"

"I asked him not to. But with Director Hane you never know."

Brenner entered and smiled at Sam as he sat a tray with three cups of steaming black coffee down. "Hey, Sam." Then at Rainbeaux, "Got the dark roast."

Rainbeaux looked at the coffee with a smile and said, "Beautiful."

They exchanged pleasantries for a moment. Obviously Rainbeaux and Brenner had talked while Sam was on the way.

Rainbeaux started to pull documents off the pile and pass them around. Sam and Brenner began to read. Rainbeaux seemed lost in her own world. Time passed as they studied and drank more coffee. Then they discussed individual bits of evidence or a report from a case file. Soon a scenario began to form between them.

Brenner observed, "It looks like the physical evidence points to different killers. But my profile suggests there was only one killer." They continued to study.

Finally Rainbeaux asked, "I wonder if they have an Ethiopian blend?"

Sam said, "Let's talk about what we do know."

"They have a Guatemalan blend," she smiled.

Sam grinned back at her, "You are pretty damn skippy. Back to the case files, it's nice to put a name to the face." Sam slid a file with a photo out so the other two could see it.

"The head we found at the Continental Club," said Rainbeaux.

Brenner read the name on the photo slowly. "Quelle Cade. Sounds damn familiar."

Sam said, "I found a lot about him in the old case files. He was a serial killer active in the fifties up around the Texas Louisiana border."

"Of course," Brenner said. "We studied Cade in grad school in a Psychology of Aggression seminar. He had a lobotomy after he was sent to Vernon State Hospital which rendered him helpless. Had to do it. He was still dangerous even inside. About fifteen years ago, someone broke into the State Hospital's lobotomy graveyard and stole the remains."

Rainbeaux furrowed her brow, "Someone could do a lot of damage with the tiny bit of brain they cut out."

"Who would take it?" Sam asked. "Besides someone crazy."

Brenner looked over at Rainbeaux, "What did you mean someone could do damage with the remains?"

"Use it in ritual magic. Bring something into this world using the dusty bits of that dude's noggin as an anchor."

Everyone stopped and simultaneously took another sip of delicious hot black coffee.

Brenner just shook his head at Rainbeaux. Sam could tell he wasn't impressed with that answer. He hoped that she didn't notice. Sam hadn't asked Rainbeaux's permission to tell Brenner anything. He knew the slip about her being a Remote Viewer was a mistake. Now he wanted her to bring up the demon she mentioned. He also understood why she didn't.

He brought up another piece of the puzzle: "There is something else about Cade. I have been going through the cold case and old case files. These ritual murders go back over sixty years. What I saw at the Red River Motel fit Cade's MO to a 't'. The Yancy's not so much."

Brenner glanced through the file in front of him. "He had some followers."

"There was a cult. The other members were tried as accomplices. A couple got off on technicalities. Get this, the defense attorney's last name was Happurstadt."

Brenner let out a low whistle. "Not our DA, I take it."

"No, his father."

Rainbeaux said, "Goes back to his old man and before. It's generational."

Sam continued, "The area where Cade operated is known as Deep East Texas. It is a strip of three counties along the Texas Louisiana border that were lawless. That's because no one was sure who had legal jurisdiction so Texas Rangers and Louisiana law men would stop at the county line. The folks who settled there still have high rates of domestic violence, incest, criminal behavior, mental illness."

Rainbeaux said, "Like I said, generational. Any grave robbers in this posse?"

Sam flipped through the file. "Funny you should ask that. There was a member of Cade's alleged cult, name of Broussard, who kept human bones hanging all around the eves of his house. But then there were human remains all over Cade's place too."

"I wonder," Brenner began, "trophies or ...?"

"Protection," Rainbeaux said. The other two looked at her. The answer had been rather definite. "One of my Master's degrees is in Folk Lore, good old Sophia University. I wrote my thesis on the study of ritual magic. He was drawing down the spirit world's power through the bones to protect his house."

Sam was puzzled, "If he worshipped a demon, why protect himself?"

Rainbeaux thought she saw an opening, "Demon worship is tricky. Demons don't keep their deals. They play you. Most of the time you look silly. That's if you are lucky. Otherwise, the results aren't pretty."

Brenner said, "I didn't see anything here about the cult that built up around him."

Sam said, "The cult didn't build up around him, he was a member. They worshiped a demon known as Baphomet."

Sam watched Rainbeaux. She was cool but he had learned a lot about her in a short period of time. He knew the name shook her up.

Brenner asked, "Is there anywhere else this cult sprung up?"

"Actually," Sam began, "there was a documented case of the Cult of Baphomet in New Orleans and in San Francisco in the twenties. Also more recently in Juarez Mexico."

"Where they found hundreds of murdered young women," said Rainbeaux. Brenner asked, "I wonder who would be attracted to this cult?"

Rainbeaux spoke again, "I studied this in grad school too. The cults like this one have been around for a long time. The empirically or what would pass for empirical documentation is very sketchy. But there are stories of very wealthy powerful political people are attracted to this cult. Men like Cade are used by them. By the way," She looked straight at Brenner, "Baphomet is usually a kind of place holder name, sort of like Adonai for the Hebrews. The initiates don't like to use the real name where other people can find it."

Sam said carefully, "You heard of this in the CIA?"

"We had a report of a coven in the DC area. Not comforting is it?"

"No it isn't." Brenner was working on something. "If the wealthy, like say Derek Yancy, are supposed to be protected by a cult like this, how do we explain what happened to him?"

Sam shook his head, "Multiple personalities, multiple people involved in serial murder with one dominant personality, cults, demons, let's throw in secret societies because of the DC connection, ritual magic and suddenly whatever internal logic is throw out by the murder of Derek Yancy."

"Only one way to figure it out," said Rainbeaux. She waited until the other two looked up at her, "road trip."

Chapter 19

"Well, technically not a road trip," Rainbeaux was happy to sit in the car next to Sam. They were on their way to the Yancy Mansion. "It's not long enough."

"All you have to do is get a car and drive a ways off some place," Sam smiled.

"Oh, the peer pressure. I do know how to drive. And I have a job." She held up a badge. "Looky here, I'm a Fed again."

"I saw that. What kind of car are you thinking?"

"What about a restored '69 Firebird convertible?"

"I figured you for a Mini Cooper or a Prius."

"A '69 Firebird is cute and practical. In a butch impractical kind of way. Actually I can walk to the store from where I live. I can take a bus to work. The Firebird will be for cruising around with you." She gave him a gentle punch on the arm.

He grinned, "I like that plan. I'm proud to be a part of it."

"I knew you would be. It's beautiful to have something nice to look forward to."

They drove along and both enjoyed that thought. Then she said, "Say, are we there yet?"

"Now kids, don't make me pull over." Sam glanced over at her. Rainbeaux clown frowned. "Almost, put on your game face."

"Sam, I never did field work."

"Now you tell me."

They were silent for a moment.

"I was creative again. I saw these metal shoes for a crippled baby. I mean, the shoes had to be metal to help the baby walk. Like braces. Then the shoes somehow led us to flowing red. Stuff."

Sam frowned, "What?"

"It's what I saw. Honest."

He thought about what she said for a minute. "What kind of metal you think the baby's shoes were made up?"

"Coppery brown. Oh, Bronze. That's a funny metal to use for ... wait."

"Bronze baby shoes." Sam laughed. "Don't beat yourself up. You did say for that for some reason you can't interpret your visions. Okay, about the red. You said it was flowing?"

"Right like air was blowing it. Only the air isn't blowing. That doesn't make sense." Now Rainbeaux frowned.

"I didn't see this picture but going from your description I'm thinking drapes."

"Right! The bronze baby shoes lead us to red drapes. Which makes a little more sense. Except not really."

"It is something we are to find in the house that will give us clues. I hoping anyway."

"So we look for bronzed baby shoes." She was holding something back.

"Yes, and beyond that a room with red curtains." Sam looked over at her and gave her a big smile.

Rainbeaux was tense. "There's something else ... I want you to be careful."

Sam wasn't sure where this was going. "Why wouldn't I be?"

Rainbeaux had been thinking about Sam reading the words on the wall. And the way an investigation would proceed. She said, "There is a type of religious literature called revelation discourse. The revelation discourse is usually a dialogue between the god or angel and an initiate of the cult."

"So?"

"The discourse requires that the initiate ask questions." She waited on him, without success, to understand what she said. She could tell he was a bit thick about it. "Detectives ask questions, Sam."

The Yancy Place was in view now.

Sam smiled, he must like that she worried about him. "Noted. It's not uncommon for the killer to idealize a relationship with the cops who track him."

Rainbeaux turned her face to the passenger side window. She was afraid for him, and he still wasn't getting it.

As they drove closer they saw The Yancy Mansion was bathed in the hot searing light of a summer day. The light was so bright that Rainbeaux had to close her eyes to slits. Within minutes she and Sam stood outside with Nancy Yancy blocking the doorway.

Sam had tried to bluff his way inside. "I have a warrant from a Federal judge."

Nancy glared at him, "My lawyer says I don't have to let you in."

Sam was steamed, "He's wrong about that."

Rainbeaux tried, "We're here to help Daisy, Mrs. Yancy. I understand that things are hard right now, but we need to come inside."

Nancy relented and stood aside. "You won't find anything in here."

As she and Sam walked in Nancy muttered something as Rainbeaux walked past her. When she turned to look at her, Nancy held her mouth closed. Rainbeaux was direct but tense. "What did you say?"

Nancy smiled showing all her teeth, "Just that you need to stop and smell the roses."

"I'm an intelligence officer, when I stop and smell the roses, I turn around and look for the coffin."

Then she turned her back on Nancy and proceeded with her work. Something about putting Nancy behind her felt right.

Inside the great room once more Rainbeaux wandered around. She stared at something in the corner. A big old fashioned video camera. She thought it inconsistent for a tech mogul. Wouldn't he have a security system that was digital? Maybe it was what he needed. The big old clunky video cameras she would find all over the house meant that were recordings of what went on in there were on video tape. Why go analog? Perhaps because you can't hack into it. Or if you could get the tape it is more difficult to play back. Although Rainbeaux knew the DID had the tech to play anything.

Meanwhile Sam kept Nancy Yancy away from Rainbeaux. "What can you tell me about your daughter?" he asked her.

Nancy clutched a handkerchief, "When Daisy was very young we knew she was different."

"How so?"

"She saw things that weren't there. Ghosts I suppose. She heard voices. She would cry and not be able to stop."

"What did you do for her?"

She appeared sad and for a moment Sam displayed empathy for her. "We did our best but nothing worked. She was in and out of various psychiatric hospitals, had many different diagnoses and was unresponsive to medication. There were times she acted so differently that her father and I didn't recognize her."

Sam thought about what Brenner had told him, "I've heard of that. Say, did Dr. Brenner's work with her help?"

Nancy looked like hate and rage boiled up from within her. She looked at Sam through eye slits. She was reptilian. Sam hoped Rainbeaux found something soon.

Rainbeaux could see an aura of energy flowing through the house. The energy was so clear she could see all its bright colors and feel it hum in her tummy. She followed a line of energy through the great room and into a library. The library was a large room with floor to ceiling built in book shelves. She found the pair of bronze baby shoes on an end table. Then she checked out a wall sized book shelf. She saw an indentation on a shelf and saw that the bronze shoes fit inside.

"Sam." She could hear him walk toward the room. It took him a minute to reach her. When he entered he saw Rainbeaux on the other side of the room. Nancy watched them from the door way. She wasn't going to leave.

Sam smiled, "Say, could you fetch me some tea?"

Nancy smiled back, "No."

"Coffee?"

She stood there and stared at him like a mean eyed cat. "The warrant means we have the right to search wherever we want." Sam knew it didn't help but he had to try.

She looked like she could bite them both, "You have the right then."

Sam didn't make this a request, "Could you leave the room. Let us work."

Nancy was defiant, "I don't see why I should leave."

Sam looked at Rainbeaux who pointed to the bronzed baby shoes.

"Don't touch that!" Nancy yelled.

Sam looked at her with real anger. He could see how this was going to play. He moved closer to her on purpose. "You'll have to stop us. And when you do, I'll arrest you."

"I'm calling my lawyer!", Nancy spun on her heel and stormed off.

Sam muttered, "Do that then."

He looked at Rainbeaux. She said, "Good on you." She gave him a thumbs up.

Sam walked over and looked at the shoes. She said, "What do you think?"

"They don't fit me."

Rainbeaux nudged Sam playfully which brought a

slight smile to his lips. She took the baby shoes over to the bookshelf. When she placed the shoes in the indentation a hidden door opened as a section of the wall moved back. She looked back at Sam.

"Ready to see how far the rabbit hole goes?"

He nodded and entered first carrying evidence bags. When he saw that she wasn't right behind him, he waited for her. He worried that she was taking too long.

When she entered Rainbeaux reached behind her back then joined him. "This is so cool."

Sam said, "This will be cool when we find whatever it is we are looking for."

At the same time in her private office on the first floor of the house Nancy got off the phone with Shneed. She didn't see Daisy trail her as she walked to the door that led to the cellar. Daisy followed her mother down the long steep staircase to the underground portion of the house. Nancy went to her household shrine with its copy of the tiny coffin like the one that holds Cade's bit of brain. Nancy began to mumble. Daisy listened and heard Rainbeaux's name over and over. She slipped away and went back upstairs. She pulled out her cell and dialed a number.

"Hey prayer buddy from church." She listened and giggled. "I gotta ask you to pray with me for someone."

Meanwhile Rainbeaux and Sam switched on flashlights and walked for a long time in silence inside the maze of corridors hidden deep within the mansion. The corridor was airless and dark. Their flashlights shone around the narrow passage on bare wood and old spider webs. They were undisturbed until they heard the distinct sound of footsteps. They stopped and listened. There was an echo that made it was hard to tell where the sounds came from. Now it was joined by the sound of voices.

"I can't make out what they say," said Rainbeaux.

"I hear them," said Sam tersely. "The sound is all

around us."

Added to the voices and footsteps were other sounds of movement. Little bumps, something heavy being dragged along the floor. "Not that I'm a fraidy cat, which I am by the way, but is somebody going to call for backup?"

Sam was concerned. "Is there a threat? This could be sound from the house echoing all through these passages. It could be the help cleaning up the kitchen."

"They're not getting closer that's for sure."

"So it maybe just echoes then."

They both heard Marilyn's voice, "They are confused by the ..." The sound of her voice became indistinct.

Rainbeaux jumped and grabbed Sam's arm. Sam asked, "That wasn't you?"

"No," said Rainbeaux as she released Sam's arm. She addressed the voice, "Talk to us again." There was silence. She asked again, "Please tell us your name?" Nothing.

"The sound seems amplified by the darkness. There isn't any light in here," said Sam.

"There is light everywhere." Marilyn's response seemed to Rainbeaux to reverberate down the corridor.

Rainbeaux asked, "Marilyn are you in here?"

Sam sneered, "Of course. She has to be. But where?"

Rainbeaux said, "These passages were built to escape or hide."

If she could have seen his face, she would have seen how worried he was. "We should have left a trail of bread crumbs or something."

"Don't you know the way back out?"

"This is going to sound really foolish."

Rainbeaux tapped him on the back. He stopped and faced her as she held up her flashlight on a ball of string with a line trailing behind them.

Sam smiled at her, "Look, I didn't know this place was going to be so ..."

"Amazing. Get it? A-maz-ing."

"I was going to say labyrinthine."

"Good thing I know my Greek myths."

"Speaking of knowing, aren't you a psychic or something? What are we looking for in here?" They rounded another tight corner and found a door illuminated in their flashlights.

Rainbeaux smiled, "You know there's this hidden room."

Sam shook his head, "Too late for that now." Sam tried the door. Predictably it was locked.

Rainbeaux looked over his shoulder, "Don't cha have a skeleton key? They aren't just for skeletons anymore."

Sam looked over his shoulder at her and grinned. The door was light and the knob and lock were made of cheap soft metal. Sam easily forced the door open with a sharp twist of the knob. "I don't know what I'd do without comedy relief."

"I don't know what you would do either."

Immediately the sounds stopped as the door opened. Sam found the light switch and flipped it on. The dull light revealed a small room draped with red curtains, a desk, a small TV and VCR on a stand and a book case with VHS tapes lined on it. And a small alter with an image of Baphomet.

"What is that?" Sam asked.

She said, "That's the old fella we have been talking about. The one with the cult of rich people, and the place holder name."

She noted his unease as he looked at it.

Rainbeaux went to the bookshelf with the tapes. She looked through the collections and loaded a tape into the VCR. She turned the TV on.

Sam started by going through the desk. He retrieved several file folders. He opened them and started to read.

Each of them were locked into what they were seeing.

Finally Sam said, "My god."

Rainbeaux responded, "Am there, seeing that, and skipping the tee-shirt."

All Sam could say was, "This is our case."

As new images appeared on the TV screen. "Dude, so is this."

Sam walked over and watched the tape with Rainbeaux. He was disgusted and he quickly turned the TV off. "Hard core porn. And he's got some family photos in here."

They moved over to the desk. Rainbeaux stood by Sam while he showed her what he found. She pointed to a blurry figure in one of the photos. She said, "This is Daisy?"

Sam flipped through several photographs. "She looks like she was quite a bit younger. See Derek Yancy stand by while his buddies take turns?"

Rainbeaux pointed to a figure in the photo, "There's Happurstadt. You know any of the others?"

Sam pointed to another figure in the photo, "That's Shneed. The Executive Director of Travis County MHMR." They continued through the photos. "There's Marilyn and Aziz. They're tied up."

"I am not liking that figure there." Rainbeaux pointed to a half formed transparent figure in another photo.

"Looks like something off a ghost hunting TV program. Probably a double exposure," Sam said. "There are a lot of these to go through."

"We're gonna be busy moving." Rainbeaux didn't mind a little hard work but she still had the sounds from the corridor in the back of her mind. The sounds still worried her.

"I think we'll get some help." Sam flipped open his cell phone.

Later that day, a line of uniformed officers carried

boxes of material out of the house. Sam stood by to super-
vise outside. Rainbeaux was in the small room tending to
the details there. "Don't forget," she said two policemen
carrying boxes, "to follow the police tape. A couple of fellas
got lost in the last half hour." There was a squawk on her
mic. "I'm here Detective Chessman."

Sam's voice came over the mic. "How's it goin' in
there? Are you done?"

"No, the more we pull out, the more stuff there is." She
stopped and pointed to shattered pages on the floor. "Get
that too." Then back to Sam, "It's like moving."

"Let me know when you see the end in sight."

"Will do. We'll keep beavering away until we move it
all out."

Outside in the waning sunshine Sam sighed, "I just
hope we get to keep it."

CHAPTER 20

Daisy was locked in her room. She went back there after Nancy was done praying in front of the family shrine. Now Nancy was on the phone. Her mother didn't know, but Daisy had a program on her computer that allowed her to listen in on phone calls. She listened as her mother pleaded for her own and Daisy's life.

Happurstadt was having none of it. His ass was on the line and he knew it. It wasn't just the Feds he had to worry about.

Daisy didn't even dare to think the Name. She had to worry too. Somehow she knew that she would be okay. That's when her savior came online. Marilyn opened a chat box.

You okay?
Daisy typed in: **yes**
Something is up
Big tyme
What is it?
Daisy typed; **You know this isn't a secure link. I'll tell you later**
k was the reply.

Daisy closed the chat. Then she restarted her browser. Not that that would necessarily help. But it didn't hurt to try. Then she went back to listening to her mother and Happurstadt argue. One thing was for sure. Someone was going to jail. Someone was going to die.

Inside the house when the recovery was done, Rainbeaux called Hane. He was pleased. She asked, "Are you going to come for the big unveiling?"

"No. Not yet. Something is up."

"No kidding."

"You know what I mean."

"You have interference too."

"Something like that. Report Happurstadt's reaction to me."

Rainbeaux was perplexed. "How come he's still out walking around? He is way implicated in this."

"He was connections too. But we'll get him."

"Say, Sam wants to get Sebastian Brenner hired as a consultant."

"If you are asking that I hire him ..."

"You know me so well," Rainbeaux laughed lightly.

"You know he has a legitimate reason not to. Doctor Brenner is too close to the suspects."

She nodded, "He treated four of them and worked for Shneed."

"Look, he will have information. It won't hurt to get that from him. But hiring Brenner is not going to happen."

"You have connections too."

Hane rang off. She hoped that Hane was hopeful.

It took a while to return to the Bureau. She joined Sam, Brenner and Virginia in a conference room. They went through the stash of evidence. Most of what they found was hard to look at. Then they got to the tapes.

Finally Rainbeaux said, "That was several hours that could made a gore hound hurl."

Sam held a tape up. "The last tape." Everyone applauded. Sam switched tapes in the VCR.

They watched for a few seconds with increasing horror until Rainbeaux broke in. "That's a snuff film. Turn it off."

Sam said, "It can't be."

Brenner asked, "Who was the victim?"

Virginia said, "I didn't recognize her. Any ideas?"

Brenner said, "Probably a runaway."

Rainbeaux looked sick. Sam saw that. "You were right about creepy. Don't worry, snuff films usually turn out to be staged."

"Why?" she asked. "Because that's what you want to believe?"

There was a moment of uncomfortable silence. Then Brenner broke in. "Observations?"

Virginia moved some of her papers around. She cleared her throat. "We need to focus on someone." Then she stopped talking.

"Honestly, this entire case is a mess," Sam started. "With so many prominent people and the DA ..."

"Our boss," Virginia cut in.

"... implicated, I think we should turn this over to the US Attorney for special prosecution."

"Why is that? So your girlfriend can take care of it for you?" Everyone turned to Happurstadt. He was standing in the door, red faced. Rainbeaux froze, Brenner pushed away from the table.

Sam stood his ground. "Sir, I don't think it's a good idea for you to be here."

"Really. You know what is not a good idea? Having this many people here who compromise the case. Officer LeBlanc was brought in for questioning and I'm still not convinced that she shouldn't be. Doctor Brenner treated several of our suspects, professionally, as their psychologist. Until he was fired for unprofessional conduct. Ms. Van Horn is the laughing stock of the city with her wild right wing conspiracy theories. Birther, my ass."

"I never subscribed to any birther ideas. Barak Obama doesn't exist, he is a thought form created by Gnostics controlled by ..."

Happurstadt yelled, "Knock it off!" Then to Sam, "And you, Detective Chessman, the things I could say about you."

"If you want us to leave, we can leave," said Rainbeaux evenly.

Happurstadt shot her a look of pure hatred. Then he relaxed his face. By then everyone was moving toward the door. "No, wait. This is a difficult time for all of us. But there is something we can do. I'm very sincere about this, we can progress the case. I want to arrest Daisy Yellow Yancy for these murders."

Sam answered for the group, except maybe Virginia, "Sir, these ritual murders go back decades. She is too young to have been involved."

"Let me tell you something, young man, I haven't been charged with anything yet. So legally I am still in command of this case. That's right, Ms. Van Horn, you are replaced. So I can still bring the killer to justice. And by the way, you still work for me."

Sam set his jaw. He knew what he'd like to say. "Very well, sir. I'll start to process the paperwork."

Happurstadt had been prepared for more of a fight. He didn't like this though. He hadn't known Sam Chessman very long but knew him well enough. He was probably buying time. "Get to it," was all he could say.

The little group quickly left the room.

Out in the hall, Virginia stopped and waited for Sam. Rainbeaux brushed by her. Though she barely touched Virginia she said, "I guess you want to protect the sweet young thing?" Virginia looked squarely at Rainbeaux.

Rainbeaux looked back and said at Virginia. "The thing is, we are made to feel like we have to protect the gentle kind people, the sweet innocent people. When in fact, I believe they protect us."

Rainbeaux walked off.

Next Sam came out. He looked at Virginia like she was beneath contempt. She was defensive, "I'm not damaged goods."

Sam shook his head, "Not here."

"How silly of me."

Sam went straight to his desk. He began the paper-work for the warrant for Daisy's arrest. Quickly, and more quickly than usual, a paralegal came and took over the details.

Sam left the office. He caught up with Rainbeaux and Brenner at their coffee hangout. They let three perfectly good hot steaming cups of joe just sit before them.

"That gave me the willies." Rainbeaux picked her cup up and then sat it back down without drinking from it.

"Still got 'em." Sam put his hand on hers.

Brenner actually got to drink out of his cup. "He's correct in that all of us are compromised. Me especially."

Sam said, "No, I wouldn't say that." He asked Rainbeaux, "Would you?"

"Yes," she said to Brenner. "You are."

"You don't have to be harsh," Sam wanted to protect Brenner.

She responded to them both, "Not harsh. Just a statement of fact. How did you feel when he brought up that you were fired?"

"I didn't think that's important."

"You were in the way. That's important." Rainbeaux smiled at him. Brenner blushed. "That doesn't mean that you can't be a big help to us."

"I don't see how," Brenner felt foolish.

Rainbeaux explained, "We need your insight from working with them professionally. Plus, Roswell said we could consult with you."

Did he? She conveniently forgot.

Brenner countered, "There are the confidentiality laws."

Sam said, "There are exceptions to protect them within the criminal justice system. Even if they aren't charged, the story is public, so their records as consumers will be public."

For some reason Brenner laughed at that. He almost couldn't stop himself. "Maybe I'm too close."

Rainbeaux said gently, "You care about them. There's nothing wrong with that. There was something about those photos. Tell me what you think."

She was right. There was something. "I did notice that no matter how ... bad ... things got, Marilyn was passive throughout everything."

Sam joined in, "Like she was there to ... do what? Stand around?"

Brenner drained his cup. "She has a 'Protector' personality. There was something else. She was front and center even if the tapes and photos don't show her participating."

"Like she was there for what?"

Rainbeaux realized what it was. She and Brenner almost said it together. "She was there for ..." "They were drawing ..." "... power" "... energy off her." They looked at each other and almost laughed.

Now Sam took some coffee, "How could she give them energy? I flunked psycho-babble in school."

Brenner answered, "She has been through stuff that would have killed most people. And has. There's too much to go into here, but her life has been a nightmare. Like what we saw with Daisy Yancy, only worse."

Sam mused, "I wonder how someone can go through all that and not do something. She must have a lot of anger inside her. And now she's been given the opportunity to act on it."

Rainbeaux squeezed Sam's hand. "Just because someone was abused, doesn't mean they are out to settle the score like some revenge movie. Sometime I have some stories about me to tell."

Sam checked his watch, "Come to think of it, she is one other person I haven't interviewed. While the arrest warrant for Daisy is being processed, I can catch Marilyn at her place if I leave now."

Rainbeaux was concerned. She didn't like him going to see her alone. "I want to go," she said.

"No, I've seen the way she looks at you. I swear it's not a jealousy thing."

Rainbeaux started to object, when Brenner said, "She does have several alters who identify as lesbian." In other words of course it was jealousy.

"Don't want any distractions, I better go by myself." Sam jumped up and charged off.

Rainbeaux and Brenner looked at each other for a moment. She asked, "If someone had some ... or been ... was conditioned to do something. How would you handle it?"

"Call it to their attention. If they become mindful of it then they can desensitize themselves to the triggers."

Rainbeaux slapped her forehead. "I knew that."

"What is it?"

Brenner knew she was worried even before she said, "Something he read."

CHAPTER 21

After Sam left he drove around for awhile. He felt confusion and didn't like it. Being a man of decision and action he wasn't used to not knowing what to do. Only the thought of Rainbeaux brought him any peace of mind. Something about her. He considered going back and talking to her. But he didn't know what he would say if he did. Quickly he decided that if he knew more about her, he might feel better. There was something too that seemed to try to block him finding out more. Something that seemed to block his thoughts. Then very depressed negative feelings of helplessness and hopelessness swept over him. He wasn't used to those feelings either. He fought against these thoughts and feelings and followed his gut.

The Federal Court Building was located downtown on West Sixth Street. Sam entered the front door like he owned the place. He had questions for Roswell Hane and he wanted them answered in spite of the internal resistance he felt.

Sam stood in front of a security desk where the guard tried to stare him down. "One more time, all you have to do is let Special Agent Roswell Hane know I'm here."

The guard was a no neck no nonsense type, "I'll have the US Marshall escort you out, sir."

Sam knew it wouldn't do any good to argue. So he was persistent instead, "I'm a detective with the Travis County DA here on official business." He had said that twice before.

The guard just looked down his nose at Sam.

Sam pointed to a couch. "I'm going to sit over here. When you get tired of me sitting there, maybe Special Agent or Director or whatever Hane will come and talk to me."

Sam walked to the couch he pointed to in the lobby.

The guard said, "Very well, Sir," as Sam sat on the couch.

He looked around at the messy pile of magazines spread on the table and couch. He picked one of the magazines up and opened it to page one.

After a long period of time, Sam yawned and closed the magazine he had been reading. He leaned over and placed it on a neat pile of magazines in front of him. He reached for another when he was interrupted by a smooth voice, "Detective Chessman, how very nice to see you again."

Sam looked at Hane. He admired his taste in suits and said, "Finally."

"Let's go upstairs. Where it's private."

Upstairs Hane occupied a nice spacious office with furniture fit for an executive of a large multinational corporation. Hane smiled at Sam, "You're quite a match for our Rainbeaux. I can see why she likes you so well."

Sam said, "Rainbeaux is the reason I'm here. She knows things she shouldn't. And I want to know how."

Hane reclined and rocked back in his comfortable chair. "Gotcha. You are here to solve the mystery of Rainbeaux Le Blanc."

Sam tensed, his face became dark. "Seems everyone can read me. Can you tell me how she knows things?"

Hane asked, "How does anyone know anything?"

"Is she psychic?"

Hane turned his hand sideways, "Aren't we all? Besides we don't deal in psychics in the Intelligence Service."

Sam thought for a moment. He wasn't going to answer anything directly. Maybe if he phrased the question indirectly, "Don't tell me you have spook lingo for psychic?"

"Remote Viewer. The short hand is RV."

Sam was slightly pleased at that response, "I see, I ask

the right questions you reward me with an answer. Okay, what is a Remote Viewer?"

Hane reacted slightly but recovered and remained impeccable. "A Remote Viewer is a documentary on the Science Channel."

"Are you telling me the whole psychic spy thing is real?"

"What is real, Detective Chessman?"

Sam thought for a moment. "What do you think about people with multiple personalities?"

"They're the luckiest people in the world." Just an hour later and now Sam sat across from Marilyn. The interview with Hane hasn't lasted too much longer after Sam got the answer about Remote Viewers. He didn't know why Hane had allowed him to know that. Sam figured out very quickly that it was a waste of time to get Hane to spill on anything.

He was at Marilyn's home in Hyde Park now. He hoped that she may give him some information that he could use to sabotage the DA's case against Daisy Yancy. He saw that she had her crib fixed up retro chic. Very sixties. Very Mad Men. Sam almost expected her to wear a Jackie- O outfit with big hair and the pillbox hat. When she opened the door she had said, "Swell of you to swing by my pad, Daddy-O."

Now Sam asked her point blank, "Do you think you have multiple personalities?"

She was nonchalant, "Sure, why not?"

Sam forged ahead, "How many?"

"How much time do you have?"

"Look, Ms. Marilyn, what is your last name?"

She giggled, "It depends on the personality you're talking to."

"Keep it serious. You're a suspect in a murder investigation."

Marilyn played him, "So what?"

"Did you know the Yancys?"

"No. Never met them."

"We have credit card receipts that place Daisy Yancy at the Continental Club on the nights you perform."

"So? Lots of other people were there, I didn't know them either."

"How did they know to hire you for the party?"

"I have a good agent."

"So how come you aren't playing Vegas?"

"Who says I don't?" Then she shook all over, and her voice changed. Now it was smoky, husky, "Looky, Daddy-O, what do you want?"

"Ms. Le Blanc warned me I'm being set up. What do you know about it?"

"Different parts know different things."

Sam recognized the same thing Aziz said. Then more changes, Sam thought she was changing lightning fast. "Let's play the game. What parts know what?"

Marilyn looked off as though listening to someone talk. Then she said, "Ask one."

"I don't know the names. You'll have to tell me." Immediately Sam knew this was a mistake. Marilyn shook all over. She smiled licentiously.

"Ja-Baaz says I can come out."

"Who's Ja-Baaz?"

She said, "A controller. I'm Misstee."

"Is there one main alter I can deal with?"

"We all work for ..." Laughing Marilyn handed Sam a popular book with Mary Magdalene on the cover. "See that red egg? It's a bird's egg she pulled out of a snake."

"I'll read it later." He tossed the book down.

Marilyn leapt up. "I got something you can read." She lifted her shirt and exposed her naked breasts. "Dude, what's your future? Can you tell?"

Sam jumped up to leave. "That's it. When I come back, I'll bring someone with me."

"How about your hottie hippy girlfriend? I'd love to get liquid on her ass." Marilyn rubbed her nipples, "She can play with these."

Sam was outta there lickety split.

About the same time Sam was at the Federal Building Aziz was sitting in his cardboard hovel in the alley behind Reading Nation watching Neddy Oldesmith approach him. Neddy was all frowned up and Aziz guessed that it was the new used pair of outsized shoes he wore.

"Hey, Aziz, man, you gotta help me." He looked like a sad clown.

"Wuzzup?"

"I got these shoes from Goodwill and now I'm feeling all discombobulated."

"That suxs."

"Sure does. I am thinking there's magic or ghosts. Ghosts in the shoes."

Closing his eyes and holding his hands over the shoes Aziz began to mumble and groan. A deep "Grrrrr" came from the back of his throat. He opened his eyes. "The problem is that someone put a spell on those shoes. Then left them out for someone to find."

"Aw, shit man, they always got to fuck with you. And just when I was getting ahead."

"It's a basic trickster spell." Then before Aziz could ask for money ...

"Or you aren't used to wearing them yet." Both turned to see Rainbeaux standing nearby. "Used to tennis shoes are we?"

"Yes," said Neddy hopefully.

"These are hard soled shoes. Plus they look like they are too big for your feet. Either one can create a feeling that you are disoriented. Walk in them for awhile and see

133

if that doesn't help. Double up on the socks while you're at it."

Neddy walked away talking to himself. Aziz looked at Neddy and back at her, "Hey that was an easy twenty!"

"He didn't have it. I'd know."

"I suppose you would."

She squatted down to eye level with him. "So as one professional to another, I want to know what you can tell me about your cult."

Aziz eyes almost popped out of his head. "What the hell, askin' me that?"

"I grok that you can't talk about it. But if you let me in, I can help all of you."

"I don't care nothing for Sam or the others."

"Then you are in a cult?"

He put his hands over his ears, "NOOOOOOOO!"

She felt a terrible compassion for him, "Oh, Aziz, what do you worship?"

"Something more powerful than you know."

"How many people have you killed? For him? Or It?"

Aziz remained mum.

"What if I tell you that I've met this Thing? Out there?"

He mumbled again, "Places you go."

"Places I go."

"Then you know how hopeless it is to fight him."

"Nothing is hopeless. We can deal with this."

"Then deal with this, I'm not telling you nothing."

"You have already told me a great deal. I know there is a cult, that you have gotten Sam involved. That what you worship is the same one I have encountered. That He, It, tries to keep you close but you have adapted ways to defeat it keeping its eye on you. And I know that you have tried to escape it."

Aziz buried his filthy face in his dirty hands. "No more, no more talking."

She sat there for a while longer. But he was shut down. She gave up and left. This might have been her only chance with him. She planned to tell Brenner and get him to help. She sensed that Sam hadn't gone to Marilyn's. At least not straight there. Things weren't going well for him either.

She went home. She took some time brewing tea and preparing for her next Remote Viewing session. After she drank her tea and relaxed she went upstairs to the Psychotorium. She laid upon the couch and started her deep breathing. As she took her mind off her conscious self the white screen buzzed with white noise and flashes. Images begin to form as the buzzing white noise subsided.

It takes a moment for the images to stabilize. On the screen she sees a darkened room. The murdered family sit together on a couch in all their squalor and gore. Odd flickering light illuminates them from the walls lined with TV newspaper moving pictures from popular TV shows, MTV style video clips, and news programs. Just as before. Only now there are steel loops with a catch and a trip wire stringing around them like a fence.

Behind the family, a puppet man in a lab coat, with vials of chemicals and multiple IV's plugged into his body, and lines that ran to a host of electronic instruments, twist knobs that controlled the TV's.

As the images slowly fade Rainbeaux feels an intense fear. And a feeling that someone was very close who could help her. As she regained consciousness she focused on one feeling then the other. She tried to hold the feelings together as one object of focus. She felt a battle between fear and light. The light felt stronger. She hoped it was.

The session ended, she sat to make notes. The images confused her. They always did. Back at the Defense Department she had a team to look at her results and interpret them. As worried as she was about trusting Sam with information, he was still the only one with whom she could process the results now. She got up to call him. After that it was time for a meeting with Roswell.

CHAPTER 22

When Sam got back to the Detective Bureau after his other adventures of the day, the uniforms were waiting for him with Daisy in cuffs. Sam eased down to the interview room filled with apprehension. Happurstadt and Virginia were waiting there for him. Sam wondered if he could pull off something as halfhearted as this interrogation and make them happy.

Sam entered and threw a thick folder down in front of Daisy. She said, "I'm Daisy and I'm in chains. Also I change. Get it? Daisy change?"

Sam said, "I get it. You want something? A cola or beverage?"

"How about ice cream. Just try to buy me off with ice cream like I'm a juvenile."

Sam apologized, "I didn't mean it like that."

Then before he could continue, "Am I the only suspect?"

Sam asked, "Is there someone else we should consider?"

On the other side of the mirror in the observation room, Happurstadt and Virginia watched. Happurstadt with a growing fury. "She's controlling the whole interview."

Virginia didn't think so. She started to defend Sam but thought better of it. "He doesn't believe she's guilty."

Happurstadt said, "Believe me, she is." Then he caught himself. He didn't want to confess to Virginia. He continued, "He has a job to do. Just ask the questions we want answered."

"Did he understand that?" Virginia asked.

Daisy was still leading the conversation on the other

side of the mirror. "Guess not," Happurstadt said glumly.

Then Sam and Daisy became more agitated. Sam's voice rose, "I want to know more about the Satanic symbols at the Red River Motel."

Daisy shook her head in fear. Her fear seemed to feed Sam. "What about the cult? What is it that you worship?"

Happurstadt in anger said, "We better get him out of there." He went to the door. But as soon as he twisted the key in the lock, the lock sprung back again. He tried the door again. It remained locked and closed. Happurstadt began to panic. His Master wasn't behind this. Then who was? Virginia watched him but didn't understand what was going on.

Sam held up a picture from the Red River crime scene. "Which one of you did this?"

Daisy shook her head and threw herself out of her chair. She went into a ball on the floor. Sam was too caught up to back off, "Who was it? Tell me!"

Daisy shook her head no. She cried. Sam was too busy yelling at her to hear the door lock. She heard. She feared who did that. She feared being in here with Sam.

"Who do you worship? What is its name?"

She shut down. He yelled again, "Is this Satan worship? Do you believe in the Devil?"

She screamed back at him, "Lies! Lies! Lies!" at the top of her lungs while she tried to push her body back against the wall.

By that time Rip came and the door unlocked for him. He found Sam standing over Daisy looking like he was ready to beat her to a pulp. "Sam! Yo, brah! We're cool, okay. We're cool."

Sam stopped yelling. He turned to Rip. He seemed to come out of a fog. He was breathing heavy. Rip patted him on the back. Then pushed Sam gently out of the room. He bent over and helped Daisy to her feet.

"Let's take you to the Infirmary." He guided her to the door.

Out in the hall Happurstadt intercepted them.

"She goes back to her cell."

A jailer came and took control of Daisy. Happurstadt left. Sam turned to Rip. "Yo, brah?"

"What? A Mexican can't live in Hawaii."

"How did you end up in Texas?"

"Family," Rip said glumly.

Daisy went back to her cell. Sam went back to his desk. That's when Rainbeaux called.

"Hane wants to see you, again. Thanks for telling me you were going ..."

"Do I have to account for every move I make?" Sam knew he sounded irritated. He didn't want her to think it was just at her.

"No, you don't. Sorry if I trespassed your boundaries."

"You didn't cross anything. I'm coming right over."

She added, "Bring Sebastian too."

Within the hour Rainbeaux, Sam and Brenner were waiting for Roswell Hane. He came in briskly with a thick portfolio in his hands and slapped it on the table. "We have a problem."

Rainbeaux looked at the portfolio and saw it was stuffed with her renderings. "Just one? What's wrong, slow day?"

Hane looked at her, "You had another vision of this family?"

"Yes. Please tell me you know who they are."

"We don't. That's the issue. I don't believe this has happened yet, as we discussed before. But our team can't place them."

Brenner offered, "May I?"

Hane wasn't sure about him being in the room. "Go ahead."

Brenner opened the folio and began to slowly pull the renderings out. As he did, Sam went through them too. They were both shocked by the photograph. "You said this hasn't happened yet."

"No, that," Hane pointed to the picture, "Came off a printer. The time it printed out matches the time with Officer LeBlanc was in her Zone obtaining these images for us."

Brenner was astonished. "Spirit photography?"

"What?" asked Sam.

Rainbeaux said, "Technically it is projected thought photography or nensha. Thoughts being projected onto a surface. You guys saw THE RING right?"

Sam was trying to control his laughter. Brenner appeared to be sizing her up for a straight jacket. Hane was sorry either of them was there.

"The thing is," she continued quickly, "I didn't do this."

Sam's silent laughter stopped. "If not you, then who did."

Rainbeaux asked Hane about the photo off the printer, "How many of us have done something like this?"

"We have people who specialize in it. Actually you did it a couple of times. I might have left that out when I debriefed you."

Sam reiterated his statement, "Who did." He began to feel a deep fear though he didn't know why.

Hane said, "If this hasn't happened yet, we have a chance to stop it."

Sam felt something grip him like it squeezed all his internal organs. Rainbeaux rubbed his back. Her touch, even through his clothes was so soothing, so gently releasing, his anxiety eased. "Let me see these drawings again."

Sam went through them. He saw something in each of them. They made no sense to him, even more so than they had before. He started with the drawing she made just before they met. "This is a representation of our situation. All these complex people and systems interconnected. This is me. This one," he pointed to the apish figure in the trench coat, hat and glasses, "is our Bad Guy. This one, of the family, hasn't happened as you said. But we are being challenged to try and find them. Like a serial killer taunting the police. Also, they are in a trap. You can see the outline of a mouse trap the way everything in the room is arranged."

Rainbeaux glanced over at Hane and she knew he was impressed. But he was disturbed too. She got an impression that he didn't like Sam, that he was jealous in some way.

Brenner said, "I recognize these people. Or the man anyway."

Hane asked, "You have a name?"

"Not yet. It is right on the tip of my tongue."

Rainbeaux addressed them, "We don't know what or who we are up against. We don't know how to deal with It. Or if we can. But if we can upset It's plans, I want to do that. Sebastian, take a little time and figure who this guy is. Roswell, I want Sam to be the one who interprets results from now on."

Hane started to object. Instead he said, "May I have a word with you? Privately."

"Whatever you say to me you can say to the others."

"It can wait." Hane was terse. He started to leave.

"If it is about Sam ..."

Hane held his hand up. "It will wait." He looked at Sam with obvious distaste. Then he left.

Rainbeaux said, "That was cryptic."

Brenner said, "May I have a copy of these photos?"

She got them for him. Then he excused himself to go study them.

Sam looked at her and asked, "Dinner?"

Later Sam was still shaken up as he and Rainbeaux sat at the best table in a ritzy restaurant. Behind them Lake Austin looked beautiful exposed through a large picture window. The full moon reflected off the water. Perfect atmosphere for a romantic dinner. He thought about telling her how unsettled he felt but decided against it. He rubbed his eyes to shake off what happened. Then winced when Rainbeaux sprinkled pepper on her French fries.

"Something the matter? She asked over an arched eyebrow that would make a Vulcan proud." She was glad when Sam laughed at her joke. He had been grim all evening. Maybe things weren't as bad as she thought.

"No. Yes. Pepper on your fries?"

Rainbeaux shook more pepper out. "Dude, lots of people put pepper on their food. You want some?"

Sam shook it off. "I saw Marilyn today. She didn't take being a suspect in a major murder investigation seriously."

"Aren't all of them major?"

Sam nodded his head. "Yeah. Had that coming." He shuffled through more drawings. He looked at the drawing of the murdered family again. He pointed to it, "Okay, what do you see?"

She looked at it. "They are in a living room. Covered in garbage. They sit in front of a picture window."

Sam shook his head, "They are in a waiting room. Like a doctor's office. There are rows of TV sets playing behind them. Different shows but there is a continuity to it. A story. This guy here," he pointed to the man with the tubes and vials that connected them, "has them hooked up. Like he's doing some kind of infusion therapy on them." He was silent for a moment. Then said, "Beautiful." He appeared incredulous. "Yeah, what's with not understanding what you see? Some kind of artist's thing?"

"The visions are all right brain. My left hemisphere

isn't involved."

"Normally I'd like that in a woman."

Rainbeaux threw her napkin at Sam. After they laughed she said, "I'm worried about you."

He smiled at her and said, "Still? No need to worry about me."

"You sure? Something is eating at you."

Sam had to really hold back here, "It's nothing. Let's skip it."

He took a deep drink of his scotch.

"Okay, I got ya. But if there is something ..."

"There's nothing. It doesn't matter." He was starting to get curt with her.

She studied him. "How seriously do you take all this?" She needed to ask this.

"I think I'm pretty serious about the case." Sam looked at her. He saw her study him with a frown. "I'm serious about us."

"Just before we met I had a series of visions about you."

"Yeah the maze in particular."

"Yes, that's it. All of them like an interconnected community, like a city."

Sam said, "Brenner describes people with multiple personalities as having a personality system. It's confusing."

She pointed to a figure in one picture, "Yet you are singled out. That is you wandering here. Then I met you at the flower shop."

He tried to distance himself from this, "Picture is kinda small but I like it better than the first lithograph I saw in your place."

Rainbeaux slumped slightly and frowned.

He asked gently, "What's wrong?"

"There is a lot going on that bothers me."

"Such as?"

She was at a rare loss for words, "Your promotion coming so fast."

"Let's change the subject."

"Let's not. Has anything changed since you started this?"

There was a buzzing noise in his ear. Sam shook his head to answer no.

"You okay?" She could almost hear it. Sam shook his head to stop the buzz. "Did you read the words on the wall at the murder scenes out loud?"

"Yes. But that's because no one else could make out what was written."

"Sam, you've begun initiation into the Entity's cult."

He snorted, "What does that mean?"

"Tell me."

"Tell me about working for the Federal government."

Rainbeaux was weary, "All I will allow; I found out some things I wasn't supposed to know." She noted that with the change of subject the pain seemed less for him.

"That's part and parcel with working for the government. They let you leave?"

"Yes."

"That's all you'll say about it I suppose."

"Think it through. Since I know sensitive information, the Federal government won't allow me to go to jail. That is why I didn't worry when I was arrested."

"What if you really did something?"

"They have a place for their own."

"How did he know to come get you?"

"There is a possibility that bothers me. The government is spying on me."

"That sounds X-Files, conspiracy theory, Virginia Van Horn crazy. Why?"

"My question, mon amie."

Sam almost laughed, "So are we supposed to go see a bunch of nerds living in a basement after this?" Rainbeaux frowned. Sam saw this. "You're not laughing." Rainbeaux looked right through Sam. "I can try to be funnier." Sam laughed loudly. He didn't know why. There was nothing funny about this.

"Don't try."

Sam continued to laugh. Rainbeaux got up to leave. "Get wise to yourself," she said. She left him there laughing for reasons he couldn't explain.

CHAPTER 23

Sam lost time after Rainbeaux left. He was back at his apartment and he wasn't sure how he got there. The sun was shining in the window but he didn't know what day it was. He tried to check the facts of what had happened. He had one scotch and no drugs. He didn't know why or what happened. The buzzing had stopped. He tried to call her but there was no answer. He hoped she would pick up if she could. Rather than sit and worry he got up and prepared for work.

His first stop was the home of one of the previous investigators listed in the case files. It had been so long ago that no one knew Detective Chuck Collins anymore. Sam pulled up in front of a house in a nice central Austin neighborhood. He double checked the address. Sam walked up to the door and knocked.

The door opened and an elderly woman peered at Sam from inside the house. She kept the right side of her face to him.

"Deirdre Collins?"

Her eyes widened as he said her name. "Yes?" She was frightened of him.

Sam flashed his badge. "I'm Detective Sam Chessman with DA's office. Is your husband home?"

"What's this about?"

"Detective Collins was chief investigator on a case we just reopened. I was hoping to pick his brain."

Mrs. Collins looked like someone just beat her over the head with a police baton. "You didn't know? My husband went insane. He's locked up at Vernon State Hospital for the Criminally Insane."

"I'm sorry. I didn't mean ..." Sam suddenly wondered

why no one knew that.

She continued, "He hurt a lot of people." Mrs. Collins turned her head to expose a deep painful scar down the left side of her cheek. "I don't have a family anymore."

"Ma'am, I am so sorry."

Mrs. Collins slammed the door in Sam's face. Sam returned to his office to reexamine his case notes. He went over to the jail and made sure Daisy got her anti-psychotic medication. Jailers tend to forget these things.

Rainbeaux finally called. She acted as though nothing had happened. Sam went over after work. She was mellow. He started to ask her about the night before but she brushed off anything he had to say. They spent the night talking. They fooled around some and then went to bed. Through all this, Sam said nothing about losing time.

The next morning at Rainbeaux's house we find a domestic scene of two people at ease with each other. Rainbeaux calmly made breakfast. Sam sat at the table and studied his notes on the murder case. She looked up from the bowls in front of her, "What kind of fruit do you want with your granola?"

Sam didn't look up, "What would the cult want with me?"

"Not sure. It's scary. We need to talk about making you safe."

Now he looked up, "Why would the Feds spy on you, Rainbeaux?"

"You don't know these people. They can be very paranoid, controlling."

He chuckled, "Believe me, if you knew my family, you would know that I know the type."

"They want to defend democracy but they are so totalitarian about it."

"There's the reason I love you." He smiled at her and she smiled back. "You know, it's hard to bring this up, but …"

"If you need to talk, go ahead."

Though he knew to hesitate, he found it too easy to begin, "There are a lot of things too fantastic to believe. Brenner talking about multiple personalities. You talk about cults and entities."

Rainbeaux shot a hard look at Sam. "What about it?"

It was against his better judgment but he couldn't stop himself, "The MPD angle and the other stuff, it's a myth."

She was calm, not defensive as he feared, "We've talked about myths before. You can take them just as seriously as any other story."

"Call it what you like, Rainbeaux, but I'm a skeptic, a rationalist." Now he was being defensive.

"You're not a rationalist, you're afraid. What are you afraid of?"

"Nothing."

"You're afraid you have a soul! You should see your soul quake at the notion."

Sam was more irritated than he was comfortable with, "Maybe I do have a soul, but I'm trying to use reason to work things out."

She was calm and measured in her response, "Reason will fail you. Rationalists forgot the lessons religion taught them. Athena was the Goddess of Reason but she was also the Goddess of Illusion. You can use a lot of things to fool yourself. Including reason."

"Bullshit! You can't use reason like that!"

"Your world of rational smoke and mirrors is catching up with you."

Sam felt hot anger rise in him. Something was wrong but he couldn't stop, "So I'm supposed to believe in ghosts and superstition and Remote Viewers and D-I-D. If someone is abused they ought to get over it."

Rainbeaux's mood changed from calm to seething to angry. "Someone who's been pampered all his life might

149

want to think before commenting on someone else's hard knocks."

Sam frowned silent for a moment. Hadn't she said she grew up on the street? What must have happened to her there? "I'm sorry. I ..."

Rainbeaux put breakfast down on the counter away from Sam. "You believe people should take care of themselves? There ya go." Rainbeaux handed Sam a piece of paper. "Here, Marilyn's last name. Hey, how did I know you couldn't get her to tell you that? Now you can say a spook gave it to you. That isn't rational is it?"

Sam looked at the paper, "Sure puts me in the demon haunted world."

She stormed out. Left alone, Sam stared after her, puzzled and perturbed.

CHAPTER 24

The weather in Austin, Texas was not a cloud in the sky clear and hot with low humidity.

Thank god for the relief of the past few days, thought Sam, *the humidity almost steamed me out of my shorts.*

The effect of bright sunlight and high clarity was to make everything look bleached out and bone white. Even objects that aren't white or even close lost most of their color.

Sam sat in his car at the Red River Motel parking lot wishing he hadn't forgotten his sunglasses. But time to face this without a filter. Time to look at as it is.

Reason and smoke and mirrors my ass, he thought.

Sam exited his car and looked at Room 462 perched as he perceived it on a ledge above his head. Just then if occurred to him that the room number made so sense in a two story building with far fewer than sixty-two rooms. Yet he had justified it to himself all these months. He stuffed these thoughts down as he walked slowly up the crumbling concrete steps to The Room. He steadied his nerves. Nothing up there he told himself. But his thoughts didn't alleviate his fear. He started to remember nightmares about the room. It was crazy. He would know if he had a nightmare wouldn't he? He always had before. Now he startled from a trance at his desk or when he was alone in his apartment to remember some florid detail of a dream. Something told him he had these nightmares for weeks.

So he kept telling himself that whatever happened here was over. It was just a room now. Nothing in there.

Sam turned the knob and entered the room. He was shocked to see a man standing in front of him. A man from the nightmares. Doctor Shneed gazing at the words written on the wall in dried blood with his back to Sam.

Sam was surprised and relieved to see him here. He didn't know what to make of it. There was a piece of business he wanted to take up with the doctor though. "I'd like to see your client's files."

Shneed kept his back to Sam. "They're called consumers."

Something about the word 'consumers' didn't sit well with him. "That because to you all they do is take and don't give anything back."

Shneed spun around, "Very smart, Detective. Why are you interested in them? Because that idiot Brenner bought into the whole multiple personality boondoggle?"

Now some of the fear from the nightmares came back to him. "I don't know what Brenner did and frankly it doesn't matter to me."

"Did you know we fired Brenner? Yeah, for trying to diagnose and treat our consumers for multiple personality disorder. It's against the law for me to tell you that. Hell, it was against Federal law to even do it. Damn government is interfering with my business."

Sam wanted to say but you work for the government. "You won't get away with it."

"Oh, you're concerned for me! Thank you so goddamn much for your heart felt bullshit threat. Don't worry, it's tough to pin me down. I'm a golden boy. I do what the insurance and drug companies and the department of mental health want me to do and I get off scot free every time." He smiled like a salamander.

Sam gazed at the words smeared in blood. "You and everyone like you gets away with it because we have become a cynical and selfish society. I think America's lost the plot."

"So I'm a sellout. I'll bet I remind you of someone else. I'll bet you were a real daddy's boy growing up."

"Don't psycho anal-ize me." Sam wanted to say something else when music from his pocket diverted his attention from the words on the wall. He grabbed his cell phone out of a pocket.

Shneed acted put out, "Getting a call from the Twilight Zone?"

Sam said, "Girlfriend being funny when she programmed the ring."

He spoke into his cell, "Chessman." He listened and answered, "Be right there."

Shneed sneered, "They are like children. They don't listen and don't know when to shut up."

Sam asked, "Girlfriends?"

"Our consumers," said Shneed offhand.

After she left Sam Rainbeaux was so preoccupied by anger and disappointment with him that she didn't think to switch the light on as she entered the almost pitch black Psychotorium. She placed a document out of her line of sight.

Printed on the document, typed in neat letters are: *The nature of the relationship between the killers and victims -Brenner*

Rainbeaux laid on the couch and went through her relaxation exercise. As she reentered the Zone the screen before her glowed again with ethereal light. Light that illuminated the room. It illuminated Rainbeaux and caused a light within her to illuminate too. So that there were two great sources of light; a ball within Rainbeaux and shining off the screen; sharing radiance with the space around them. The radiance from the screen comingled with the radiance from within her. There was a flare of supernal light. Then ...

Up on the screen: a hologram image of multiple layers of wheels within wheels. Eyes, not necessarily human eyes, line the sides of the wheels. Rainbeaux tilts her head so the perspective on a wheel changes. The wheels spin like records; the grooves emit an eerie light. Appearing on the spinning wheels she sees a decrepit dark graveyard with a flowering tree leaden with heavy golden blooming flowers. Dark human shapes also hang from lines of rope in the branches. Everything in shades of gray, black and white. Except for the golden flowers which are open and fragrant.

Go to the tree. Rainbeaux's hand reaches out to touch a flower. The flower falls into her hand. It burns. She grabs her hand in pain. Then the flower falls from her hand to the ground. There the flower morphs into a human corpse. She can't help but stare at it. Leathery skin stretches over dull white bone. Empty eye sockets. Frazzled hair sticks up straight. The mouth open in a permanent rictus grin. Two hands stick up as it to grasp at her.

All around her the flowers turn into hanging people who scream and flail around on the branches.

PANIC! She pushes through the HANGING SCREAMING PEOPLE. See Happurstadt swing back and forth. See Shneed swing. See Derek Yancy with his bloody hole in the center of his torso and his guts hanging out. See Nancy Yancy. See Aziz fight the noose as he swings toward and away, again and again.

A soft glow creeps into the scene. The light grows stronger and brighter as though someone is entering the garden graveyard. Rainbeaux turns to see Marilyn shine in bright full color compared to the dull grey colors of the scene. Marilyn sits in a tall tree away from the hanging tree. Bright red flame encases her. The tree doesn't burn! The flame's illumination makes her appear as the only living person there. She holds out her hand to Daisy. See Daisy take her noose off. See Daisy hold the noose out to someone off screen.

See the Entity in heavy trench coat and floppy hat move among the dark heavy branches. Crouches over like a movie villain from the twenties or thirties. He breathes heavy. He turns toward Marilyn and runs away.

The light on the screen and within Rainbeaux grew dark. She woke from her trance holding a series of pictures she drew while she was under. She carefully placed these down on the couch. She turned a light on. She looked down at her hand and rubbed a mild burn in the shape of a flower in the center in her palm. "That's never happened before." She worried about Sam. And what did this vision mean about Marilyn?

CHAPTER 25

Sam turned off his cell phone as he entered Hills Cafe on South Congress Avenue. He scanned the few late night patrons in booths and on stools. He saw Aziz at the bar hunched over on a stool at the counter surrounded by the debris of coffee and cigarettes. Odd, the City hasn't allowed smoking in a bar or restaurant in years. Aziz glanced at Sam at the same time. He turned away in an attempt that would surely fail to keep Sam from seeing him.

Sam walked over. "I got a problem."

Aziz didn't look around, "Go see Jesus."

Sam said, "Everyone I know is telling me things I can't believe."

Aziz said quickly, "Choose to believe something anyway."

"It's not just that I believe, I want to know what happened in the Red River Motel."

Aziz said, "Getting down to it. Alright. I don't know. Have to ask the parts."

Sam was firm, "Then ask them."

Aziz turned toward him now and shook all over. "Different memories with different parts. Have to put it together." He was quiet a moment. Then, "Aziz diseased. Aziz diseased. Aziz, Aziz, Aziz. Diseased, please Aziz."

Sam asked, "Are you Joe Bear?"

"Can't be Joe Bear now. He saw too much."

"It's safe to tell me."

"Not here. He'll die away from the tree."

"Die? Someone threatened him?"

Aziz rasped out, "He falls from the tree and burns like a flower in the hand."

Sam alarmed. His first thought ran to her. He whis-

157

pered, "Rainbeaux." Then to Aziz, "Is she in danger?"

Aziz jumped up. Sam reached for him. Aziz pushed Sam out of the way and ran out of the dinner. Sam sprinted after him.

Behind Sam the waitress reacted to Aziz's booth. He had put a glamor on his booth so no one would see him smoking there. She looked as though blinders were taken off and she saw that Aziz had been smoking in her section. She ran to clean it up before anyone noticed.

Outside Sam had to stop and look for Aziz. He saw Aziz jump on a city bus headed north. He dashed to his car and followed the bus. Unaccountably, it began to rain. Not unwelcome in draught afflicted Austin. But it was difficult to see who got off the bus through the rain and the dark.

Then he had an idea. Sam cut over to Lamar via Oltorf Road. He drove up to Fifth Street, turned toward Congress Avenue and parked downtown close to the Warehouse District that went down to Second Street. He walked to the alley where he caught Aziz a few days ago. Sam was right on. Aziz was there as though waiting for him.

Aziz turned to run but Sam ran Aziz down in the rain splattered alley. Sam held him up and said, "Talk to me. I can help you."

Aziz shook his head, "I have many different people living inside me. Not all of them trusting."

"I really don't have time for this now. Why don't you come down to the station with me? I'll get Brenner."

Aziz trembled and shook, "Not Aziz anymore."

"Who are you then?"

"Guess."

Sam pulled at him. "Let's go." Aziz pulled back. Sam thoughtful and though it pained him to do this. "Can I speak to Aziz please?"

Whoever this was now said, "Aziz is tired and must rest."

Sam continued to go along with it, "I want to speak to Joe Bear."

Aziz went through another visible change, "It's me. I wasn't tired. I was hiding."

"Why?"

"You know too much. Joe Bear says that you must do as he does, not as he says."

Sam firmly but gently took Aziz by the coat collar. They began to walk. After a few steps Aziz slipped out of his coat leaving Sam to hold that and his medicine bag. "Hey Aziz, you forgot ..." He held it up but Aziz was gone. Sam dropped the coat and bag and took off the general direction that Aziz must have fled.

Behind them a hand appeared out of the darkness and took the medicine bag.

They ran through the warehouse district. Sam chased Aziz into an abandoned building by rusty railroad tracks. Aziz disappeared inside. SLAM! A metal door clamped closed behind him just as Sam caught up. He jerked at the door; it was rusted shut. "Naturally," he said to himself. But then it didn't make sense that was rusted shut if Aziz just went through. He moved to a window. He broke the glass and climbed inside.

Once inside Sam stopped to listen. He was rewarded with the crunch of broken glass. Sam followed the sound. Then he heard the sound of footsteps in a fast run. Sam began to run toward the sound. The walls around him began to distort and bend. He stopped and tried to reason this away. He was tired, ill, dizzy from lack of breath. The walls continued to change and shift around him. He saw Aziz looking back at him from a distance away. Sam began the chase again. He ran after Aziz through a disorienting labyrinth filled with strange LIGHTS and passages that twisted and turned at odd angles. Sam stopped when he hadn't seen Aziz for a few minutes.

159

Then he heard Aziz address him from out of the dark, "You got to learn to be an honest man."

Sam was breathing heavy, "What?"

Aziz continued, "An honest man respects a locked door."

Sam heard Aziz run again. He tried to keep up.

Aziz shouted to him, "Reason the doors locked. Stay out of the maze."

Then Sam saw Aziz and the chase was on. Aziz led Sam through rooms that changed in size and made Sam and Aziz appear that they changed in size; larger to smaller then smaller to larger. Sam felt like he had run a marathon in ten minutes.

Finally Aziz got to a door that led to an intersection of the mazes.

Sam found himself standing on a catwalk above Aziz. He tried to talk but the words wouldn't come out, "Ten minute road race, marathon."

He stopped and tried to force himself to catch his breath. "We seem to have come a long way in a short time."

"Here, my son, time turns into space." Aziz had stopped in an open area surrounded by mirrors that led into more mazes. Aziz raised his arms. "Follow the maze and you become lost, see? They have you in the maze."

"This is crazy. Come with me Aziz."

"You have your way out to a world beyond flesh. Strings attached."

Sam pulled his firearm. "Put your hands on your head. Step toward me."

"I'm not afraid because we aren't real. Just parts of the Dreamer's mind. But the Dreamer is dead, undiscovered and hidden. We are just the figments of a Nightmare waiting to wink out."

Sam cried, "That isn't true. I'm good. I'm okay."

"You haven't learned anything. Not even that you are trapped."

The buzzing rang in Sam's ears again, "Liar. Lies. All lies."

"If only you believed what was happening to you." Aziz appeared terrified. "It's time."

Sam squeezed his eyes shut. A rumble felt through the air and through the cat walk as the mirrors shook. Sam opened his eyes. Sam reached for Aziz with his gun hand. "Aziz!" The Deep rumble caused the mirrors to wobble.

Aziz appeared more peaceful than he ever had and said with total acceptance, "I enter a World Beyond Flesh."

Then the mirrors exploded sending shards of glass flying in a tornado around Aziz. He covered his body with his hands and arms. The flying glass sliced Aziz into a thousand gory bloody pieces.

Sam looked at his hand, saw the gun, smoke curling out of the barrel. Sam dropped the weapon. It fell to the floor of the catwalk. He had a hard time looking up. And when he did, all that was left of Aziz was a bloody pile that was not recognizable as human anymore. All of a sudden they were ...

Outside the warehouse. Sam stood on the ground close to the remains of Aziz's corpse. Crime Scene Investigators and police officers worked the scene. He saw Hane direct some officers into the warehouse. Then Hane waved Brenner through. He frowned at Sam.

Next thing Brenner handed Sam some coffee. Had he lost time again? Sam said to Brenner, "All I wanted him to do was come back with me."

Brenner was calm and soothing as he spoke. "And you say you were somewhere else?"

Sam trembled he must have told Brenner something about what happened. He couldn't remember what he had been saying. He knew he had to be careful about what he said. "I can't explain it. I don't think we were in the warehouse. We weren't out here."

Brenner was worried about Sam. He changed the subject slightly, "I haven't heard from Ms. Le Blanc yet."

Sam looked at the bottom of his empty coffee cup. "We're not talking."

Brenner asked gently, "I see. Everything okay between you two?"

Sam shook his head and turned away.

He went back to the office. It was six in the morning and he had been up all night. He wanted to go home but there was a message from Happurstadt to come see him at eight. Sam went to the cafe and ate a small breakfast with coffee. Then he cleaned up in the locker room showers.

Soon he was before the man. He didn't want to be there. Happurstadt was unpredictable and Sam didn't know what to expect. This time Happurstadt was fatherly. He sat with a kindly frown on his face. They discussed what happened with Aziz. Sam paced around the room as he argued for a new theory in an effort to tie this case up. Sam ignored the issue that he may have murdered Aziz. Best if Happurstadt brought that up.

Happurstadt didn't appear to be concerned about Aziz's murder or whether Sam did it. He said, "Well, okay, I buy your story about what happened in the warehouse. But I'm sorry, I don't make Aziz as the killer."

Sam reached the barrier of a large bookshelf. He turned and walked back across the room, "What about using the words the killer wrote on the wall? The World Beyond Flesh."

"Good try, son, but no dice. We need to push on with the case against Daisy Yellow Yancy."

Sam was unhappy to hear that, but unexplainably relieved too, "One more thing. Yancy's pornographic material disappeared from the evidence room."

"I'll have someone look into it."

"You'll keep me informed?"

"Naturally."

Sam started to say something but Happurstadt gave Sam a look. Sam felt confused as the buzzing in his head started again. He simply left the office.

CHAPTER 26

After Brenner got home he was so worried about Sam that he couldn't sleep. Specifically he didn't want to believe that Sam could kill anybody. It was true that Sam's behavior and demeanor were in conflict with someone who had killed another human being. Sam had called him to come out to the crime scene, not something a guilty person would do. Then Sam didn't appear to remember that he had called him. He also appeared confused as to what he had said. Brenner could discern that Sam was confused about what happened until the other detectives explained it to him. He displayed appropriate remorse at Aziz's death.

On the other hand Aziz was shot dead and it appeared that Sam had done it. Sam didn't remember shooting Aziz. Brenner felt and thought everything in a jumble. There was shock, doubt, pity. This situation felt worse and worse to him. He wondered if he had trusted Sam too quickly. He knew of one person who could help him understand Sam.

He returned to Rainbeaux's house. He liked it, her house, he immediately felt comfortable there. But he felt bad that Rainbeaux was uncomfortable. Upon hearing what had happened with Sam she started pacing around. Her thoughts became more scattered the more she talked. Brenner looked at her drawings from her session the night before. He didn't have an opinion other than the artwork was beautiful.

They talked about what had just happened with Sam. He tried to explain that this is why he sought her out. He wanted to help Sam and knew they were close. She said, "Once Sam was initiated into the cult he was compromised." He didn't have an opinion on that either. He didn't

165

believe in magic or the supernatural. He believed that people deluded themselves about certain ideas. But he wasn't going to bring this up with Rainbeaux. He kept silent mostly. When she said, "Why are you so quiet?" He had to say something. "I'm thinking," he allowed.

She picked her drawings up again. "Because I go so right brain in session, I can't make heads or tails of what I see."

"Your analytical skills are shut down." A self check. Not only did he not believe in what Rainbeaux said, or did in her Psychotorium, he knew that Chessman didn't either. He felt like he was hiding something from her. And a part of him wondered how long he could. A curious thought: If she doesn't have extrasensory powers, why worry ...?

"There has to be something here to help us." She had her first drawings of the labyrinths too.

"Rainbeaux, Sam just shot Doug Jamison in cold blood. They were out in public and there were civilian witnesses."

"I thought you said you couldn't believe that he did it?" She put her drawings down. He thought she looked more than defeated. He felt his terrible compassion for her. She continued, "What did he say about what happened?"

"He said they were in a warehouse. He was chasing Doug, Aziz, whatever alter was present. There was some kind of wild explosion of glass. But the witnesses said Sam just walked up to Aziz and murdered him."

"Sam didn't announce that he was a detective? He didn't try to arrest him first? But what about the differences in the two stories? If Sam said ..." Her voice trailed off. She was exhausted.

He waited then said, "Clearly he was in a Dissociative Fugue."

She was silent. She didn't say anything so he picked up

her drawings and looked at them again. "How do you get interpretations on these?"

She said, "Back at Fort Meade we had a team who looked at them. Recently Sam has been able to see the patterns or whatever in them." She let out a small "Ha." Then, "I wish I could talk to Sam."

"I don't know if we can do that anymore." It occurred to Brenner that maybe this wasn't his call to make. He felt protective of her and of Sam. He felt even more sympathy for her in her desperation.

She dropped the paper on the table. "Roswell said that we couldn't trust Sam. I refused to believe it but after this. Do you think maybe I've been putting Sam in more danger by including him? I don't want to hurt him anymore than he is hurt already. But I want to talk to him."

"I would like to help him too."

"That's it." She gathered up drawings. "Sebastian I don't want to lose him. Not to anything but especially not this thing that follows me around."

"It may be more complex than the Entity just following you around. This is something that, if it truly exists, is intruding on our world. I get that it isn't comfortable for you but Sam is either a homicidal maniac or about to twist off. I don't want to believe that. Or he is connected to this Entity on a very deep level. Which I doubt." Ouch. His protection of her wasn't helping him edit what he said.

She suddenly realized that she hadn't heard Brenner talk this way before. She knew suddenly that he doubted her. She pushed it aside. "We need to talk to him. Let's do it together. That will make us all safe."

Brenner agreed. This may be the best way after all. Maybe now they would know for sure.

A cell phone call and Sam met them in the conference room down the hall from her office at the Federal Building. Rainbeaux sat down beside Brenner and across from

Sam. She spread several sheets of paper out on a table. "Here are the results of my session last night."

She looked at Sam as he studied the drawings. That he wouldn't meet her gaze made her more uncomfortable being in the room with him.

Finally Sam commented, "This isn't a pattern like the labyrinths. This is a deep organic connection. And Marilyn. That is a striking drawing of her."

Brenner offered, "I was looking for connections between the killers and their victims. That often leads to us to the killers motives and builds a profile. I was thinking that we set a behavioral trap for the killers before they strike the family."

The three looked at the pictures for a moment. Then Sam said, "There is an organicity here that is missing from the first set of drawings about the labyrinth. There everything was part of an interconnected but artificial system. Here we are part of a living system. This goes back to what Aziz said about how he would die apart from the tree. Like a flower dies when it falls from a tree and rots. He said he falls from the tree and burns in the hand."

Rainbeaux glanced down at her hand. The burn in her palm was still visible. And a little painful. What Aziz said shocked her.

Sam continued, "Comparing the first sessions with this latest one. It is almost as though the artificial system is imposed on or wait, no, make that modeled after a created order. As though we are being manipulated by this system into doing things we don't want to do. We are fooled by the similarity of the artifice to the organic. Then there's Marilyn here. Something about that rendering is so familiar to me. I've seen it or lived it at sometime in the past. I don't know where. Okay, I get it now. To us she is this abuse survivor. But she has this outlandish show where she performs and struts on the stage."

He stopped so Rainbeaux took over. "But here she is a divine figure. Like what Jung said about how we choose to be and our shadow self. Only Marilyn has a positive shadow from the looks of it. And together with the photos and video we recovered, a person to be followed. Or kept repressed." She furrowed her brow.

Sam picked up again. "Also I see a pattern here." He pointed to features of the tree of corpses and the labyrinth. "A numerical pattern based on twelve."

"Wow, twelve?" she drew that out. She smiled a little surprised at this.

Brenner saw what Sam meant and did some quick calculations. "Adds up to one hundred forty-four."

She bit her lip. "Of course. Twelve in a coven. Twelve covens. But also twelve signs of the Zodiac. Twelve tribes of Israel. Twelve months in a year. Add it up."

Brenner got up and began to pace. He kept an eye on Sam, "When I first met you we discussed how the killers were part of a cult of assassins."

She said, "A long lived cult it seems like."

Brenner continued, "And it seems to come back to Happurstadt, the Yancys, Shneed."

Sam appeared doubtful, "No, this doesn't make sense. If they are in some kind of conspiracy why commit murder and then get us involved in the case?"

Rainbeaux said, "I've been thinking about that. It's a difficult nut to crack." Then the idea hit her, "They play us because they need us to track another murderer down for them. A rouge assassin in their coven."

That stopped the conversation for an moment while they processed that. She continued more hopefully, "Sam, was Aziz the rogue agent in their coven? Is that why he died?"

Sam became defensive, "I didn't kill him."

"Sam, they are using you." She almost said that she

had been trying to warn him. But she didn't want to come off like she was saying I told you so. While she was stumped about how to proceed, Sam traced his finger along a pathway in the picture of the young man in the labyrinth. He was solving the puzzle of the maze. Then he was stumped. He said, "You left the CIA because of something you found out."

"Before I left, they hypnotized me, so I'd repressed the memory. But now I feel like a memory is coming back. Something about sleeper agents. I can't be sure."

Brenner's voice was comforting, "I can offer to use a mild hypnotic trance to guide you through your memories for clues."

She nodded. "Okay, but not here."

"Where then?"

"At home. My home. Get ready, Sam. I'm gonna school ya," she said with a smile. Sam liked it, the first smile she had given him in days.

CHAPTER 27

When they arrived Sam saw that in her living room, Rainbeaux moved the couch next to the love seat. A papa san chair and a rocking chair opposed the couch and love seat. Rainbeaux sat on the love seat. Brenner moved the rocking chair in front of her and a little off to the side. Sam hung back on the other side of the room. He looked at Rainbeaux like she was someone he couldn't touch. That same feeling of desperation that something or someone you want is beyond you now. That you will never have them again. He worried that Rainbeaux watched him with suspicion as he sat.

She stood in front of Sam and made a little speech. "Thanks for coming over. There are things I don't know. Or I did but don't know now."

Brenner asked, "Things about the Entity? About your federal service?"

Sam watched her answer, "Yes. They wouldn't let me waltz out of there knowing what I know." Sam felt her eyes on him as she said, "I want to know for certain what happened. Why I really left."

He watched as Brenner gently refocused her attention to him. Sam moved out of her line of vision. Brenner said gently and evenly, "This won't be a remote viewing session. This is basic hypnosis."

She nodded, "I can induce it myself. I'll raise a finger when I'm ready." She leaned back in the chair. Her head nodded slightly. Sam thought it was too fast when immediately one finger went up.

Brenner said softly, "What memory is important to you now?"

Rainbeaux furrowed her brow. She began to speak and

told this story:

"My most salient memory was from the night I left home. I was just ten years old. I remember my childhood home in New Orleans Louisiana. I don't remember specifically what happened. I do remember I stared at a large tree limb outside my bedroom window that partially obscured the view to the outside. I sat on my bed, my face wet with tears. I stared down in shock. My clothes torn. A broken doll and a music box lay at my feet. My stomach churned waiting for something to happen. I didn't know what would happen, but wanted it to be over as soon as possible.

"Visible through the open door, AC, my asshole father, and Cheramie, my mother, argued in the living room. In a far corner, my Uncle Nate sat and stared and smoked a cigarette; a bottle of cheap beer at hand. The dim light from a cheap lamp made him look yellow and cast a long shadow from him across the living room.

"While AC yelled in the other room I fell over on my bed and wept bitterly. The music box played a sad children's lullaby; my favorite. And it kept playing while everything was going on.

"The words I could make out when AC hollered loud enough, 'It ain't nothing but a thing. 'Sides, she brought it on herself. It's her fault.'

"Cheramie yelled back at him, 'Stop.'

"I tensed up as AC burst into my bedroom. He was yelling at me, 'You told. You ruined everything. What're you gonna do now, cry? Come on, cry for me.'

"I shot up straight and fought back the tears. I didn't want to let him see me cry. Just then Cheramie forced her way in. With great effort she pushed him out. I was hopeful this was almost over. I raised my hands to Cheramie, 'Mommy?'

"Cheramie took a hard leather belt and lifted it over

her head."

Sam saw Rainbeaux's features hardened then a single tear that drifted down her cheek. She said, "After that beating I waited until everything calmed down. About four AM as I recall. I slipped out the window and split and pretty much lived on the streets of New Orleans with my friends. I raised myself. I spent most of my time dodging pimps, cops, drug dealers, social workers and homeless men. I would sneak back from time to time and nick a few dollars off my old man when he was too drunk to notice. My granny would give me something to eat. So would the nuns at Saint Louis church.

"One of them, Sister Amelia Agnes, tried to get me to come to school. I refused. I didn't want to have the sisters call the cops on me. I knew enough to stay out of juvie.

"But one day she offered to show me how to paint. She said she saw some doodles on my cloth bag. I was intrigued. I followed her into the school. I picked up a paint brush. In no time at all I was painting. It was a liberation. It was like lightning struck me. Then I noticed that several hours had passed. No cops.

"So I went the next day and the next. Sister Amelia couldn't spend all her time with me so after showing me some basics, I was usually left to myself."

Brenner asked, "Did they give you instruction on anything else?"

"I went to church but didn't attend catechism class."

"I meant to ask if you went to school?"

"Yes, I went to classes. During the day it was almost like I was a normal kid. The good times with friends at the school and the painting lessons were enough to provide a needed respite from the bullshit on the street. Plus I was fed at school. And the sisters would give me personal items like a toothbrush or a comb."

"Is there a memory of anything that happened on the

street that is important now?"

"Naw," here Rainbeaux almost sounded like a teenager. "It was dangerous though. I mean it wasn't just pimps, regular guys, dudes who came into town for a ball game or to party tried to pick me up even when I was eleven or twelve. It disgusts me that the younger I was the more turned on they were.

"There was this one time when I was about fifteen. I was hanging out in the City Park, late at night. I think I had four friends with me that night. We had a little cash so we bought some food. Then we thought someone was chasing us. So we ran down the street together. Then we all stopped under a street lamp. We shared some Chinese fried rice out of a paper container. I was getting thirsty. Just as I said, 'Now I want a coke,' four preppie pieces of shit drove up in a big convertible. I remember a little kid with them. Couldn't have been more than eleven himself."

Sam heard this and was wide eyed almost panting. He would have been eleven then. And he went into New Orleans with his older cousins all the time.

"They looked us over and started to smirk. The Preppie Driver sneered at me. He hopped out of the car and grabbed my shoulder. 'Look at this. Prime stuff, gentlemen.' His friends laughed.

"I stood between my friends and the preppies. I said, 'Fuck off, asshole,' as brave as I could.

"The Driver made a face like he couldn't believe I talked to him like that. He was like, 'You know who I am? You know what you are?' And stuff.

"I turned my back on him, I don't care.

"The Driver grabbed my arm which scared the shit outta me. He was laughing when he said, 'You're just a dirty kid.' Then he pushed me down and stood over me. 'Beat it, dirty kid, don't make me fuckin' puke all over you.'

"I pushed up off the dirty sidewalk. I was crying and

backing away when he said, 'Whenever I want you, I'll have you.' He laughed at me as my friends ran away. We escaped to the park. I never saw him after that.

Sam felt a quietness all around him for a moment. He looked at her and Rainbeaux just breathed.

Brenner said, "We can stop now if you want." She shook her head no. He asked, "How did you get money to live?"

"I made spare change painting street portraits in the French Quarter in the tourist areas. Most of the time now I could scrape up enough to rent a cheap motel room. It wasn't nice but it was a place to sleep where I didn't need to keep one eye open. So no matter how bad things got, and they could really suck most of the time, it also got better. The day it got amazingly better I was out on my usual corner. It was a bright sunny day. I had just rendered a painting of a classy dressed woman. The classy dressed woman smiled at her portrait. She asked how working outside affect my technique.

"I told her that it helped. Working fast sharpened my style.

"She said, 'I don't know. I think a more thoughtful approach is the best way to go for you. I'd like to talk to you about your education.'

"She handed me a business card. The name on it was Betsy Carnahan. I don't know even today if that is her real name or not. My friends said I made a 'cho co' face. She had written a sum of money on the back of the card. She said it was to pay for my education. I wondered what she wanted for that money. But for all I knew, it was also my ticket out. I called her and said I'd take her offer."

Brenner was thoughtful. "This was a big step for you. You didn't trust many people. How did you know to take her up ?"

"I did talk to some people about it. My friends agreed

with my suspicion that she wanted something for that money. I knew girls who were lured into the sex trade. I didn't want that. Sister Amelia had a different set of concerns. She didn't say what they were. But she said that this woman had been poking around for months. She said this woman was a recruiter. Again not for what or who. But as long as I wasn't gonna end up hookin' I wanted out of there so bad I took a chance. I took the money and the Amtrak to New York City."

Brenner asked, "Did you see your family before you went away?"

"Sure. AC wasn't home when I went by that last day in New Orleans. Cheramie was there. I told her what happened. I told her I had already chosen a school in New York. I had the money in a bank account. My first bank account ever. We stood outside our old house. She watched me put my bags in the trunk of a city cab.

"She was anxious and asked, 'What you reckon a sixteen year old girl like you is gonna do in that art college in New York City?

"I snapped, 'Dry up, Mom' at my old lady. She said that no good will come of this. I told her that someone liked my painting and I've got a chance. Either be happy for me or go to hell. I was snappy. I was still just a little girl but didn't know it.

"I remember getting to New York. I was worried that someone would throw a bag over my head and I'd end up a strung out hooker on Times Square. But the money Betsy Carnahan gave me was legit. As long as nothing bad happened I quickly took advantage of my situation and made a lot of new friends. But my strongest memory was meeting someone who would make a great impact on me."

"Who was it?" Brenner asked though Sam could guess who it was.

"Roswell Hane started out as one of my classroom instructors. Art Appreciation 101 instructor if you can believe it.

"After a year I had already started to get some attention for my work. Roswell kept up with me. Not in a creepy way. But in an interested professor way. I had become addicted to coffee and was sitting outside covered in paint fresh from an all night painting marathon. Roswell walked over and offered me a cup of New Orleans style chicory. We hung out on a bench in a common area.

"He said, 'I found your latest work, Ghosts in Old New Orleans, to be quite interesting.

"That was actually a painting that other people seemed to ignore. I said I paint what I see.

"He said, 'You see ghosts?'

"I told him for sure. Ghosts are real to me, so is clairvoyance, so are dreams of the other places. So are my visions.

"I saw him take extra interest in that statement but didn't think anything of it. Not until later. He was very interested in my visions. What kind and how often I had them. Under what circumstances.

"I told him they could be spontaneous. That they came in dreams. Sometimes I felt that nothing was real, the world around not real but all a dream. Then I could have a vision. Visions of the past, the future, where things are. When I said 'what people hide', he smiled mysteriously. I couldn't make it what that smile meant either.

"A few months went by. All was well. Then during a student exhibit everything turned inside out again. At the student art exhibit people milled around and looked at work in a variety of media; oil paintings, sculpture, conceptual pieces and what have you. I was there with my boyfriend of the weekend, Felton. I walked arm in arm with a pale skinned young dude sporting an ironic late eighties style Mohawk haircut with blonde and green streaks through it. We enjoyed checking everything out. Of course Felton was checking me out too. When he finally just happened to look at my arms he saw the scars from razor thin cuts that went with my self-mutilation. He wanted to know if I had an accident.

"I told him, 'it ain't nothin' but a thing, dude. Sometimes, you cut just to know you're alive.'

"He was saying that he wanted me to cut him too when I saw something that sent a chill down my spine. I stopped by a piece that featured a broken doll with a music box. A sign on the sculpture read PRESS ME. Next thing I knew Felton was waving his hand in front of my face. He said I stared at the piece transfixed, what he said was I was in a trance. I hesitated then pressed the button. The music box played a sad children's lullaby, the same song on my music box back home. No surprise when the piece triggered all the painful memories I had locked away. I freaked out and screamed and ran around the gallery.

"One doesn't normally say that time passes quickly in a psychiatric hospital. For me it seemed that time accelerated. I passed that time in a room with pale green and yellow walls in an uptown facility.

"Good old Felton was there. He said I was running and screaming 'I'm not falling!' And that everyone in the gallery was staring at me. He said he tried to cover for me. That it was a performance piece. Within thirty seconds men in uniform carried me out while I fought them and screamed profanity. My fellow students, gallery visitors and instructors watched in horror.

"When some nurses came in he argued with them about whether he got to see me or even stay. He told them he was my boyfriend. He was still at it when Roswell appeared on the scene. He looked at Felton and with a shake of his head Felton was carried out. It took two burley staff to remove him. I heard him yelling but his voice grew dimmer as he was shoved and pushed down the hall. The last I would ever see of him.

"In a daze I watched Roswell present documents to a male nurse. The nurse nodded his head. Then he patted me on the shoulder. Somehow I wasn't reassured. He led me away with two other men in plain clothes with Federal Marshall badges pinned to their jackets.

"In no time at all I was flying, the only passenger, in an Air National Guard C-130. I sat strapped in a seat facing Roswell. Just the two of us and I didn't even know enough to wonder why I got such special treatment. He sat across from me with a bemused smile on his face. I wanted to kick his ass and wipe that smile off. But I was still and quiet not sure what had happened or what was going to happen next.

"Finally I said, 'It's cool, no one in my family finished college. I'm just one of the dirty kids; we don't amount to much.'

"He replied, 'Don't worry, Ms. Le Blanc, you will finish school. You will finish a lot of things you have started.

"I thought about that for a moment not sure what he meant. I asked slowly, 'Where are we going?'

"I remember when the three large sedans carrying us pulled up to the guard gate at Fort Meade, Maryland. I remember when he said, 'Home.' He must have said it earlier when I asked. But I associated home with Fort Meade.

"After entering the base we took a winding road toward the back of the military reservation. The sedans stopped in front of a set of small indistinct concrete brick buildings.

"He announced, 'Project Danse Star, the US Army's Remote Viewing program.'

"I didn't understand what that meant. Yet. So I asked, 'The what program?'

"Roswell turned in his seat to face me sitting in the

back. I sat between two large Federal Marshals. He asked if I ever heard of psychics being used as spies. I was puzzled, but intrigued.

"After resting in a small bare room overnight, I started with breakfast, which I didn't feel like eating. I enjoyed the coffee though. I asked if it was Maryland Club. Roswell was amused at that.

"Then I met a psychologist and took a battery of psychological paper and pencil tests. Then interviews about my experiences. From the abuse at home, to my visions, to my art, and how I survived on the street.

"According to my shrink I was diagnosed with Dissociative Disorder Not Otherwise Specified and Borderline Personality Disorder. The shrink explained to me that the BPD was a specialized adaptation to Post Traumatic Stress."

Sam wondered if Brenner agreed with that diagnosis, having made it many times himself at the community mental health clinic against his boss's orders.

"I began two year's worth of psychotherapy. I learned meditation. How to relax instead of cut myself, how to tolerate distress and boredom without seeking excitement. How to distinguish between my thoughts and feelings and those of other people; boundaries in other words. I learned impulse control. One by one my dysfunctional behaviors faded. Some things I experienced didn't.

"I remember the day I officially entered the program. It was two years later, I was sitting on a couch in Roswell Hane's office. He sat in a chair next to his desk. He said, 'Your psychological treatments have gone very well. Your symptoms are fading. Yet you still report that you see spirits and foretell the future in dreams?'

"I told him I grew up in New Orleans believing the spirit world is right next to us all the time.'

"That's all well and good but there is more to your talent than culture. We have a position for you. You will be well paid and receive full benefits while continuing your college education.

"In no time I picked up the skills they taught me. It was typical that I would lie upon on a couch. I was medically monitored though for a long time I didn't know why. A large mirror on one side of the room. I knew it was a two way mirror. Later I learned that Roswell used to brag about me. He and the other managers in Danse Star had determined I had an accuracy rate of ninety- five percent against the typical RV's seventy-five."

Sam saw Brenner writing this down furiously on a note pad. Brenner asked her, "I'm interested in why they put you through so much psychotherapy?"

She remained passive. "They didn't explain. So I read literature from Russia, Brazil, China, Israel, anywhere a government has a Remote Viewing program. I discovered there was a problem with RV's going insane. Most RV's have traumatic childhoods. But it was our native dissociative skills and creativity that was interesting to the men like Roswell who ran RV programs. They wanted us to develop coping skills to keep us grounded. Of course, things still went awry.

"It didn't happen all the time, but I remember the handful of times it did. One incident was especially bad. And led to my leaving.

"I was in the office monitoring an older RV who was sort of my mentor, we called them spiritual companions; Margot Haliwell. Margot had more advanced training than I. She and Roswell wanted me to enroll in her program. I had thought about it but I didn't know much about it and wanted to learn more first.

"She was using her special skills that day. It seemed like a safe session when she began to spasm and the medical monitor's red light flashed. Then she went into a full seizure. Roswell and I rushed into the room together. By then Margot was fully convulsing and screaming on her couch. Roswell didn't look at me. He simply said, 'shit', under his breath. I thought about that later. It wasn't important at the time. But later as I reflected on it, it seemed he knew something and he was afraid I would find out.

"Meanwhile I tried to help her. I tried ground her, "Margot? Are you okay? Margot, listen to my voice. Follow my voice back.' I said a lot of things I was taught to say. Distressingly it didn't work. I feared that she was lost to us. I had never seen it this bad before.

"Roswell and I escorted Margot to a large stuffed chair. She began to whimper, 'He saw me! That face! Not human. From nightmare.'

"I tried to listen to what she said. 'What's she saying?' I asked.

"I knew him well enough now to know that even though he was playing cool for me, he was scared shitless. He tried to dismiss my concern, 'She's babbling. Get the doctor on call. We'll have to commit her.'"

To Sam Rainbeaux was clearly agitated, squirming in her papa san chair. "Understand that by this time any misgivings about the government; the CIA and DD were past. On one level I had finished grad school, had two master's degrees, had nice things, I had money put away. On an emotional level, this was flowers in a vase with a nice dinner instead of eating out of a trash can or begging the Sisters. It was a frosty beer stein full of premium bock instead of warm coke with some strangers spit in it out of a can.

"On yet another level, this incident reminded me how dangerous our work can be. Mostly I was concerned about Margot. I did remote viewing sessions on my own. I didn't have anyone I could trust there. So I took them to Margot while she was in the hospital. She didn't want to talk at first. Then she looked at my drawings. She directed me to the records room. She told me the code to get in. I went there and I came across a document called the Velvet Morning File, the official agency report on what happens when Remote Viewers go insane. They wanted to use that information in unorthodox and creative ways."

Something in that statement stirred Sam. It hit him in the gut and seemed to shake something loose within him. Something he fought. He got up and stepped back. "My god. If we could prove that." He started to feel as though he were waking up after a long hard sleep.

Brenner ignored Sam. He asked her, "How were they going to use the information?"

Rainbeaux relaxed again, "I'm not sure. I had a bad feeling about it."

Brenner appeared angry and said, "Promoting corporate interests over the welfare of the people."

She continued, "There was a related report on the Mabuse Project. But when I got into that, I encountered ... what Margot saw."

Then she doubled over in pain. Sam ran to her side. Brenner asked, "What is it? Rainbeaux, are you with us?"

She said, "It's hard for me. It's so blocked." Sam came to her. Rainbeaux looked at him in fear. "Get away from me."

Sam looked down and saw his arms reflexively ready to punch ... Horrified at himself he backed away.

Brenner was soothing, "Let your body relax." He waited a moment. "If you need to stop, we'll stop."

From behind them Hane said, "I need you to stop."

Sam turned, alarmed that someone could sneak up on them. Rainbeaux was still under and not entirely aware he was in her house.

Roswell Hane stood in the entrance to the living room. His agency badge worn on his coat pocket. He was terse. "Put a stop to it, now."

Sam was defiant, "You aren't going to come in here and order us around in Ms. Le Blanc's home."

Hane smiled cruelly, "You are naive. I like you."

Brenner tried to negotiate with him, "Special Agent Hane, I'm sure you know that we need to bring her out of this gently."

He nodded, "By all means. And it's Director Hane."

Brenner returned his attention to her. "Rainbeaux, when I count to three, you will gently wake, feeling refreshed as though you had a restful sleep and pleasant dream. One. Two. Three."

Rainbeaux opened her eyes as she came out of the trance. She opened her mouth and screamed as loud as she could. She put her hands to her face and sobbed uncontrollably. Brenner and Sam were jolted by this. Even Hane was concerned for her. As she continued to scream, her eyes wet with tears, Sam moved to her. He reached out to touch her shoulder. When she felt his hand on her shoulder she yelled, "What the hell are you doing?" She screamed, "Get away from me."

Sam jumped back.

Brenner sat on the floor in front of her. "Is it okay if I sit next to you?"

She nodded her head yes as she broke into a sobbing fit. Brenner continued while Director Roswell Hane watched him like the German shepherd guard dog Sam had as a child, "What do you need us to do for you?"

She was blunt and direct and sounded angry through her tears, "Leave me alone."

Brenner said softly, "We can do that but we want to know that you are safe."

Rainbeaux gulped air as she tried to relax. She struggled to slow her breathing, "I'm okay." She looked at Hane, "What's he doing here?"

Sam spoke up accusingly, "He just showed up. Wanted

us to stop."

Hane stepped toward Rainbeaux. He said to Sam and Brenner, "I don't owe either of you an explanation." He directed the next to Rainbeaux, "Remember our agreement, Special Agent Le Blanc." Hane turned to leave.

She said, "You're using another RV to spy on me."

Hane wagged his finger at Rainbeaux, "Keep your nose clean, mind the rules, trust me not to violate your rights."

As Hane left, Rainbeaux gathered herself, she began to calm down. She even got some of her sense of humor back, "And to think I feel absolutely no reassurance as he says that." She almost kind of laughed.

Sam offered, "Maybe I should stay. I'll sleep on the couch."

She said to Sam, firmly, "No." She said to Brenner, "Will you call and let me know both of you made it home okay?"

Brenner said, "Sure. And I'll check on you too."

Sam picked himself up. He left in a hurry. He hoped it hurt Rainbeaux. He stood in the yard while Brenner spoke to her at the door. She held the door open and asked, "Stay while I check the house?"

"Sure."

Rainbeaux ran toward the back of the house. He listened for her footfalls but he was too far away. When Rainbeaux returned she appeared sheepish and vulnerable. "It's, I'm, okay."

Sam waited for Brenner on the front lawn. He fought the consuming jealousy that welled up within him when Brenner was allowed to bid her a good night. As Brenner walked to Sam, Sam was very loud. "Brenner, what the fuck was that all about?"

For the first time Brenner was angry with Sam, "Chessman, keep you voice down. This isn't about you."

Sam said, "I didn't think it was."

"There is a reason she repressed the memory."

"I'd love to argue that but Hane showing up was too creepy."

"At least we agree on that."

Sam looked down, "I'm going to worry about her all night."

Brenner walked past Sam to his car, "Maybe you should."

Sam's head snapped up, "What's that supposed to mean?"

Brenner got in his car started the engine and drove away. He left Sam on Rainbeaux's front lawn. Sam looked at the house until the buzzing started again. He grew even more tired. He finally got in his car and went back to his apartment.

CHAPTER 28

Rainbeaux slept fitfully for a couple of hours. She woke as she began tossing and turning in bed. She opened her eyes and stared at the ceiling. She hated the fact that she was too tired to sleep. Irritating.

Then she went over her list of troubles. Something evil from beyond this world won't leave her alone. Her boyfriend isn't the coolest guy in the world anymore. She's wrapped up in a murder involving mentally ill assassins and pieces of a dead serial killer's brain. She corrected herself on the assassins. These people aren't mentally ill, she thought, they aren't crazy, just survivors. They went through an adaptation to the violence of their family of origin. Just like she did. Or tried to do.

Then it really hit her. She, and Sebastian and Sam, hadn't given enough attention to the lobotomized remains of Cade's brain. Why did the cult want it? What did they get out of it? And the Entity who walks Worlds Beyond Flesh, what is his/her name? Is this the Entity she saw back in Maryland? And is it what Margot saw?

She trudged up the stairs to her Psychotorium. Went through her ritual and reentered her Zone.

Up on the screen before her:

Ants with oversized heads crawl around an ant farm. The words, MABUSE PROJECT in red letters beneath the ant farm. Then it all changes to the intricate complex labyrinth again. And the trees with the gold flowers overlaid on that image. Was this vision or memory? Or? As she realized she was trying to interpret the images she had come out of the Zone and the light on the screen had grown dim.

She went back downstairs to her kitchen. She brewed some tea and sat down to make sense of her newest drawings. She couldn't, yet. It was too soon after the session. She wished she could talk to Sam but didn't dare. By now the Entity would know who she was and what she knew if It didn't already. At least Sam knew more about her past. She hoped it would help him to humanize her. That was her plan to keep him from hurting her if that is what the Entity wanted.

In the meantime he hadn't wanted her to see Marilyn. But Marilyn was featured prominently in the evidence recovered from the Yancy home and in her visions. So going to see Marilyn. She put it on her to do list for the next day.

In the morning aftermath of another sleepless night she felt rather lobotomized herself. She trudged out the door to catch a bus. On the street a large black sedan pulled up to the curb next to her. When two Federal Marshals got out she threw her hands up. "Okay, I'm coming."

Soon she was in the Federal Building sitting in front of Roswell Hane. He tried to look more pissed off than he was. She didn't have to pretend. "So, givin' me the hairy eyeball?"

He replied, "Come on, you knew we'd be watching."

"Watch this: I want the Mabuse Project Files."

"That program doesn't exist."

She was firm, "I still want to see it."

He remained relaxed in his chair, "The file is classified."

"I'm employed here again. So classify me and hand it over."

"This is useless. You know I can't admit it exists much less let you see it."

"It has bearing on the case."

"If it does, then I'll obtain the necessary intel from the file and incorporate ..." (that into our plan.)

"Spare me the Big Brotherese." Rainbeaux let her fatigue show to Hane.

He said in response, "This is why we let you go." Then he frowned.

Rainbeaux was shocked, "WHAT? You let me go! I quit!"

Hane nodded, "All the more reason to not let you see it."

She paced around the room. Angry. Sullen. She hoped Hane knew he was in trouble. He asked, "So did you have any effect on Chessman?"

"I don't think so. Some maybe." With her answer she let him change the subject.

"Has he hurt you?"

"Not yet. The potential is there."

"You seem unusually rational about it all. Considering."

Now Rainbeaux felt her energy leave her. "I'm worn out with worry. Listen, I appreciate your concern, but let's progress this investigation. If I can't see the files that will help us solve the case, I want to interview Marilyn."

"You don't do field work."

"Make that will do. I intend to interview her."

Hane thought about it. Or pretended to. "She isn't at home today. She's recording. May not be the best time to question her ..."

"Doesn't matter, I'll get it done. Address?"

"I gave you her last name for a reason," Hane said as he slid a card with the recording studio address over to her. She knew the place. A studio on the east side, mid-town. "Thanks. I feel a little girl chat over coffee coming on." She gathered her things.

Hane tapped a pencil on his desk. She knew what that meant but ignored it. Hane was going to have to talk.

"One of the most distressing things we discovered, after you left, was that all that Christian stuff about cosmic powers fighting a battle inside our bodies." He stopped.

"Yes?"

"It's true."

"I know. Maybe not exactly as they said. That is what is going on with Sam. I know he wouldn't hurt me if it were just him, you know, alone in there." She sat her things back down.

"You can tell me more if you like. You have been closed off." He tapped his pencil then confessed, "We both have."

"This doesn't go back a couple of generations. It goes back centuries."

Before she could explain that it was just her opinion, Hane said gently, "We don't know about the old man. We do suspect that he is part of a coven in Houston. But then there are many powerful people in the US and throughout the Western countries who worship the Beast. The Beast protects them. They protect him."

Rainbeaux understood what he was talking about, "It's the old patron client style relationship from the ancient Mediterranean societies. Like in The Godfather. Only we're talking gods of a minor order. Demigods."

Hane smiled weakly and shook his head. "Exactly. You know what's in the file already. You have any idea what's going to happen when we try to tackle this Thing?"

"I haven't thought it through. But then, I'm, you know, terrified."

"I have. This could cause us to lose everything."

"Even our lives."

"Especially our lives."

She picked up her purse again and stood. "And Goodbye to the United States as a major power."

"Do you have any idea what THAT will mean?"

"At least we'll own our soul again. Clean and clear. There's power there too. The most important kind."

She left.

The black sedan dropped her off at the recording studio. It was located in the part of town known as East Sixth Street, where gentrification was started but not finished. She walked through overgrown weeds pushing up through the concrete sidewalk. She stopped and regarded them for a moment. She turned and pushed a buzzer at the front door. Someone inside unlocked the door. There was a loud CLANK. A breeze of air con. She was in.

A receptionist directed her toward the back of the building. Rainbeaux walked down a long unlit hall. She could hear music. As it grew louder, she could pick out a tune from the sixties. The door was open and she entered the studio. Marilyn was singing Some Velvet Morning the old Lee Hazlewood and Nancy Sinatra song. Rainbeaux thought of the documents she saw back at Fort Meade. Was more of her memory coming back? Was this a trigger? The producer and recording engineer hardly looked up at her as she entered and sat down.

Daisy was there. She was hanging back against a wall. Her head nodding and keeping time with the music.

Rainbeaux saw Marilyn smile at her while she sang. Marilyn sang both the male and female parts. Perfectly. She even seemed to be switching personalities while she sang. Rainbeaux walked back to stand by Daisy.

She looked up at Rainbeaux and winked at her. Soon the music stopped and Marilyn came out of the booth. She hardly looked at Rainbeaux. "I guess you want to talk."

Rainbeaux looked over at the piano player discussing something with the producer and engineer. "Let's get some privacy."

Then the recording engineer turned and looked at Rainbeaux. He quickly turned back to the discussion.

Marilyn yelled over her shoulder, "Takin' a break." The producer waved her away. "There's benches and a table out back. Stop by the soda machine?"

191

A short walk and a visit to the vending machines. Rainbeaux ran her credit card through the card reader. "Grab what you want from the Skinner box."

Daisy and Marilyn laughed as they pressed buttons. "Thanks for tha can o' diabetes, baby," said Marilyn.

They sat outside under an awning at the long wooden tables. Marilyn motioned toward the studio, "I like it here. Art reveals things you know? Reveals your soul, your innermost thoughts."

Rainbeaux asked, "What does Some Velvet Morning reveal about your soul?"

Daisy giggled, "What a question!"

Marilyn pointed to her nose. "Depends on I open your gate, right?"

Rainbeaux said, "First, whatever you spill to me you spill downtown, agreed?"

Marilyn said sharply, "No."

Rainbeaux replied, "I'll find people you can trust."

Daisy said, "That sounds like a threat."

Marilyn elbowed her and said, "Like your hunky stud muffin; Sam the He-Man?"

Daisy took her finger and wiggled her nose. Suddenly more grown up she said, "You know he's like a closet? Walk in."

Rainbeaux saw Daisy fiddle with her nose. "Figured that out," was all she allowed.

Marilyn pushed closer to Rainbeaux, "We'll get to that later. Right now let's talk about you and me."

Daisy almost yelled, "Marilyn, that's enough."

"Jealous much?" Marilyn shot back. Her hands seemed to cramp. There was pain on her face. Then her hands released their tension. Her face relaxed.

Rainbeaux noted that too. She pressed on, "About Sam being walked in on?"

Daisy changed again, now she was completely child-like, "We better not say."

Rainbeaux lowered her voice, "This Entity who possesses you, is he or was he once human?"

Daisy whispered, "No. Never human. But he wants to be in human flesh."

Rainbeaux remembered what Hane said, "And Sam? He didn't just blunder into this, did he?"

Daisy's eyes went wide, "He wants Sam pretty bad."

Rainbeaux could have cried. She remained stoic, "Why?"

Marilyn was matter of fact as she answered, "Given to Him. Poor daddy, so deluded. They all are. They ain't gonna get what they think they're gonna get."

Rainbeaux choked back her tears. It was true. Offered up as a human sacrifice from the time he was a child.

Marilyn reached out to stroke Rainbeaux's face. She was seductive as she spoke, "Does it matter why He wants Sam? You've put yourself at risk, too."

Rainbeaux grabbed Marilyn's wrists and pushed her away. She demanded, "Tell me more about this Entity."

Marilyn turned away. Daisy touched her lightly on the back. A soothing gesture. "Our cult worships an Entity who commands angels, or demons maybe, who each created different parts of the human body."

Then Rainbeaux snapped to the idea about different parts of their bodies being activated when they switched personalities. You could see it when they changed.

Marilyn looked at Daisy. She continued, "He says his worship is very old. Older than written history."

Rainbeaux knew she was pushing it now, but she was getting somewhere, "I need the name of the Entity that you worship."

Daisy put her fingers to her lips, "Shush. We can't say the Name. He comes if you say His Name."

Rainbeaux asked hoping that they weren't too at-

193

tached to this Entity. "Does the Entity have to leave if you use His name to order Him away?"

Daisy nodded her head.

Marilyn turned back around, "Hate to rain on your party but He's gone by different names. Hell, He's been worshiped as both male and female."

That was something Rainbeaux didn't foresee, "I hate it when a god can't decide on a gender."

Daisy said, "Finding an identity is His or Her quest."

Marilyn burst out laughing wildly.

Rainbeaux was thoughtful then she realized something. "Of course. He has to ..." She thought, *differentiate.*

Daisy said, "He hears us. The walls can't keep Him out forever. We have to go."

Rainbeaux said, "Please, let me help you."

Marilyn leaned over and quickly kissed Rainbeaux passionately on the lips. "Meet us at my place in two hours."

The door opened and the producer stuck his head out. They broke off their meeting and Rainbeaux left before Marilyn got back inside.

On the way back to the office, Rainbeaux called Brenner and Sam. Then when she got to the office she debriefed Hane what happened and invited him to her house too. She told him that they were going to include Sam and Sebastian in the planning.

Hane said "I have to object."

She was firm, "I have to say I don't care. They are part of this. They can help."

"But," Hane said.

She cut him off, "Even if Sam is compromised he still has insight into my visions."

She let Hane win, sort of, the debate on not letting her see the Mabuse File. He didn't argue this matter now.

CHAPTER 29

When she got home, Brenner was waiting there for her. "I recognize one of the people from your picture."

"Brilliant," she said. "Can the big reveal wait until the others get here?"

Brenner answered affirmative. It wasn't long until Sam and then Hane showed up.

While Rainbeaux led Sam, Hane and Brenner into the living room Brenner said, "The man, the father of the family in that photo and from the drawing; it's Michael Fong Torres. He was an investigative reporter. In the mid-nineties, he wrote some scathing articles about Satanic Ritual Abuse, DID, that's multiple personality disorder, not your agency. He's a professional skeptic. That's how I know him."

Rainbeaux said, "Why didn't an internet search of his picture give us his identity?"

Hane said, "He's protected."

She said, "Until now."

Hane picked the picture up. "I'll call the man at the desk and have research find out where he is. We'll figure out the rest later."

As he left the room to make the call Rainbeaux said, "I won't be surprised if he is anywhere but here."

Rainbeaux waited until Sam sat on the large couch, then she sat cross legged in the middle of the love seat.

Brenner took the rocking chair. He leaned forward.

Rainbeaux started, "While that cooks, let's talk about how to deal when we find this guy and his family. Things look mighty bad. But I think there is a way out of this. Are you willing to listen?"

Brenner said, "Yes, I am."

Sam looked at the floor, "To be honest, I find I can't trust anyone but I trust you."

"I'm in." Hane appeared behind them again. He had already finished his call.

Rainbeaux nodded her head and relaxed. "The memory of the Mabuse Project is clearer. An Entity, a demon or a fallen Angel, whatever, entered the minds of the RV's."

Sam blurted out, "That must have been helpful." Then he hung his head. He knew he shouldn't have said that.

Rainbeaux continued, "The Entity caused them to go insane. We watched It build a system of people He can inhabit, much like someone with multiple personalities."

Sam laughed inappropriately, "Only he has multiple persons."

Rainbeaux thought, *and He, She or It seeks a physical identity*, as she got up and walked to a book case. She selected a book bound in leather, with iron hinges and an iron clasp. She placed the book on the table. She took a heavy iron key, placed it in the lock on the clasp and twisted it. There was the scrape of metal on metal she unlocked and opened the book.

"I went to see two of the inhabited people today. We don't have the name, but I learned how to discover the Entity's name and cast it out of our world."

Sam sneered, "That quite a book."

"I'm being pretentious. I have the paperback copy right over there."

She motioned with her head to a bookcase that leaned against the wall.

Sam went over and retrieved the paperback. "I hope I don't have to do any VooDoo shit."

Rainbeaux tried to control her reaction to Sam. She said simply, "Knowing the Entity's name will give us power over It."

She saw Brenner nod his head and look like he wanted to say something. She thought he would say this Being is symbolic of something or other.

Rainbeaux flipped through the book, "From my interview and research I learned that the assassins' cult taught their followers that different demons made different parts of the human body." Rainbeaux pointed to a picture and related passage in the book. The passage was a demonology, a list of demon names. "The name of the Entity may be similar to one of these names."

Hane said, "That's quite a list."

Sam said, "Not too precise either."

Rainbeaux said as evenly as she could, "This isn't a science as you understand it, Sam. They may have the name translated incorrectly. Or it's a local variation of the name."

He asked, "Is there an English version of the name?"

She replied, "Most likely."

Brenner joined in, "Any ideas on how to confirm that name?"

She said, "We know The Entity has a way in and out of His worshipers that allows Him to possess them for a time." She watched Brenner react. "You have a synch. I just know it."

Brenner said, "In my therapy with people for DID, they sometimes associate a sensation in a particular part of their body to a memory. That memory triggers an alternate personality to take over. Similarly the Entity entering the host may elicit a mood state associated with a certain part of the body and a corresponding sensation."

She smiled, "I saw that today actually. So as a tactic calling attention to a person's somatic pain to find out the Entity's name isn't perfect."

Hane had been silent until now, "But it's a shot."

BEEP Sam pulled his cell phone out. He looked it and

frowned. Then he put his phone away.

Brenner asked, "What is it?"

Sam said, "I have an appointment with Ms. Van Horn to discuss her conspiracy theories. I can cancel."

Rainbeaux was thoughtful. "It couldn't hurt to pick her brain. I would like to know if she's a player or a scene chick."

Sam said, "Really, I can cancel."

"Why don't you two go ahead," said Brenner.

Sam shrugged, "Hey, it's not too late to cancel."

Rainbeaux shook her head, "I want to hear."

Sam was defeated, "Time to hear about the government cover up of UFO evidence and the Trilateral Commission and whatever." He got up to go.

Rainbeaux got up to follow him out the door, "I think the Trilateral thing is passé now, Sam. Try Bilderberg Group."

Brenner looked at them and said, "Be careful."

Rainbeaux turned and looked at him. She smiled slightly, a bit puzzled.

Brenner answered her, "People into conspiracy theories tend to identify with them. If you challenge the theory too much they take it as a personal affront."

Now Sam nodded his head toward him as a sign of acknowledgement.

"Report back to me," said Hane. Brenner looked at him. Hane looked back and shrugged his shoulder.

Soon Rainbeaux and Sam were sitting in front of Virginia Van Horn. She seemed a little put off that Rainbeaux was there. They met at an East Austin eatery. A funky place that recalled Austin's hippie era.

"The thing is," she started. "Democracies fall under their own weight. It was only a matter of time before it happened here."

Sam smirked, "Who's taking us over? The Illuminati?

The Gnostics?"

Rainbeaux elbowed him on his arm the only place she could reach.

Van Horn had seen it of course. "The super-rich." Van Horn took them by surprise. This sounded half way possible. She continued, "Certain wealthy individuals are rigging elections. Buying influence."

Sam laughed, he thought of his father and his friends taking US Senators from Texas and Louisiana out for cruises on their yachts, use of private jets, private boxes at the stadium and that was just a start of what Sam knew. He had seen it as he grew up. "Sorry to break it to you but that has been going on a long time."

She shook her head. She was used to this. "People in the US make jokes about it. We have assumed it was true. But now it's happening. It's not a joke and not something we can laugh off anymore."

Rainbeaux sensed that Sam was more agitated that usual about this. She was worried and anxious because she literally didn't know what Sam would do next. She came out of her mild daze to hear Van Horn say, "They have coalesced around something. I don't know what. But it brings them together in a way, well, they haven't been united like this."

That hit Rainbeaux like a gut shot. She had been wrong about the patronage thing. This made more sense. The Entity wasn't just being worshipped by these people, S/He/It was actively leading them. And the influence was getting stronger; just like with Sam.

Van Horn continued, "As bad as it's been, it started getting worse in the early seventies. That's when lobbyists started gaining more influence on Capitol Hill in DC."

Rainbeaux said, "Right, I remember seeing something on TV about that recently. As the lobby organizations got permission to spend more money on elections, they got a foothold with Congress and the President."

"Now it's gotten to the point that they actually own at least four members of the Supreme Court. I mean in their back pocket own. And that isn't all. We are on the verge of a financial melt down."

Sam laughed and Rainbeaux interrupted him. "This wouldn't have anything to do with wanting to believe that the trust fund is safe until you can ruin it?"

She saw Sam fight the urge to slap her. She regretted bringing that up in front of a co-worker. She had been unkind and she would beat herself up over it later. He was irritating her more than she allowed herself to admit.

Van Horn continued because she wasn't paying attention to them, "They have gotten the SEC regulations relaxed to the point they are comatose. The regulators too. And don't get me started on the oil industry."

Rainbeaux let out a long, "Hmmm. Okay, let's think global and act local. How is that playing out here? In terms of what are the local actors doing to prosecute this group's agenda."

Van Horn took a moment to think. Then she spoke very rapidly with pressured speech. "They did something that is so horrible I dare not speak it. A blasphemy so egregious it cannot be forgiven. The Beast was at least transcendent." Here she lowered her voice, "He could not operate on the material plane. He was beyond it. But they used unholy magics to open the door so that He could live here physically. The Beast wants to live here like a man."

Rainbeaux thought her a bit melodramatic but, *if this were true ... damn. Who did this? How to hold them responsible?*

Van Horn blathered on, "The Beast and his followers used them. They were just four kids. One of them was a young man you'd know, Douglas Jamison." Here Van Horn breathed hard and slowed down.

Rainbeaux saw Sam react. He felt what? Guilt? They hadn't discussed it but Sam was there when Aziz died. She still wondered what happened.

"As a young man, Douglas got involved with an archaist group."

Rainbeaux interjected, "You sound like you knew him pretty well."

"I did back then. I defended him in juvenile court. He was charged with murdering another student in his high school class. Now I regret getting the charges dropped."

Rainbeaux said gently, "That was your job then. You did your best for him."

Van Horn almost cried, "I managed to move heaven and earth for him once."

Rainbeaux continued, "Surely you know about some of the more esoteric activities."

Van Horn nodded her head as she began to cry. "I do."

"And your opinion?"

Sam became more agitated, clinching and unclinching his fists but kept to his seat.

"He was an angry young man. He reached out into the ether and something reached back for him. From the Abyss."

Sam suddenly got up knocking his chair over.

"It overtook him."

Sam paced frantically around. Rainbeaux didn't know what to do. She let Van Horn continue.

"He met others with the same, erm, interests."

Sam slammed his fist down on the dining table so hard he should have broken every bone in his hand. "Enough!"

Van Horn was startled but continued. "They met often. At midnight in the graveyard."

Sam looked like he would explode. Rainbeaux said to him, "That's enough. Let her finish."

Sam pushed off the table. He ignored the patrons of

the restaurant staring at him as he glared at Van Horn then Rainbeaux. "Don't forget to breathe." She really shouldn't have said that, the veins on Sam's head throbbed.

Van Horn was still talking. "They met at midnight. Trying out their spells or whatever."

Sam stormed around the table. Rainbeaux thought that the manager was going to kick him out. She thought of ways to get him out of there. He was too dangerous and unpredictable. Then she picked up on the next part of Van Horn's story.

"There were two other boys and a girl. Douglas led them out into Asylum Street's Lobotomy Graveyard. The Daemon that led them out there took them to the grave that held the remains of Quelle Cade's brain. Cade was a murderer who served the Beast in his day. The howling wind, the pouring rain, the others wanted to run away. But Douglas was a good disciple. He convinced them to stay. They fought the growing madness, dug through the muddy ground and brought the box up."

Sam yelled, "Lies! All lies! There was nothing there!"

Now Van Horn shouted back at him, "What happened there drove them all mad."

"They knew what they were getting into!"

She cried back, "They were just teenage kids! They didn't know! They didn't know what that was or what it would do to them!"

The restaurant manager, a gentle man with a pony tail came up to them. "Uh, guys, is, uh, everything cool here?"

Rainbeaux nodded at him. She gently put her hand on Sam's arm. Then on Virginia's. "Sam," was all she said.

Sam seemed to gain some control of himself. He pushed away from them and ran out of the joint.

The manager asked, "Is he okay?"

Rainbeaux nodded again.

Van Horn was sobbing now, "The girl died. Douglas told me how she was killed ... He never forgave himself. The image of her and what was done to her never left him. He wanted to die because of that. He wanted it. The release of sweet, sweet oblivion. But he isn't going to get that is he? Will he be punished forever? Oh, the burning ..."

"I don't know. There must be a goodness out there that we can trust." Rainbeaux wondered if Brenner knew this. She had been in therapy for years. And knew that for all the good it did, there were times when you let the therapist lead the session such that some subjects were never discussed.

"The others?" Rainbeaux gently prodded her.

"Their lives were ruined. The other young men died within a few years. Drugs, no surprise there, huh. Still I'm suspicious. One died of an overdose, the other in a deal gone wrong. But I wonder. It's easy to get rid of someone with that identified problem. The police practically collude with the killers to cover it up."

Rainbeaux stayed with her and let her talk for a few minutes. Virginia was heavy into grief but okay, so Rainbeaux went out to find Sam.

He was sitting in the car holding the steering wheel with white knuckle intensity. His eyes were squeezed shut and he was breathing heavy. The first thing she saw was that every vein in his head and hands looked ready to pop. Immediately Rainbeaux felt a love for Sam that was stronger than her fear. She opened the driver's door and touched him lightly on the shoulder. "Buddy? You okay?"

Sam looked at her with anger, "So I'm just your *buddy* now?"

She was reassuring, "Yes, we are friends. But never doubt that I love ..."

She couldn't finish. Sam began to cry and turned to her. They put their arms around each other and cried together. Sam said, "I'm so lost don't leave me."

Rainbeaux finished her statement, "with all my heart."

So there they were, she squatting beside the unmarked car. Sam half turned in the seat with the police radio blaring.

It was awkward even humorous if you were in the mood so she said, "Hey look at us."

Sam released her and turned from her. "We better go."

She didn't argue. She got in on the other side. As Sam started the engine, "Listen," here she almost said *buddy* again, "Sweetheart, maybe you should take a couple of days off."

"You really think they will let me do that?"

"Maybe the best thing for you now is to ..."

"I'm not quitting." Sam was tense. She realized that she was ordering him. This wouldn't work.

"You know me so well. I just want to look out for my boyfriend."

Sam smiled at the word boyfriend. Rainbeaux took it as a good sign. "Right on. If we're gonna work, tell me what you want me to do."

"I like that attitude. Now." Then Sam was silent. Rainbeaux didn't take that as a good sign.

She said, "Virginia Van Horn knows a lot more than we suspected. You know that makes her a target now."

Sam turned up Red River Street. "I'll take you home, see if you can dig up anything on those other kids. I will go back and check on Ms. Van Horn."

Rainbeaux didn't think this was a good idea. She was afraid of Sam's potential for violence toward Virginia and he was in enough trouble already. However, she knew better than to cross him. She would deal with this another way.

"Alright, it's a plan," she faked being pleasant and agreeable.

After Sam let her off at her house, she didn't go in right away. She watched him drive off. Then looked across the street looking for Daisy. She hoped that Daisy was there watching her house. She wanted to protect Daisy now that she was the target of Happurstadt's wraith. She wasn't there. Rainbeaux hated the thought of her in jail. After that she went inside and called Roswell. He said he would send a couple of agents to watch Sam. Nervous, she rang off. Then began her internet search for the other kids in Aziz's coven.

CHAPTER 30

After Brenner and Hane discussed Michael Fong Torres role in debunking multiple personality disorders among other things, they left Rainbeaux's house. Hane went back to the office to find the Fong Torres family and try to effect a rescue.

Brenner drove to Marilyn's house. He sat outside a few minutes. This was really against professional ethics. He tried to justify it and couldn't. Then he said to hell with ethics.

He walked up to Marilyn's door and rang the bell. He was surprised when Daisy Yellow Yancy opened the door. She jumped and clapped when she saw him. Then she ran off leaving him unsure of what to do. He stuck his head in the door. "Daisy, may I come in?"

Daisy ran back around. "Yes!" she called out. Then ran away giggling again.

"I'm glad to see you out of jail. What happened?" he said as he entered.

Daisy yelled out from another room, "Momma got me out. She still has money. Don't know for how much longer though. That's what she says."

Brenner looked around the place. He saw the French door leading to a dining room. He looked at the furniture and the paintings on the wall. He wasn't big on the style. It struck him how unlike it was for someone with Marilyn's diagnosis to keep her house so clean. Or to put so much thought into how she decorated it.

Then Marilyn slowly opened the French door and came into the room. Brenner realized he wasn't familiar with this alter. She wore her hair in a beehive do, a little black dress with a pearl necklace and high heel shoes. She smiled licentiously at him. She strutted into the room taking a step with each word she uttered, "How utterly exciting that you are here." Now she stood almost toe to toe with Brenner. "Whatda think of the place?"

"A bachelorette pad from the swingin' sixties?" he said weakly. Now he remembered why his profession had ethics. And boundaries.

She saw how uncomfortable he was and this excited her even more.

Just then music started blaring out of speakers hidden around the room. Daisy reentered the room and began to dance around. Marilyn joined her and they lip-synched the song. They danced their asses off in front of Brenner. Jumping up on the couch or a chair. Jumping off and dancing in a circle around him. It was a happy upbeat song and Marilyn's face expressed every sweet emotion.

Brenner was embarrassed and struggled to find words. He couldn't so he stood there and looked as embarrassed as he felt.

Sam decided he didn't want to deal with Van Horn again. So he drove to the county building on Eleventh and Guadalupe after dropping Rainbeaux off. It was getting late but he thought it was odd that the building was empty. Usually there was someone here 24/7.

But not tonight. No one worked late getting their case ready for trial. No other weary DA Office detectives returned from late night interviews or record searches. No security guards. This was not like the county DA offices at all. He didn't like it.

As he rounded the corridor to his office he heard a loud scream. Sam ran down the hall. He recognized Van Horn's voice as she screamed again. He got to her door. He grabbed the handle but it was locked. He put his shoulder to the heavy reinforced door and forced it open.

When he entered the room he saw Van Horn sit in the corner crying. Then the masked man who stood over her. Sam pulled his weapon but the masked man turned with lightning speed and knocked the firearm from Sam's hand with nunchucks. Goddamn nunchucks. Sam couldn't believe it but the sudden sharp pain in his hand told the story. The man faced Sam and he saw that he was a ninja. The unreality was replaced by the reality of physical trauma as the ninja kicked Sam in the midsection. Sam stepped backward as the other's foot connected with his midsection and absorbed the blow. He stepped in and swung at the ninja and connected with his jaw. Then had to dodge those nunchucks. The ninja swung the nunchucks again and a row of Van Horn's UFO conspiracy DVD's exploded over Sam's head. Sam threw a half shelf of books at the ninja. This caught the ninja off guard while Sam body slammed him. The ninja fell to the floor.

Sam looked for his firearm but when the ninja started to get up Sam kicked him on the knee. There was a spine tingling snap of bone. The ninja pulled a knife and came limping at Sam again. Sam saw his firearm laying close enough to Van Horn that all she had to do was pick it up.

Meanwhile over at Marilyn's place, Daisy took a swing with an imaginary katana, a Samurai sword, in the her dance for Brenner.

Back at Van Horn's office, Sam yelled, "The gun, throw it!" But Van Horn huddled in the corner in terror.

As the ninja thrust the blade at Sam he dove to the floor. In one motion he retrieved his firearm, rolled to a kneeling position, turned and fired.

The ninja dropped to the floor as Happurstadt burst through the door. Sam aimed at Happurstadt.

Happurstadt stood looking at Sam. When he said, "Put that away. Help me."

Sam looked at the floor where the ninja lay. There was

no one there. He looked at his hands. His knuckles were bloody.

"You have splinters in your hands," Happurstadt said.

Sam looked at his hands and saw wood splinters. Sam looked at his weapon. As he was examining his knuckles, he had the firearm pointed at Virginia. "I said put that away. It does no good now. They're coming, hurry."

Sam holstered his firearm.

Sam was still shaken by unbelief. But then after everything else, why not? "What happened?", he asked Van Horn.

Van Horn was shaking, "He came at me. I called for help. But no one responded. He started flailing around. He punched through the book shelves. He was in a trance. Then ...." She stopped talking and started crying.

Sam didn't like it. *Why weren't there county sheriff deputies or APD all over the place? How did Happurstadt know to be here to save the day? That one wasn't too hard to figure out; he wasn't. He was there to make sure she died.*

"I better call EMS and the police."

Happurstadt was grim, "Take care of the clean up. I'll back you up that someone attacked her. And see to Assistant DA Van Horn."

Sam almost said that was what he was afraid of. He knew he couldn't cross Happurstadt yet. "Let's get her to a safe house. Since they are after her."

"Of course," was Happurstadt's terse reply.

Sam made the calls. He expected to be there for hours but he hardly turned around when Rip came through the door.

Off Sam's look Rip said, "You called and I came. What's up?"

"Assistant DA Van Horn was attacked. Someone's making a statement." Sam knew he wasn't making sense.

How had Rip gotten there so quickly? "You must have been outside the door."

"I was just coming on shift. Plus, I always keep my ears peeled for you."

Sam wondered if he could trust Rip but was glad Rip had his back. Still he had to be cautious.

"What happens now?" Rip asked.

"Take Van Horn to a safe house. If she doesn't go to hospital first."

"No prob."

"Thanks man," Sam said.

Then the deputies finally arrived along with EMS. They gave Virginia a quick once over while Sam and Rip talked.

"Listen, don't tell anyone where you're taking her." Sam thought about it. "Not even me." Rip slapped him on the back, "It's not that. Don't let the info out."

Van Horn was released to Rip. Happurstadt stayed behind to answer their questions. Sam helped secure the crime scene. Then he returned to his office to write a report.

Later Rip told him how he quickly escorted her out and to a police safe house. Virginia cried all during the ride there. When they got to the safe house she wanted Rip to stay with her. Sam was surprised by how torn he was to do that. "How did you get out of it?" he asked.

Rip smiled, "I finally made the excuse that I was a patrol officer and that the job of staying with her was for the homicide bureau detectives. I left in short order. She was clinging and needy but then she was just assaulted."

"Attempted murder," Sam said. Then he snapped to the fact that he was genuinely empathetic to her. That pleased him. He felt hopeful. For himself and Rainbeaux and everything.

He and Rip parted. Rip had his shift. Sam filed his report and left for the night.

CHAPTER 31

Rainbeaux pushed back from her computer. She had just confirmed Van Horn's account. Or most of it anyway. She called Hane.

"I was about to call you," he said. "We are having a problem locating Michael Fong Torres. Every time we try to recover an address, the computer goes back to the search engine. The IT guys say they haven't seen anything like it."

She bit her lip. "Weird. We must be closing in on the Entity or Beast or whatever. Have your other RV's come up with anything? You want me to try?"

"No, and don't try anything yourself. This is getting more and more dangerous and I don't want to lose you. We'll keep at it with the computers."

She brought him up to date. "I found out that there were three other young people who helped Doug Jamison steal the pinch off Cade's brain. All of them are dead. The girl was a suicide. The other two young men were murdered but had their deaths covered up."

Hane said, "And maybe if we find who helped with the cover up, we will find more suspects. And use them against the Entity. There is something else. Several million dollars are being moved around in certain bank accounts we are watching. It's a wet work account. I'll keep you in the loop on that too."

They rang off. She could tell he was worried. As if all that weren't enough bad news, Sam called. She couldn't believe it when he told her, "Get this, a ninja tried to kill Virginia Van Horn."

Rainbeaux said, "What are they getting weird for? I'm not grocking this at all."

"And Happurstadt was there when I shot the ninja."

Just then Rainbeaux had a vision of Daisy making the cut with an imaginary sword as she danced for Brenner. "Sebastian is in trouble too. He's over at Marilyn's. And Daisy Yancy is there. I'm sorry I forgot to tell you she's out of the joint."

"Don't worry we're cool. I'll be right over." She thought it sounded like Sam threw the words into the cell before he ran out the door. Within minutes he screeched up to Rainbeaux's with the siren blaring. She ran out of her house and they took off.

When they got to Marilyn's Rainbeaux got to the door first. Daisy opened the door, sweating and breathing heavy. She looked them up and down, turned her head and shouted into the house toward Marilyn, "Company!" Then she slammed the door. Sam started to go around back when Marilyn opened the door very slowly. She led them into her home.

They entered the living room. Daisy was sitting cross legged on the couch. Brenner sat in on a dining chair. He was sweating too but not from exertion. Daisy laughed at him. "He got an eyeful."

Brenner turned to them. "It wasn't like that."

Sam said, "I would understand if it were."

Rainbeaux looked at Sam somewhat surprised. She addressed the two women, "So kids, what you been up to?"

Daisy was in five year old mode. She stretched her leg out, took her foot in her hand and pulled her leg over her head. Reveling the fact that she was panty-less under her dress. Rainbeaux pushed both Sam and Sebastian out of the room. To Daisy, "You go put some britches on, little girl." To Marilyn she said, "I never thought I'd say that."

Marilyn flicked her lighter on, lit up a smoke. "Kinda tough bein' a mom ain't it?"

"I wouldn't know."

"Not yet."

Something about the casualness of that remark struck Rainbeaux. She sniffed. "That wouldn't be that thar wacky tobaccy would it?" Marilyn blew some smoke right at her. "There's an officer of the court and a Federal agent in the house," coughed Rainbeaux.

Marilyn smiled when Rainbeaux coughed a couple more times. She shrugged, "I'm up for murder. What else are they going to do to me?"

Daisy reentered the room. She hiked her dress up. "I got on some breeches now. See?"

Rainbeaux went to open the door to let Sam back in, "Indeed, you have five pairs."

Sam said, "We can handle her from here." Before realizing what he said.

Rainbeaux arched her eyebrows and said with a smile in her voice, "I don't like the sound of that. And even less now that Miss Show-off can't keep her dress down." She said to Daisy, "You go to your room." Daisy left.

Marilyn appeared triumphant, "That's how a real mother acts."

Rainbeaux took Sam by the arm, "Why don't you take Sebastian home. I'll call you later."

Sam nodded and he and Brenner left.

Marilyn looked at Rainbeaux with a know it all smirk. "You aren't helping yourself," she said.

Rainbeaux tried to maintain her composure. "This is for Sam, and Daisy. And you."

"And you," Marilyn shot back. "It's all about you isn't it?"

Rainbeaux half squinted her eyes. "Excuse me? If you're talking about how I want to live, that is the good selfishness."

Marilyn snorted, "Whatever."

"No you don't get away with a 'whatever'. We need information. Members of your cult keep getting whacked. What do you know about that?"

"I don't know what you're talking about."

"How about Virginia Van Horn. She was snuffed tonight."

Marilyn glared at her. "She isn't part of ..."

Now Rainbeaux smiled. "Gotcha."

Marilyn turned red with anger, "She isn't dead anyway."

"Correcto-mundo. So it turns out you do know quite a bit. You know I can find out what you know. I'll bet you even know how I will."

Marilyn's eyes closed and she glared at Rainbeaux through slits. Her personality changed to a gang moll from the nineteen twenties. She had a Brooklyn accent. "Get wise to yourself."

"I can go home right now and ..."

"Get wise to yourself," Marilyn repeated.

Rainbeaux played prosecutor, "One word to my boss and you go down for the a whole bunch of murders." Marilyn glared at her. Rainbeaux continued, "But I want to help you avoid that."

Marilyn almost laughed, "Get wise to yourself."

Rainbeaux was frustrated and furious. She yelled, "How about you get wise to yourself?"

Rainbeaux saw the change in Marilyn's demeanor. As though a mask she was wearing broke. Her face relaxed and her expression changed. It was as though she woke and was seeing the world for the first time. Rainbeaux followed her powerful intuition. "When you say, 'Get wise to yourself', where do you feel it?"

Marilyn withdrew from her and moved around the room. She was trying to get her bearings.

"Where?" Rainbeaux pressed. "Where do you feel it when I say it to you?" Marilyn raised her hand to defend her face. "Please don't. No one goes in there."

"Why, because no one has spoken to your core personality?" Marilyn nodded her head. "Who is it?" Marilyn shook her head. Rainbeaux tried again, "Get wise to yourself."

Marilyn deepened her voice when she said, "No one is allowed here." Then she broke into a string of high pitched gibberish.

"Am I talking to Reburta? It's okay. You know me. Rainbeaux Le Blanc."

Marilyn slowed down her speech as she withdrew further to the other side of the room. "No one can come in."

"Get wise to yourself. Where do you feel it?" Marilyn touched her nose. "Of course," said Rainbeaux, "this is where breath, the spirit, enters the body. It brings life."

Disco, she thought, *this is where the demon goes in and out*. She said, "When you feel it in your nose, what name comes to you?" Marilyn shook her head in terror. "You can tell me."

"No I can't," Marilyn said.

"Some call it the Beast. Is that good enough?" Marilyn backed away. She didn't want to lose her. Then Rainbeaux followed her powerful intuition. "Is there someone inside you who can protect you from the Entity?"

Marilyn responded by placing her trembling hands over her heart. She reminded Rainbeaux of a statue of the Virgin Mother she saw as a child in Saint Louis church back in New Orleans. "Go with that. Follow it. If I can't go there, you go there. Tell me what you find." Then Rainbeaux said gently almost tenderly, "Get wise to yourself."

Marilyn was still. Almost without breath. Then it was as though a cloud lifted off her. She was puzzled but she kept her hands over her heart. Now Marilyn's demeanor and personality changed. Unlike the other hard physical transitions to different alternate personalities this was a

peaceful transformation. She smiled simply and beautifully. Her eye color changed from deep green to slow light
green. She was radiant as though a clear bright gold tinged
light streamed out of her. She looked at Rainbeaux with
complete love and acceptance.

Rainbeaux was overwhelmed by that radiance that
flowed from her. A powerful psychic aura that she felt
went right through her. She felt that could carry her away
to paradise. And to a place of power. "Who are you now?"

"You made it, Rainbeaux. I am the core personality."

"Beautiful. And you are?"

"I am Mary Magdalene."

Rainbeaux was taken aback. For a moment she didn't
know what to say. Finally, "You're who?"

"Mary Magdalene."

"Okay, Mary. That, that's what I would call progress.
And we can tell Doctor Sebastian." Mary Magdalene
laughed at her awkwardness. She continued anyway,
"What I need is the name of the Entity."

Mary let it roll off her tongue like it was nothing to say
it. "Gadfan."

Once again, Rainbeaux was stunned. "That's it?"

"It isn't a name in the sense you are looking for. It's
Hebrew. It means 'The Blasphemer.'" Rainbeaux was puzzled. Mary said gently, "This isn't turning out how you im-
agined it, is it?"

"No."

"Here's the story, I really am the Mary Magdalene
from the Gospel stories. I return in a new incarnation each
generation to help people along their path." Then off
Rainbeaux's continued puzzlement, "Their path to salva-
tion and enlightenment."

"And the Entity, Gadfan, is here to stop you."

"Gadfan is here for a lot things. I'm in his way. So I
have to be killed off. Again."

"This has happened before?"

"Each life ends, Rainbeaux."

"Of course. To forestall that today what name can we use to defeat Gadfan?"

"He, and she, have many names as you were told before. I'll remember them all in short order."

"How can I help make that happen?" Mary looked at her simply with purity and grace. Rainbeaux felt like she should explain her hurry. All she came out with was, "We don't have much time."

Mary said, "I have countless lifetimes to remember. And all my alters from this life to reintegrate. I don't know how long it will take."

"Okay, multiple lifetimes and personalities coming right up. We'll hide you in the meanwhile."

Mary asked, "Where can I hide? This radiance you experience looking at me is a beacon to Gadfan and His Demon Army."

Rainbeaux was overwhelmed. This was indeed more than she expected. And if what Mary said were true about her being a beacon ... She replied, "I suppose my place is out. The DA's office have safe houses, but those are known to our enemies. I don't know."

"As it happens, I think I have several credit cards in various names. I could use one of those to get a room."

Rainbeaux wasn't sure it was that easy, "Unless they know the names."

"I don't have my memory on that yet. What do you suggest?"

Rainbeaux was thoughtful. "You use the alters, alternate personalities, to hide from them don't you?" Mary nodded yes. "Do you have a performance coming up? Or a town where you've performed before? You could check into a room there. It's not going to hide you for long but if they think you are going to perform you may move off their radar. For the time being."

Mary grinned, "I see what you mean. I know just the place. Daisy! Let's go!" There was no answer from Daisy. She grabbed a gym bag with her things in it. She held it up, "I have this for emergencies." Over her shoulder she called, "Daisy!" There was no answer. "Where is she?"

They looked around the house. As they got to the bedroom she used when she stayed with Marilyn, they saw that the bed was made. The room tidied up.

Mary said, "Her bag is gone."

Rainbeaux frowned, "It doesn't look like she was taken. Unless some neat freaks nabbed her."

"No, she must have left while we were talking. I'm sure it scared her."

Rainbeaux said, "I'll call Sam and Sebastian and see if she breezed out with them. If you're ready, let's skedaddle."

Mary turned and headed for the front door, "I just hope she's okay."

Rainbeaux said as she brought up the rear, "How long will it take you to remember everything?"

"It depends on everything," said Mary.

"And everything depends on you," said Rainbeaux as the door closed behind them.

CHAPTER 32

After Sam dropped Brenner off. He went back to the DA's office. Sitting at his desk but his mind was a million miles away.

A female secretary he had seen around the building came up to him. She said, "It's time." He got up and she led Sam to Happurstadt's office.

Shneed was there. He sat in a chair at the furthest point from where Sam would possibly sit. Happurstadt was behind his massive desk.

Sam took his seat. Nervous. Anxious. He sensed the tension in the air. As he looked around Shneed wouldn't meet his gaze. Happurstadt kept a steady bead on him.

"Detective Chessman, you have been a potential asset. It is time to put you into play."

Sam replied, "I don't quite know what you mean, sir."

"It is time for you to kill the enemies of our Lord."

Sam tried to buy some time by not responding right away. He was aware that Shneed was muttering. Sam followed Shneed's line of sight. An imagine of Baphomet, the same one he saw in Yancy's hidden room, casually sat among bric-a-brac and law books on Happurstadt's shelf. Sam thought that Happurstadt's gaze was boring holes through him. He almost laughed as he thought of his soul as Swiss cheese.

"I don't know who that would be, sir."

"Our coven has experienced problems as you and your friends have surmised. We need to rebuild. First we cut the dead weight. Starting with terminating Daisy Yellow Yancy, her mother Nancy, Marilyn LezElvis and your friend, Rainbeaux Le Blanc."

Shneed looked at Sam at last. "Not to forget that idiot

Brenner."

Sam shifted uneasy in his leather covered chair. "Sir, I don't know ..." He started to protest that Rainbeaux and Brenner weren't part of the coven.

Shneed grimaced and looked as though he could kill Sam right there. Happurstadt smiled. "I understand, son. I really do. You are surprised that I know so much. There isn't a thing in this world that you can keep from me. So if you are copacetic with me, I'll go easy on you."

Sam recognized phrases and phrasing his own father used. Suddenly the fear of the old man from his very young childhood returned.

"You remember how things are for her, your Rainbeaux. She is suffering. She is in pain." Suddenly the memory of every time Rainbeaux frowned or looked the least unhappy came flooding back to Sam. He felt foolish for not noticing sooner.

Now Shneed took over, "You do agree that she is in pain? Only you can make it stop. You want to help her don't you?"

"Of course. Anything I can do for her."

Shneed continued in soothing seductive tones, "No one else can do this for her. She won't accept it from anyone else but she will from you. To take it. All. From you. Only you."

Sam nodded his head. He understood.

"It must be you to end her pain. It is terrible for her. And only you can stop it. Out of love. You must stop her suffering because she loves you."

This went on for some time. Shneed repeating everything over and over. Sam being inundated with the thoughts of how happy she would be to be released by his hand. And of course the others would welcome it too. It was the only way.

They were interrupted by a call. Sam answered with

trembling lips. It was Rainbeaux. She needed Sam to come to her. It was just as they said! She was calling to him. She needed him. He was going to do right by her. And her pain would cease. She would be grateful to him and love him even more.

Sam took a pen and paper and wrote out where she would have gone with Marilyn. Happurstadt and Shneed watched him write the apartment's address down. He saw that they read what he wrote. He stood up, "Are we done?"

Happurstadt smiled and said, "You have something to do. Go on."

Sam left the office. Happurstadt lifted the phone handset off the cradle. He them talk. "I'm going to send some back up."

"Good idea," agreed Shneed.

"The Lord's power hasn't failed us before."

"This is just in case. It's smart." Shneed nodded as Happurstadt made the call.

Sam left, walked down the hall and out the door. As he started his car, he made another call to Rainbeaux. She gave the him the real address this time. A motel near San Macros south of Austin on I35. Sam was glad that they had worked out this precaution beforehand. The gun in his holster felt like it weighted a thousand pounds. He hated using it. But knew that he must end her suffering. He couldn't stand the idea that she was hurting for one minute longer.

CHAPTER 33

Mary drove them in her car down I35. She was singing the words from Some Velvet Morning. The road was crowded but they made good time.

Rainbeaux called Roswell. There was no answer. She was more than a little concerned. "That's never happened before."

Mary seemed to ignore her while she concentrated on driving in heavy traffic. After they got out of Austin and she couldn't see anyone following them Mary said brightly, "This is that Velvet Morning. From the song."

Rainbeaux thought about the project back in Fort Meade. She hoped it wasn't that kind of Velvet Morning. She asked, "I can't help but be as curious as a cat about your life with Jesus."

Mary laughed. "I'm still getting those memories back. It's the first memory since that is the central part of my soul evolution. What do you want to know?"

"There is so much I could ask, I don't know where to begin."

Mary laughed again, "We used the local Aramaic version of his name, pronounced ish-oo-WAH."

"That is interesting. What would that even look like in English?"

"It's Joshua but in Aramaic J is Y. Y is either silent or pronounced as a soft *i*. In English it is spelled as capital Y, then an apostrophe, then s-h-u-a."

"I suppose that's a good start. Was he as good a man as we are led to believe?"

"When you know someone in person it's different but yes, he was an amazing man. Natural leader. Wise. Funny too. Go on, hit me with another question."

225

"Dang we are almost there. And I want to know all of it."

Mary glanced over at her. "I want you to know. And I promise we will make it through this and I will tell you everything."

Just then she had to exit off the highway. What Mary just said gave Rainbeaux hope. Just the idea of learning more from Mary helped her feel better. She thought about if she could trust Mary. Was this really Mary Magdalene? She didn't know for a fact, but her gut told her to trust this woman. She looked up and out her window. A short trip down the frontage road and they were at the motel.

Rainbeaux lightly touched Mary's arm. "Let's make sure no one is here waiting for us. I hope you chose a no tell motel."

"They haven't exposed me in the past. I've always been fairly anonymous here." Mary winked at her which caused Rainbeaux to laugh.

"If it's no tattle then let's rattle." They laughed as they got out of the car. "Say, how do you say Gimme Shelter in Aramaic?"

Mary said, "They don't speak Aramaic here." They laughed again.

In spite of her joking around she was vigilant as they went into the motel office. Mary checked in as Misty Autumn. Rainbeaux observed how composed Mary was. She either choose well or Mary was leading her into a trap.

They rented two motel rooms adjoined through a common door. As they entered Rainbeaux said, "You were cool as cool could be out there, Misty Autumn. Whereas I'm about to shit my pants."

Mary put her purse and a small bag down. "I could tell. Remember we'll have time for me to tell you everything. There's a lot you can teach me too."

Before Mary Magdalene sequestered herself in one

room, she and Rainbeaux sat and talked for a few minutes. She asked Mary about what going to happen now.

"Well," started Mary, "the process of recovering all my memories has begun. Kind of like I am waking up after a thousand years." Mary double blinked her eyes and made a face that got Rainbeaux to laugh.

Rainbeaux said hopefully, "Now you have to settle in and let it happen."

Mary reassured her, "Baby, it just pours in from now on."

Rainbeaux nodded, "Nice and easy, cool and breezy. Sorry, still a little scared. I get a little weird when I ..."

"I wouldn't be surprised if you weren't a lot scared. So am I."

Rainbeaux was sheepish as she asked, "One more thing, what happens when I go out into my Spook Zone?"

"What do you think happens?" Mary asked.

"I don't know. I thought for a long time I was just meditating, an altered state of consciousness. But I wonder, am I going somewhere else?"

Mary beamed at her as though that was all the answer Rainbeaux needed. "This helps me get my process started. The doors are opening." Then she closed the door between rooms.

Rainbeaux sat down and waited. For what she hoped for, what she feared and for who she loved. It had all come down to this; the bottom line on everything.

Within minutes Brenner knocked on the door. Rainbeaux carefully looked out the window and then let him in.

"Hi," he started. "I got here as fast as I could." He sat a bag of groceries down.

"I am so glad you are here. And right on mah brotha you brought munchies. Good on you." She sat on the bed and looked in the bag.

Brenner reached in front of her and dug a few items

out of the bag. "Sorry to be rude, these'll ruin," he said as he put them in the mini-fridge.

"I thought you'd like to know she is doing fine," said Rainbeaux.

"Glad to hear it."

"Have you heard from Daisy?"

"I called Mrs. Yancy. She said she couldn't talk to me since I wasn't employed at the clinic."

Rainbeaux knew that Brenner was hurt by that. "Maybe if Daisy was hurt or in trouble, she would tell you."

Brenner smiled a little. "I hope so. Guess I lost my professional bearing in all this."

Rainbeaux touched him lightly. "Don't do that to yourself. After all that has happened ..." She couldn't finish. There was a loud knock at the door. Loud. Insistent. A cop's knock.

Rainbeaux stepped lightly to the window. Brenner looked out the peep hole. Just in time, Rainbeaux grabbed him and pulled him down. There was a 'phffft' sound and the peep hole exploded.

Next Rainbeaux made a dive for her purse. Brenner asked, "What was that?"

"Goddamn it," she stammered, "he has a silencer."

Brenner gasped out, "A what?"

She was patient with him, "This is a professional hit." She pulled her service weapon from her bag.

Brenner looked at her firearm. "You'll attract attention."

"We need some." She thought that Brenner nodded that he understood. "When I count three open the door. One, two, three."

In the meantime Brenner moved off to the side of the door. He quickly opened it.

Sam stumbled in. A smoking silenced automatic pistol in his hand. Brenner had shut the door as fast as he opened it when he saw it was Sam.

Sam sat on the bed. He sat still, breathing heavy.

Rainbeaux studied him. She was concerned but cautious. She kept her weapon on Sam and moved slowly toward him. Brenner shook his head and signaled with his facial expression that this was a bad idea.

She returned his gaze with a self assurance that said she was in control. Even if Sam was not. "Sam, can you hear me?"

Sam began to mumble. He was staring off into space. "Sam, what do you hear?"

Rainbeaux glanced over at Brenner. He had slipped by them. Now he tried the door to the other room. It was locked. Sam said nothing. Brenner returned his attention to Sam.

Sam stopped mumbling. He appeared confused or perplexed. Then he spoke, "You have to get out of here."

Rainbeaux said, "We will."

Brenner was alarmed. "Sam, be clear. Did you come here to kill us? And ..." He stopped and appeared to pity Sam.

When Sam didn't answer Rainbeaux said, "Sam, we have to scoot. You are coming with us. First give me your service weapon." Sam looked at her terrified. "What are you afraid of?" she asked. Sam returned to mumbling. "Talk to me, Sam. What are you saying?"

Brenner leaned in and was shocked at what he heard. "He is mumbling that he must kill the one he loves ..." Brenner looked up at Rainbeaux who was moving toward the door. "He's in a trance."

"He's not in control of himself."

Brenner said, "I'd say he is. To a degree."

She was so worried that she couldn't think. "He could have killed us by now. Poor sweetheart he's fighting it. What can we do?"

Brenner was fast, "We leave and we leave him here."

"Not gonna happen. Anything else?"

Brenner answered just as quick. "We try to bring him out of this trance."

Rainbeaux said slowly, "Enchantment."

Meanwhile Sam's finger was still on the trigger of his silenced automatic pistol. He continued to chant, staring at a fixed point on the floor.

Rainbeaux blanched white with fear. She mouthed the word *Gun* and pointed at his finger moving lightly over the trigger. Brenner shook his head to not try. But Rainbeaux moved quietly to Sam. She started to move her hand to the pistol, when Sam's hand reached out and grabbed her. She froze in terror then gently moved her hand out of his grasp.

Brenner led her away from him. "He may be in a trance but he still has his ability to defend himself."

She shook her head, "No joke. I want to find a way to reach him."

Brenner said, "If we can. There is one way to find out." He moved around to speak to Sam face to face. "Sam, can you hear me at all?"

Sam turned his face away from him, "Of course."

Brenner continued, "I want you to hear and understand what I'm going to say. I want to speak directly to Sam. This is trance logic. There are words or phrases that are repeated over and over that keep you in a hypnotic state."

Sam looked back at Brenner.

"Sam, please, are you aware of the chanting? The repeating of the phrases? If you think about them, they don't make sense. How does loving someone and killing them fit together?"

Sam was confused. He tried to answer but only gibberish came out.

Brenner continued, "You have to repeat it over and over so you can ignore how little sense it makes."

Sam startled a little bit. He started to look around the room as though he was surprised to be here.

Brenner took that as a hopeful sign. "That's it. Keep looking around. Notice where you are. Focus on Rainbeaux. And on me. On the feel of the breeze on your skin from the air con. The feel of the bed covers under your hands. That weapon is heavy. Too heavy to hold. Put it down and notice the relief in your hand and arm."

Sam appeared to start to wake up. Before he could say anything they heard a moaning that came from the next room. Then a cell rang. Rainbeaux recognized the ring and she searched frantically through her pockets. Her cell stopped ringing just as the moan changed to a wail. As Brenner went to the door between the rooms she said decisively, "We'll be right there."

Then there was a cry of alarm. She said, "What now?" Rainbeaux rushed to the door. It was locked. Then her cell rang. Rainbeaux searched through her pockets for the key. "Mary do you hear me?"

Another cry of anguish from the other side of the door. The cell kept ringing. As Rainbeaux dug the key out, she slapped the door. "Mary Mags! Is someone in there with you?" She fumbled the key into the lock. In seconds she and Brenner, followed slowly by Sam, entered the room.

Mary Mags sat cross legged on the bed. Her mouth was open and a long low "Oh" came out. The others stood in a small crowd by the door and looked at her. Her appearance had changed. All her tattoos were gone. Her leathery skin was now supple and smooth. She looked twenty-six again.

Finally she looked up at them and said to no one in particular, "We have to go to the church and talk to the Gnostics." Off their look that she was talking crazy, she said, "We can ask the priest or priestess help us find them." She looked at the others and their surprised expression on their faces. "Abwoon, the Heavenly Father, the Source of All, has taken pity on me. I'm restored."

Rainbeaux said, "Wow, well, I was going to ask about that." Then Rainbeaux, who in particular was just as surprised at the reference to a priestess in a church, asked, "What do you mean the 'Gnostics?'"

Mary explained, "The wise ones in the church. Father or Mother can ..." She stopped and put her hands to the sides of her head. "I remember. No, no it wasn't supposed to be like this."

Brenner approached her slowly and carefully. "It's okay ..."

She interrupted him, speaking quickly, "No, it is not okay. Things were different. Things were better. But the bastard changed things."

Brenner spoke softly, "Who changed things?"

Mary Magdalene continued, "Things weren't perfect but they were better. I mean, we fought World War One or WW Seven as we called it. WW Eight too. I mean also. WW Eight also. But we could talk. More, I don't know, rationally."

Rainbeaux asked again, "Who?"

She waited as though listening to something far away. Finally Mary Mags spoke, "Gadfan."

"How?"

"He is called 'Blasphemer' because he shifts boundaries. In cultural terms he used wicked priests and men of mockery to infiltrate ancient Judaism with ideas and laws there were not part of the pure worship of God. That's what Y'shua and I and the others were reacting against. At first. Along with Roman occupation. But Gadfan can shift other boundaries too."

Sam spoke up, "Boundaries of time."

Mary Mags said, "Yes, the boundaries of time. He can't or isn't allowed to change things to his liking directly. But he can shift events around. Events that change our world." She fell into silence and stared into space.

Rainbeaux grew alarmed. "So we aren't just trying to save our lives, we are trying to save our lives as we know them."

Mary Mags looked at her. "You have true Gnosis, Rainbeaux Rene Le Blanc." Off Rainbeaux's puzzled look, "That was a blessing."

Brenner jumped in, "How does this integration you are doing work?"

Mary said as though teaching a pupil, "All living things are surrounded by a sphere of light like a halo. There is an opening in my halo above the crown of my head. This allows the supernal light of The Eternal Our God, Blessed Be The One, to enter and bath me in illumination. The power of the light then opens portals between all my selves creating passages for the light. This is what integrates my past with my present with my future and attending memories of each lifetime. Then each incarnation of each lifetime becomes enlightened. And this will start of wave of enlightenment and salvic, that is, healing, energy that sweeps over this world and the world beyond flesh; the Imaginal Plane; Rainbeaux's Spook Zone. And brings our reality back."

Rainbeaux let out a long low, "Whoa." She looked at her cell and pushed a button. While she waited for the message. "Thank you. For the blessing." She listened. "That was Roswell. He says the Fong Torres live here in Austin. Bad news is there are a team of assassins on their way to ice them right now."

Brenner was lost. "They need a team?"

"Now we need to start to push our own end game." Rainbeaux walked around the room. "I know that you can't

233

rush these things ..."

Mary Magdalene answered before the question was asked, "I'm not finished yet. It could take years or hours, I don't know."

"We just heard that the bad un's are on their way. Arrive at the Fong Torres by dark. And it's getting dark."

Brenner asked the woman he knew as Marilyn, "Is it safe to move you?"

Rainbeaux said, "We better not separate. Better if we are all together. Now let's split."

Mary Magdalene asked, "Where to now?"

Rainbeaux said with assurance, "We're going to find Daisy and bring her with us." She looked over at Mary. "We need her don't we?"

Mary Magdalene nodded her approval. "We need everyone."

Rainbeaux said, "Let's move."

Brenner looked at Sam who was clearly still under the spell. "Even Sam?"

Rainbeaux said, "Everyone."

As they grabbed their things and headed out the door Brenner said, "It would be nice if we had some back up."

Outside on the way to their car Rainbeaux dialed Hane on her mobile. He didn't answer. She rung off. "Let's all ride together in Sam's car. We'll Trojan Horse our way there."

Brenner drove, Rainbeaux rode shotgun. As they settled in, Brenner asked, "Is there anyone else you can call besides Director Hane?"

"Yes," Rainbeaux said. She dialed a number as Brenner drove out of the parking lot. Then another and then another. She closed the cell. "No answer, not even the man at the desk."

Brenner couldn't help asking, "Who is the man at the desk?"

"Something like an emergency operator."

"Oh," said Brenner.

"Sorry if that took the mystery out."

Just then Sam moved quickly forward between Rainbeaux and Brenner. He pushed a button on the dash computer.

Rainbeaux sucked in her breath in shock and sat there open mouthed. Sam said, "Turned the GPS off. They can't track us that way now. Unless any of us have our cells on."

Everyone busied themselves turning their cells off. "If they have the number," Sam finished.

"I'm leaving mine on in case of a message from Roswell," Rainbeaux said to him.

Mary said, "After we warn the Fong Torres, we should warn Happurstadt. The System is angry with him. The whole coven here was handled poorly. They'll send a hit team to take them out."

Rainbeaux said, "So he's dead. And Shneed too." Mary nodded yes. "Why am I not broken up by that?"

Mary touched Rainbeaux lightly on the arm. "Mercy, Rainbeaux. We all deserve it."

There was a ping on Rainbeaux's cell phone. She read her message as she continued the conversation. She was good at multi-tasking. "Of course. Then will Gadfan still answer them if they call?" She furrowed her brow at the message.

Mary shrugged her shoulders. "Don't know. Even with the System mad at them Gadfan may still want to use them. For something. Who knows what."

Rainbeaux said, "That was a text message from Roswell. Daisy and Nancy are going to the Red River Motel. He thinks the Fong Torres family are being moved there too. Sebastian, how much time will it take to get there?" Now she powered down her cell phone.

Brenner grinned as he gunned the police cruisers engine. "Depends on the traffic. Which this time of day shouldn't be that bad. Except when it is."

Rainbeaux looked at a car ahead of them accelerate and match their speed too. "Crap. We're being followed."

Sam shook the fog from his head. "Not surprising is it? They used an old trick of staying ahead so we wouldn't notice them. Got it from the Dick Tracy comic strip."

Brenner yanked the wheel and they shot across the grassy median onto the frontage road. The other car raced ahead to the next exit ramp. Brenner said, We've half a mile before they can turn around." He turned down Breaker Lane going east. Then down a side street. He stopped. Everyone took a deep breath and looked around.

Rainbeaux seemed to shut down. She didn't but was lost in thought over what happened to Hane. There was no answer. That worried her and the more she thought about it, the less she liked what she was thinking. He couldn't be part of the Entity's system. He had too many chances to betray her to It. Still the plan was too elaborate for a whacko religious cult. It could be that he was caught or dead. She thought that she would know: they were close, since he was her handler. She looked over. Brenner was studying his phone too.

"I'm using my maps to find a back road route to the ..."

Mary Magdalene began to moan.

All this distracted Rainbeaux, "Good plan. We can't dally too much ..." Rainbeaux looked at Mary Magdalene. "Are you okay?"

She looked like she was having an orgasm. Then she smiled saucily and relaxed. "I've been a lesbian in this incarnation. I forgot how much fun men are. Until now."

Sam looked over at her although still struggling to wake from the trance. He cocked his head to the side.

Rainbeaux saw Sam reacting to his surroundings. She wanted to try and get that gun. "Sam, give me your firearm."

He clearly didn't want to do that. He pulled his coat closed and held it tight.

Mary Magdalene said, "You should have taken it back in the room."

"No joke. Okay, Sam, I really need that gun." She bit her lip. "That may be a poor choice of words."

Mary waved her hand in front of Sam's face. When he didn't react she said, "I don't think he noticed."

Brenner turned up another street. It was a cul de sac. He stopped the car and shut the engine down. "I think if he was going to use it he would have by now."

Rainbeaux turned and sat in her seat. Then took a chance and sent Hane a text. Then she switched her phone off. She looked back at Mary and Sam.

Mary said, "He's okay."

Brenner started the car and they began to roll.

Rainbeaux said, "I hope he is. We need the help."

Mary said, "We have you."

"Thanks for the support. But I'm thinking machine guns and stun grenades. Which I don't have."

Mary turned her head. Rainbeaux figured she had said enough. Of course, Mary Magdalene was their big gun to get rid of the Thing that held so many followers in Its thrall.

Rainbeaux said, "Sometime I'm going to have to confront this Entity. Gadfan."

Mary nodded, "I'm glad you said it. I don't envy you."

Rainbeaux said, "I ran from It before. But if I'm going to face It, what do I do? I mean, I know we use the name. But is there a ritual or do I just order Him away?"

Mary asked, "What do you know about it."

Rainbeaux looked pensive, "It is the Beast worshipped all over the world. Especially by the wealthy and powerful ..." She was lost in thought.

Mary prodded her gently, "This reminds you of ..."

"Those passages in the New Testament. Paul's letters. We are opposed by spiritual wickedness in high places."

Now Mary knew she got it, "That wasn't a poetic reference to highly placed people."

"It was the Rulers, the Archons in ancient Greek, the gods who have, or had, power over our world." She turned to look at Mary, "I'll bet you had your differences with the Apostle Paul."

Mary began, "Well, we had words ..." But she was cut off when-

-Brenner turned suddenly down another suburban side street. "Our friends are back."

The four of them watched the black sedan drive past on the main road.

Brenner turned around in the street and he sought a back way out to I35.

Rainbeaux said, "I guess I had my cell on a little too long. Mary, how many are looking for us?"

Sam answered her instead, "They are making a show of force. They know where we are going. It isn't too hard to figure out. They intend to catch us there."

Rainbeaux turned to Brenner. "What if we do the unexpected?"

Brenner's hands shook. "Like what?"

"I don't know. Mary how else can we hurt them?"

Mary said gently yet firmly, "This is about you facing Him. I can't endorse you doing anything else."

Brenner said, "I want to get Daisy out of there. I'm supposed to keep a professional distance but ..."

Rainbeaux said, "It's okay. You're human. And you got into this because you are compassionate."

"I just don't want them to hurt her. Anymore than they have." He looked in the rear view at Mary Mags. "You too."

"We know." Then Mary smiled again.

Rainbeaux looked around. "So we agree. We intercept Daisy. Get her out of that place."

"She is mostly likely with them already."

No one said anymore. Brenner changed direction and they headed north. After a few minutes Rainbeaux said, "I'm not familiar with this part of town. How much further?"

Brenner said, "We're getting there."

Something about that caused a change in Rainbeaux. Or rather a change in her perceptions. It seemed a darkness came over her. Lawn shadows jutting out into the road from the tidy suburban houses around them took on menacing shapes. There was a pain in the pit of her stomach. She felt a cold mistrust of everyone especially Sam.

CHAPTER 34

Within minutes they rolled up to the front of the Red River Motel. They all looked around at the empty parking lot. No cars, no sign of anyone coming to welcome them.

Rainbeaux said, "No Daisy. No Roswell Hane. Damn."

Brenner pulled up to the front door. "So we are ready for anything?"

"No. But let's go anyway," said Rainbeaux.

Mary said grimly, "I feel presence here. He is here. I feel Daisy and the other surviving members here. I feel death here."

"Great. Let's get this funeral on the road." In spite of her bravado, Rainbeaux was still strung out on anxiety.

They all exited the car more or less at the same time. Sam climbed out a little more slowly than the others. "Pushing in," he said as he got out.

Rainbeaux was the first to the lobby door, which opened with a mere push. Spooky. She looked back at everyone then entered. The others followed her.

It was eerily quiet. Still. The cheap motel smell of mildewed carpet and rotting moldy ply wood. The air was chilly as though the air conditioning was turned way down. Mary rubbed her arms. "Cold," she said.

Rainbeaux said, "It feels like no one is taking care of things." Her breath came out in a fog caused by the cold.

"Empty," said Mary Magdalene.

Brenner looked around. "Daisy!" He called her name several more times. There was a distant sound. They followed it toward long hall leading out to the back of the building. The hall was tiny and as empty as the lobby. As silent as a tomb except for a child's humming.

They walked up to the backs stairs leading to the rooms above where Daisy Yellow Yancy hopped up and down four of the steps at a time. She barely looked at them.

Then in a childish voice she said, "Antigonish by Means. Yesterday, upon the stair, I met a man who wasn't there He wasn't there again today I wish, I wish he'd go away ...

"When I came home last night at three The man was waiting there for me

"But when I looked around the hall I couldn't see him there at all!

"Go away, go away, don't you come back any more!

"Go away, go away, and please don't slam the door ... (slam!)", she clapped her hands.

"Last night I saw upon the stair a little man who wasn't there, he wasn't there again today Oh, how I wish he'd go away."

She stopped and smiled at them. Brenner stepped forward. "Daisy, we have to leave. Want to come with us?"

"Not leaving my mommy." Rainbeaux thought she sounded like Shirley Temple.

Brenner gently continued, "It isn't safe here. We need to go. Why don't you come?"

Daisy pointed at Mary, "That's a bad girl. Named Lily. Lily does bad things. And I ain't goin' with her. NO. NO. NO!" Daisy stomped her foot.

Mary walked forward a couple of steps. Brenner side stepped away from her. "Daisy, is that who you are?" Daisy didn't respond to her. But she was listening. "Who told you I was bad?"

Daisy shook her finger at Mary, "Nobody. I just know you are bad. I saw what you did, bad girl. And changing back into someone else doesn't help."

Mary continued, "Of course it helps. Please come with

us we are worried about you."

"My mommy said I can't go anywhere."

"Where is your mommy?"

Daisy smiled brightly as her mood changed. "Mommy's in there."

She pointed to a room back down the hall, the way they came. There was a small room off the lobby that could be used for a breakfast buffet.

Looking at that room, Rainbeaux felt that darkness from the street swirl around her around her again. She felt like fainting. She fought the sensation. She pushed it down.

Mary said, "Let's go see her. I want to say hi."

Daisy bounced down the stairs. Brenner tried to angle around behind her. He and Rainbeaux locked eyes. She shook her head no. It was no use trying to grab her. They followed her back down the hall.

Rainbeaux's dark feelings became more intense. Now a suffocating dread that almost overcame her as they reentered the lobby. As she peeked around the corner into the breakfast room:

The first thing they saw was the blood that covered everything. Nancy's body was ripped apart and laid out like the other ritual murder victims.

It was too much. In a panic, Rainbeaux ran to the lobby door. It was locked. A heavy chain with a padlock kept them inside. How did that get there? Wouldn't they have heard?

Daisy walked over to her mother's corpse. "Mommy, wake up. Get up Mommy. We have company."

Rainbeaux watched in sorrow as Daisy tried to wake her dead mother. She stopped. It seemed that she realized that Nancy wasn't coming back. She was overcome with loss and started to cry. Brenner moved forward. He gently put his hand on her shoulder. "There are things we can do for Mommy. Let's go and we can take good care of her."

Slowly they walked Daisy out of the breakfast room. He looked at Rainbeaux. She used her eyes to direct him to the chain and lock on the door. Rainbeaux slowly became aware that another pair of eyes were looking into hers. She followed Brenner, Sam and Mary's gaze to a group of men surrounding and watching them. One down the hall, two of them behind the desk now. One more in the breakfast room. One more outside standing in front of the car.

Shneed stepped out from among the men, clapping his hands. Somehow he didn't look himself; his facial features had changed. When he spoke, it wasn't his voice. "Sorry about the sign, there's plenty of room for ya. Gotcha."

No one said anything. They were too petrified.

Finally Rainbeaux said, "What about the Fong Torres family?"

"Long dead I'm afraid. At least a week." He turned to the men in black. "It's been a week, earth time, right?" Then he let out his whopping barking laugh.

Rainbeaux knew that laugh from her visions. She stepped forward. "So you're ..."

The more he talked the more his words slurred. "I know my name. Your curiosity will kill the cat, Officer Le-Blanc. The cat being you."

She mustered all her courage. "Gadfan, you have to leave."

The Blasphemer smiled, "You don't know everything you need to know about how this works. Do you have a place you'd like me to go?"

Mary whispered to her, "Careful, he's the Deceiver."

Rainbeaux felt her bowels turn to water. She kept it together enough to quip, "So many jump up your own ass-hole jokes, so little time."

"Less than you can imagine. I'm not going anywhere. Least of all ..." He held up his hands, and smiled with all his mouths.

"How about you go to Hell then."

Gadfan looked around. He held his arms out wide. "Still here." He nodded at the men with him. "Not so with you."

Shneed and his men all put gas masks over their faces. Quick as a wink, Rainbeaux and everyone with her fell to the floor.

Rainbeaux didn't know how long she was out. She vaguely became aware of her surroundings. She quipped, "Rusting Eastern European factory. How cliché."

Her head dropped back down on a soft pillow. She heard mirthless laughter. Struggling to open her eyes, she only saw multiple outlines of everything around her.

Then Gadfan's voice in her ear. Soothing, low, hypnotic. "You have the worst case of psoriasis imaginable."

Rainbeaux could see her head misshapen by piles of skin that wouldn't flake off. Red and white splotches. She was horrified at what she saw. Sam would hate her. "Yes, he would. So we are putting you in a special bath." She felt and then saw herself being lowered into a bath of warm water by a dozen hands.

Quickly hundreds of little fish came around her. They started eating the dead flesh off her head. She could feel the tug of the fish nibbling at her scalp. Eating and eating at her head for hours until it was a normal shape again.

She mercifully blacked out.

She woke again. Groggy. She was in a soft comfortable bed. Someone was taking a feeding tube out of her mouth. She was hooked up to an IV. Gadfan spoke to her again. "The skin on your feet is rotten. The red flesh itches so bad you can't stand it."

It was so. She couldn't move but wanted to scratch her feet. The itching and burning were so bad her eyes watered.

"Uh, uh. You will cause an infection."

It didn't matter. The itching was unbearable. She felt her hands reaching down to her feet. Then she was dimly aware that her feet were lowered to the floor.

"Careful. You'll fall if you try that. Let us purify you. Open your eyes. Have a look."

She looked down. Her feet were covered in raised red dry skin eruptions.

Then. Worm creatures, repellent and unwholesome, the likes of which are not seen on earth came crawling to her feet. Within seconds they opened their eel-like mouths of concentric rows of sharp teeth. There were dozens of them latching onto the ugly red raised blisters on her feet. They began to suck and chew the itchy red flesh off. Again the feasting went on for hours. Finally she was laid back on her bed. She looked down at her feet. They were red but not damaged. She had feared the worms would have chewed her feet off.

Gadfan in her ear again, she could hear the whiskey soured smell of His breath. "We have cleansed your mind and your experience. " He reached over and felt up her breasts. "There is so much more for us to do."

Rainbeaux lost consciousness again.

This went on for a period of time that she couldn't perceive. It was either months or years or thirty minutes. But systematically each part of her body was attacked by some hungry mutant creature. Sucking or eating infected, cancerous, pimply sores off her body. Or out of it. Hungry little mouths biting and chewing the blisters, open wounds, warts, acne, moles off her tender skin. No matter where they were found.

It was torture.

Then she awoke. Or thought she did. She couldn't breathe. Her nasal passages were clogged. Through her panic at being suffocated, she saw weird cockroach-like bugs surrounding her. They crawled up her nose to chew the material blocking her nasal passages. The bugs had sharp little claws and tiny hands that touched her all up her nose and sinuses. She could feel big hard chunks of hard dried snot worked loose and pulled out of her nose by the insectoid creatures. From time to time they ripped out nasal hairs which caused weird stinging vibrations. At that point she wanted to sneeze and then scream. She could do neither.

Then she was aware, if dimly, that she lay in a white fluffy bed. She wore a thin almost transparent gown. She was surrounded by very small horrid repulsive primatoid creatures. They crawled all over her. In their tiny human-like hands, they held a tool that looked like a metal can opener. But it had a long single sharp edge blade. The tiny primatoids scraped and scratched her skin until it came off in long strips.

Soon they exposed the layer of skin underneath. She was aware that this skin underneath was hideous. She was covered with hairy black and brown warts and huge discolored moles. More horrific alien crawling things climbed all over her to eat the cancerous eruptions off her skin. First stinging the warts and moles with poisonous fangs, injecting venom. Then biting them with sharp mandibles so that they broke open. Finally their long proboscis sucking the matter out of the open wart or mole. Cleaning out the hole and leaving an endomorphic rush surging through her body in its place. Followed by intense mind numbing pain.

She knew it was insanity and psychosis inducing. She worked to keep her mind anchored. The techniques worked. But the hallucination wouldn't stop. She knew she was crying and screaming. Submitting to whatever they wanted. But becoming more aware that she was hallucinating. There was small reassurance there.

Suddenly Gadfan was next to her ear. "Now that's a problem." She could see the colors in his voice.

Then everything stopped. Merciful oblivion; a compassionate blackness spread over her.

Finally she was aware that she was being moved. It felt like a long ride. She was in a box. She was scared but now knew that if they wanted to kill her they would have by now. They could have at any time. She tried to think what they wanted. But that was in the midst of all kinds of crazy thoughts. Random patterns played in front of her eyes. Strange noises. Memories of dogs barking in the yard from her childhood. Smells of food. She wanted to talk to her grandmother again. She remembered painting someone's portrait in the French Quarter. Finally a rational thought; that must have been when I was living on the street. I was just a teen.

Finally she awoke in a motel room. She was disoriented and didn't know where she was though it was familiar. Then it came to her; she was still in the Red River Motel. She was becoming fully aware. Her eyes popped open wide. She saw the others positioned around the room to her right. Around them were men in black suits.

Then a face right in hers. It was the face she had seen in her visions; Gadfan. He was closer than he had ever been. His head and eyes and apish preposterous face covered by the thick dark glasses and wide brimmed hat. His lower face and jaw were exposed. Something not quite right about his jaw. His teeth. He looked directly into her eyes and shook his head.

"You are one tough nut to crack. I gotta say, girlie, you impressed me."

He backed away from her and walked, crablike, around to the others. Sam, Sebastian next to him. They were still and unconscious. Daisy lay whimpering on her side, not fully awake. Mary Mags between she and Daisy.

She didn't like the look on Mary's face. Her thin white tattooed skin bruised. She took it hard. They all had had it hard though.

Gadfan's eyes shone through his dark glasses now yellow now red eyes toward her. "We threw it all at you. Nothing. Wow. You feel like you just woke from a nightmare?"

"Just tell me what you want. There's no need for all these games."

"These aren't games, girlie. They were purification. We were cleaning you out. Getting you red-eye for ... What would you call it? Oh yeah, the Qilopothic version of the Sacred Marriage. HA!" The more he talked, the more he slurred his words. Then his eyes glowed red like octopus eyes through the darkness of the glasses.

Rainbeaux pretended she was irritated that he wouldn't get to the point. The truth was that was she was looking out her peripheral vision at the minions. They were bound to have weapons. She knew He could most likely read her thoughts. But she still thought about what it would take to make a last stand. She wondered if she could reach one of the guns the men in black kept in their shoulder or ankle holsters.

"Look at you. After all that you took, you still want to play hero. Ha! Fellas, don't give her any guns understand?"

The Blasphemer nodded at her. That answered that. "Yes, I do read your mind. This is no escape from here. Tell ya what. I'm gonna show ya."

She took the opportunity to look around the room. The dimensions didn't seem right. The room was too big. She thought that he might have knocked down some walls to make the room bigger. None of that seemed to make sense to her. Then she realized she wasn't fully awake yet. Immediately a suffocating drowsiness came over her. She shook her head and blinked her eyes. Not just to wake up but to stay alive.

He might have waited for her before he motioned for the men to undrape a large coffin shaped box. The drape came off and then the box opened. Shneed was inside. He was beaten up; black and blue and lumpy. His face was a bloody ruin. Gadfan took off his glasses and hat. The skin of Shneed's face was draped over his. He took the skin off his face and threw it in the coffin. "Don't need that any-more." He said it carelessly.

For the first time she could see what went for his real face. It looked like lumps of clay busts of several people smashed together like some insane sculptor might have done for a high concept decadent art piece. The grouping of the eyes reminded her of spider eyes. There were teeth jutting out of the face or faces at odd angles. When he opened his mouth to speak there were two tongues that forked out. And more eyeballs that peered from his open mouth.

"Why torture me with creepy crawlies when all you had to do was show me what you look like?"

He was proud. "Yep, this is me." He pointed to part of his face. "Recognize this guy?"

She did. Through the fog of waking up and her torture she knew it was the remains of the face of Doug Jamison.

"It's Aziz," was all she could say.

"That's right. Now if you were one hundred percent you would figure out that I am using parts of all these peo-ple who worship me to manifest here in your space time continuum."

Rainbeaux struggled to regain some of her strength. She wanted to make the most of this. "How about Quell Cade? Innocent after all?"

"No, he committed the murders. This," here he circled around his face with a long grubby nailed finger, "came after Doug and the Teen Wicci Gang dug me up. They are all here." He laughed though she didn't know why.

Then the smallest hope sized her. "Sam didn't kill Aziz did he?"

"Nope, it was me. I made sure to frame good old Sam for it."

"I'll guess you do that a lot."

"I do. But I'll fix it so he didn't now that he is with me. I do take care of my own."

"I see that."

"See that guy?" He pointed to Shneed lying in his coffin. "You know why I did that?"

"He wasn't any use to you anymore." It was the most Rainbeaux could do after using her fading strength to speak.

"He was a fuck up from the word go. He didn't play well with his peers. The people we selected he treated with contempt. Useless!"

The Blasphemer threw a paper coffee cup at Shneed's prone form. The cup landed on the skin of his face that rested on his chest. Shneed spit some blood out in response.

Rainbeaux tried to buy time. Maybe one of the Men in Black kept a gun in an ankle holster. If she kept Gadfan talking. "He let things go. He didn't discover Mary Magdalene in your coven. She was there all the time. He was so arrogant he missed the most obvious spy in your organization." Rainbeaux was proud she could muster enough to throw that at Gadfan.

Gadfan shook his head. "Not organization. We have a system. You do remember your own visions don't you? But you're right, you got the right idea. Now we're down in numbers because of this useless cocksucker and Happurstadt the fuckwad."

She became more aware of a certain sloppiness in His

speech.

"It must hurt to have someone so close to you fail like that."

"Then you understand why I have to kill him."

Rainbeaux was frightened. "Not here!"

"Why not? This room costs me a bundle. We'll wake your pals here then get on down to the thing."

Rainbeaux recognized *get on down to the thing* as a phrase her father, AC, used when he was happy or drunk. But not both at the same time. She struggled to think how to buy time. "First tell me why. What do you get out of all this?"

"I get power. What? You surprised that I am that transparent?"

"Don't you have enough out there?" She asked. He laughed mirthlessly again. "We can't mean that much to you. Please just let us go."

The men in black drug Shneed out of his coffin box. Someone opened a curtain further back in the room. Impossibly the room seemed to grow. A ritual space was set up. There were zodiac symbols drawn on the bare floor around an alter where six candles were arranged in front. They unceremoniously dumped Shneed there. The Blasphemer gave the men some orders.

With his back turned to her Rainbeaux took the opportunity to nudge Mary Magdalene. "Hey, Mary Mags. Wake up, girl. Come on we need the big guns now."

She stopped when Gadfan turned to look at her. Then he went back to his supervision. That worried her more than if he had tried to stop her. He wasn't threatened by her. Then another thought worse than the other came to her. That all the cleansing may have cleaned Mary Magdalene out of Marilyn. And for that matter all the alternate personalities too. Marilyn had been a target of abuse so severe that she stayed submerged under the alters. She remembered that Sebastian said that he hadn't met the core personality. This could have left Marilyn a hollow shell now. She used her shoulder to nudge her and try to rouse her again. Nothing. Then a more hopeful thought. Maybe they cleaned Gadfan out of Sam. Anything was worth a try now.

Especially since none of the men in black were close enough to make a grab for a gun. Especially since Gadfan came over to Mary Magdalene.

"The Lady said for you to wake up!" He yelled at her his voice booming impossibly loud. She didn't move. He looked over at Rainbeaux and said sardonically, "Kids these days."

Then he kicked her with all his might. Rainbeaux saw Mary's limp body flop across the nasty moldy carpet. She lay there. Unmoving. And from the look of it not breathing. He kicked her again. It was like kicking a rag doll along the floor. He shrugged his shoulders.

"Oh well that's the way it goes. You know I had plans. Now I'll just have to ..." His words became indistinguishable. He didn't look at Rainbeaux as he walked back to the alter.

Time to try to get to Sam. She tried to move but her limbs felt like lead. Whether from any drugs they may have given her, or who knows how long she was under and her muscles atrophied. She couldn't walk that was for sure. She strained to crawl toward Sam. She stopped when some of the men in black moved another coffin shaped box to the ritual space.

Gadfan saw her. He looked toward Sam. "Go ahead," he said. She continued her slow crawl gasping for breath the whole way.

"Sam! I need you. Come on, buddy, Sweetheart, open your eyes."

She reached toward him. It took all her strength.

Thankfully he stirred. He opened one eye then the other and looked at her.

"Honey, there you are. Thank God. We gotta get moving. Do something." She strained to move toward him.

Then his hand reached out for her fast as a snake strike. He grabbed her wrist and yanked her across the floor. His other hand took hold of her throat. He squeezed with inhuman strength. She was choking. Her eyes watered and she was close to passing out.

"Hey, Sammy boy! Let her go," Gadfan called to him. She looked over at the Blasphemer. "Yeah, that's right, Miss Rainbeaux. It's the worst case scenario. He has joined us completely now."

Gadfan walked over to her. "Did I steal your boyfriend? Sorry about that. Wait, no I'm not. He's going to rebuild the coven here."

She coughed. Then shot back, "How many more do you need?"

"Just the few."

Something occurred to her, "Somewhat shy of the one hundred forty-four thou you need? Thought so."

He cocked his head at her, "You can read minds too. Shame to waste you." He said it off handedly. He turned back to directing Happurstadt and Shneed's demise.

Rainbeaux looked pleadingly at Sam. His return stare was cold and hard. He didn't see her with love anymore. She was something to be manipulated. Like a tool or a utensil. This sapped more energy than anything else they could have done to her. She tried not to cry but the tears rolled down her face in little rivers of sadness and pain. She was dimly aware that somewhere behind her the men in black were chanting in Latin. She looked for any sign of life in Sebastian or Daisy. None. Daisy had stopped moving. The chanting behind her grew louder.

The Blasphemer walked over to her. "We gotta cheer

you up." He snapped his fingers. "Know what we're missing? A baby. Don't you think a nice baby would liven up the ritual right now?"

Rainbeaux said through gritted teeth, "Your laugh doesn't sound like you are enjoying yourself very much. Of course you are laughing at your own." She stopped before she said the word *joke*. It hurt to talk. It hurt to breath. It hurt to stay awake. If only she were in her own bed. She could sleep for a week. She promised herself that she would live through this. And that's what she would do; sleep for a week.

"Survive to sleep? There's a certain poetry to that." He turned his attention to the others, "Wake up!" Gadfan yelled at Brenner and Daisy. "You will want to see this." As they opened their eyes, there was a piecing scream from the two men on the alter. Happurstadt and Shneed were stripped naked. The men in black suits craved arcane ideograms into them with ritual knives while chanting the same Latin phrases over and over. Rivulets of blood poured out of them. The blood flowed into channels on the alter where it flowed further into vessels for collection.

Gadfan walked over to Marilyn. "I said get up." He kicked her. Her body quivered on the floor. "No time to sleep." He nudged her with his foot. She was motionless. "Well, isn't that that. She gone and died again." He kicked her hard this time. Her body slid across the floor. "Don't worry about her. She'll be back. Be- otch." Gadfan left her with her head pointed at an odd angle. She couldn't be alive after that.

Then Sam got up and walked over to the two victims. He removed his coat, tie and shirt. Gadfan pointed to his shoes. "Unholy ground and all that." Sam didn't move. "Take 'em off," Gadfan barked. Sam removed his shoes and socks. Then he stood before the alter.

Rainbeaux watched helplessly as Gadfan waddled

over. He dipped his dirty filth covered fingers in the blood pouring from Shneed and Happurstadt. He then painted half forgotten obscene ancient symbols on Sam's face, neck and upper torso. When he finished Gadfan commanded Sam, "Finish 'em off."

As Sam raised his knife, Rainbeaux screamed, "No!"

Gadfan laughed, "No one can hear you in here. Least of all, Sam."

"Sam! Remember who you are. Don't cross ...!" She wanted to say *this line* but she ran out of energy.

Just then the two victims on the alter stopped moving. Gadfan held up his hand. "Dead. No value any more. You can relax, Chessman."

He looked at Rainbeaux. He mocked her, "You lucked out. The other side must have taken them so good old Sam wouldn't be defiled."

Now Rainbeaux laughed, "This won't be easy for you, Blasphemer. I want this to be harder than hell."

"What an odd turn of phrase, Officer Le Blanc. It seems to me that pretty soon you will find out how hard Hell is."

Rainbeaux realized one of her assumptions may have been wrong. "You don't want to turn me?"

"This isn't a silly fantasy story, Officer Le Blanc. I don't turn anyone to anything. All of you do what you want to do. I simply manage things from there. You have free will and you, most of all you, didn't choose me. Now how am I supposed to feel about that? Yes, that's right it's all about me. And I'm hurt. Deeply."

Yes. She had been wrong alright.

"Cat got your tongue? If not, I will soon."

Gadfan yelled at the men in black. "Grab her next. Time to get this fucking bitch out of my misery."

Rainbeaux was dimly aware that three men with doll dead eyes grabbed her and began to remove her clothes.

She saw Sam stand back from the alter. He began to chant something she couldn't quite understand. Then, before she knew it, she was dragged up to the alter naked. She felt the men in black look at her nakedness. She saw how men looked at her on the street, but she never thought she looked good naked. Reflexively she was afraid of the judgment of men in general about her appearance. She looked at the men in black again. Their cold unappraising stares meant that they didn't care. These were dead men; only shells remained of them. The demon had overtaken them, in so many ways they no longer existed.

Mechanically they tied her to the alter. She tried to pull against the binding but couldn't move. No more last stands she thought sadly. Maybe she could come back too and kick Gadfan's ass.

At Gadfan's gesture Sam walked forward, his mouth moving and his eyes staring unblinking at her. He was enchanted and behaving according to his trance logic. He held a ritual knife like the one he found in the dumpster. Maybe the same one. Rainbeaux worried that he would find her unattractive. Then she saw his bulging trousers. His cock hard and ready. He was turned on by her, naked and tied down. He looked at her with longing, desiring her completely. She hoped beyond hope that he would use that knife to cut her free. Then he leaned over her and she heard what he was chanting, "I must kill the one I love."

Then he raised the gnarly looking knife to her throat.

"Sam," she squeezed out. "Remember that you love me. Come back to your senses."

Gadfan said offhandedly, "His senses are all he has. It is what he responds to now."

Sam's trousers were fully tented. His cock was so ready to plunge into her he was about to explode. That's when he pressed the knife down and began slicing into her flesh. Rainbeaux was afraid and she could feel the blade cutting into her throat. Slowly. Going deeper and deeper. Her heard him a little louder now, "I must kill the one I love."

She said to him, "Sam, trance logic."

Gadfan the Blasphemer smiled his lopsided smile as he said, "No, Sam, you don't love her. You cannot love. But you are obsessed. Stop your evil sick obsession for this woman. You are better than that."

Gadfan stopped smiling, "Now speed up. We have a lot on the alter today." Rainbeaux felt her blood running down her naked body. She tried to say something but couldn't. It felt like the knife had cut her vocal cords. He cut deeper and faster, yet still slowly decapitating her. She knew it and she stopped looking for a way out. She wondered if she would be grateful for death. She wasn't now. She felt cold, she was about to black out.

Then ...

Something caught her eye. She saw movement toward the back of the room.

Mary Magdalene's lifeless body stirred. She stood crookedly with her head bent to one side like her neck was broken. Not dead at all she was fully animated and alive as her body seemed to repair itself. She straightened up behind Sam, Gadfan and the men in black. Rainbeaux saw her deathly white face with dark circles under her eyes and a trickle of blood dripping out of her mouth. Her skin was pale. Her jet black hair a tangled mass on her head. She looked pissed off. She moved with catlike stealth up behind Gadfan.

Sam stopped pressing the knife as hard. He stopped cutting her because he seemed to sense something. There was a sharp CRACK as Mary's neck straightened. Sam and Gadfan heard it. As the Blasphemer turned to look behind him ...

Mary Magdalene said in a loud command voice, "Walk

behind me all you men in black."

The men dressed in black collapsed to the floor.

She continued as they fell, "Samuel Elliot Chessman, drop the knife."

And the ugly ritual knife bounced twice to the filthy carpet.

By now Gadfan had turned, had seen her, had understood what was happening. He seemed unsure of what to do, either attack her physically or run.

"You. You!" Was all he could choke out. "YOU!"

Mary Mags smiled a Mona Lisa smile. "Walk behind me, Gadfan, Blasphemer!"

Gadfan screamed a sound that could have, and may have, pierced the walls of the Outer Abyss. It was so loud that Rainbeaux, unable to cover her ears, almost passed out from the jet blast of sudden roaring noise. Next thing she knew Mary Mags stood over her untying her bonds. "Sorry, this happens sometimes during an exorcism."

Rainbeaux mouthed weakly and without sound, "So that's what that was."

Mary Mags motioned toward Sam with her head while she untied Rainbeaux. "You, over here and carry her out."

"No." It was hard for Rainbeaux to speak but she got that out. She could feel the steady stream of blood pouring out of her and down her chest. What he had done confirmed her the fear of the past few days and more. No, it was worse than what she had feared.

Mary Mags was sympathetic, "Sorry, dear, we have to hurry." Simultaneously Brenner and Daisy rose up and tried to walk on unsteady legs.

Mary touched Rainbeaux's throat. "Be well," was all she said.

Rainbeaux felt a delicate sense of comfort at that touch; a deep healing that came with it. Starting at her throat a feeling of warmth and well being swept over her.

Mother love. She could breathe easily now. She knew she could talk again. She knew she the cut was closed and she was going to be fine. Mercifully she went to sleep as Sam stooped over her to carry her away.

CHAPTER 35

When Rainbeaux awoke, she was in a large comfortable bed. There were freshly cleaned sheets. The wallpaper reminded her of something. As she came out of her daze she realized she was home and this was her bedroom. This was her bed. She could keep her promise to herself after all.

Then she saw Sam was beside the looking down at her. When she opened her eyes, Sam looked away. He refused to look at her again. She could tell he was worried about her. She started to tell him it was alright but then remembered the events at the Red River Motel. She had a sick feeling. As she grabbed her stomach, Sam left the room.

He returned in a moment with Mary Magdalene. As Mary walked up to the bed, Sam left them alone.

"Oh, good, you're awake," she said cheerily.

"Never better," Rainbeaux threw the covers back and looked all over her body.

Mary Mags looked her over. "You're going to be okay."

"Wanna bet?"

She smiled gently and lovingly as she said, "There's a remedy for that too."

Rainbeaux covered herself and turned her head away. "I don't want to know what that is right now."

"Of course not," said the other. "When you're ready."

"What about ...?"

"Sebastian is awake. He is taking this hard. Daisy, I don't know if we will get her back."

"We need everyone."

"And Sam. Poor Sam. Yes, we do need everyone." Then off Rainbeaux's look of disgust. "Like I said, when you're ready."

"What if I'm never ready?"

Mary Magdalene looked at her with complete love and acceptance. "One thing at a time."

"Gadfan?"

"He's still a problem. The main problem. Still in the body he inhabits in this world. I am working on a plan."

Rainbeaux strained to sit up. "Let me in on it. Believe me when I say I want a piece of that motherfucker."

"Of course. I will always need you. What would I do without my Rainbeaux?" Mary Magdalene had the gentlest sweetest smile.

Rainbeaux felt overwhelmed with love. Including love for Sam. She quickly shut it off. The good feeling disappeared. "Sorry I said, you know, M F."

Mary guided her to lie down again and tucked the covers under Rainbeaux's chin, "Finish getting your rest. Then come downstairs."

Mary got up and walked soundlessly out of the room. Rainbeaux felt the warm indent on the bed to remind herself that Mary wasn't a ghost. That this wasn't some dream. Then with a great deal of pain she remembered what she shared with Sam in this bed. She was dizzy with grief yet relieved to be home after what happened. She fell into a deep restive sleep. In her dreams, Sam is healthy and happy. She is too. They meet at some large convention hall. It as though they hadn't seen each other in a long time. They apologize and laugh that no apology is necessary. They are in love again and as they bend their heads together to kiss ...

She awoke after a long time. She went to the master bath and washed her face and throat. She examined her throat where he had cut her. Not a scar, just some dried blood which she wiped away with a towel. She cleared her throat and knew her voice was normal. That's right, she had been talking to Mary hadn't she?

When Rainbeaux made it downstairs, she found Mary in the living room. She was rocking slowly in the chair, a faraway look on her face. Still lost in thought, she reached over and gave Rainbeaux a glass of ice cold orange juice.

Rainbeaux gratefully drank it down. She said, "Good to the last drop." Then, "Thanks."

She took the empty glass to the kitchen. She filled it with filtered water. She gulped the fresh clean water. She felt it enter her and refresh her. Energized now, she was hungry. She saw that someone had been baking and knew that it was Mary. There were cookies, a pie and a wonderful loaf of fresh bread. Beside that a large bowl of butter and another of strawberry jam. Rainbeaux shook her head. Mary had also laid out fresh sliced fruit and vegetables. Rainbeaux filled her plate and feasted like she hadn't eaten in days. As she ate she thought that nothing tasted so good in all her life. There was healing in this food prepared by kind loving hands.

When she returned to the living room where Brenner was on the couch staring into space. She stood in front of him for a minute before he saw her.

Sam was not there.

Rainbeaux addressed Brenner's dual state of mind, "Sebastian?"

He looked at her with tear stained eyes. She moved over and hugged him. "How are you?"

"It's hard. My conceptions. All upside down."

"You want to talk?"

"What do we say." It was more than a question. It was his statement of their existential situation.

Rainbeaux looked around. She addressed Mary, "Thanks for the food, Mary Mags."

Mary nodded her head still lost in thought.

"You said Daisy may not recover?"

"She's stirring around. She's tougher than we all

think."

"She would have to be. Sam?"

"He's out back."

Rainbeaux thought of her paintings, sketches, lithographs and all her art work. She felt protective then realized she was irrational. There was nothing he could do to her out there. Nothing more than he had already done.

Mary said, "Just stay in here with us." She looked over at Mary. Then she thought that he could destroy her artwork. Mary watched her. She said grimly, "Gadfan will hurt you anyway he can."

Rainbeaux started to go out there.

Mary finished what she started to say, "He can hurt with unnecessary worry. If you stay in here, you can stop him from hurting you."

Rainbeaux turned toward the back door that led out to her studio.

Then Mary said simply, "Your clothes."

Rainbeaux looked down. She was dressed in a thin tee shirt and short shorts. "I'll get dressed."

"Let's talk about this."

"What is there to talk about?"

"Safety. Don't go out there alone."

Brenner spoke up, "I'll go with you."

Rainbeaux went back upstairs and put on some jeans and hard boots. Then she slipped a heavy blouse over her tee. She went back downstairs. Brenner appeared more energetic. He even smiled. Mary slipped out of a spare bedroom. She smiled too.

"At least she's sleeping. It's good, peaceful. Restful."

They all went out to the studio. They found Sam studying a large canvas on which Rainbeaux was painting her first vision. The vision of the labyrinths piled on top of and next to each other. Nothing seemed disturbed.

Brenner spoke first, "How are you doing, Chessman?"

Sam continued to stare at the painting. He spoke to Rainbeaux, "Are you going to finish this?"

"When I have the time. Something else important came up."

He looked at her with all the guilt that was swimming around inside him. "Finish it, please."

Rainbeaux stifled a curse, instead she asked, "You see something there?"

Mary nodded her head to affirm that she saw what Sam saw. Rainbeaux wondered what that was.

"The thing with the trees. The painting about the trees. That painting is about relationships and revels character." He nodded toward Mary. "But this one reveals a path. Back in Yale, I took a Greek mythology class. The prof used a phrase that just came back to me: Sacred Geometry."

Mary breathed, "Of course." Off Rainbeaux and Brenner's puzzled looks she explained, "Sacred Geometry traces a pathway through the stars for the souls of the dead to follow to their destiny; their angelic or star companion."

"A way out," added Sam. "I'm trapped in a labyrinth. Lost in it. This painting shows me the way out. I don't know why I didn't see it before."

Rainbeaux looked and now she saw the pattern. "It shouldn't take me long. First though. What about Gadfan? I doubt he's toothless and certainly not going to wait around for us to do something."

Mary spoke up, "Unfortunately, he still has all his power. That's not just supernatural power but his earthly political power as well. He's waiting to strike when it suits him."

Brenner asked, "Any ideas?"

Mary closed her eyes. Then opened them. "A few. Let me work something out."

Rainbeaux put her painter's smock on, "Can't you do a

remote exorcism and take him out first?"

"I could but functionally, I am still integrating; that is, forgetting my amnesia. If I could have at the Red River Motel, then I would have gotten rid of him first."

Sam said under his breath, "We're all stuck at the Red River Motel."

Brenner looked at him with horror.

Rainbeaux picked up her brushes, paints and a charcoal pencil. "In the meantime whatever I can do." She began to work on the painting.

Sam said softly, "I really appreciate this."

"Guess I'll take one for the team, huh?"

Sam hurried away. She was already sorry. Mary touched Brenner's shoulder. He went after Sam. Then she said, "It doesn't have to go down like this."

Rainbeaux began to work. "Well, I did."

Mary considered something. "It's not that you should be okay with what happened."

She left to let Rainbeaux know that she wouldn't belabor either point.

A while before this happened, Daisy laid in bed with the covers over her head. It was just before Rainbeaux came downstairs when Mary came in and checked on her. Daisy laid still like she was resting. She felt Mary pick up each of fingers looking at the tips. Daisy knew she was bruised on both hands. She felt a warmth as Mary touched the fingers one by one. Daisy felt her reserve of blood restore. Then she heard Mary leave and gently close the door.

After a little while Daisy got up. She quietly walked to the door. She tip toed out to the bathroom down the hall. She carefully closed and locked that door behind her. She could tell she was alone in the house as the others were out back with Rainbeaux and Sam. She bent over the sink and put her finger down her throat. She gagged and choked until she vomited up the small coffin shaped box wrapped in a plastic baggy. She washed the plastic off. Then she opened the plastic baggy and took the tiny coffin out that contained Quelle Cade's bit of Brain.

After washing her mouth out and gulping water she clutched the box close to her heart as she returned to the room. She put on the clothes Mary had laid out for her. She slipped the coffin shaped box into her jeans pocket. She crept down the stairs.

They were back in the house. She heard the woman she still knew as Marilyn telling Brenner that she was getting more of her memory back. Uh, oh, thought Daisy. Marilyn, or whoever she was now, said more had changed. Daisy allowed herself to laugh silently. Mary was *on the rag* about how Pope Gregory the First changed her story. She protested, "I was never a prostitute! I worked with indigent lepers when Y'shua came along. I joined him. We supported each other's work. That bastard Gregory!"

Brenner asked, "Didn't you say Gadfan had changed things?"

"Poop Greg was his human agent! One of them."

So she may be Mary Magdalene after all. Daisy was aware of the change in Marilyn but hadn't considered whether it was true or just another deluded alternative personality. They said something about Rainbeaux finishing a painting in the studio. At that Daisy smiled. She thought, *She uses her paints and pencils. I paint my spells and memories in blood. I give my memories and spells weight and power a common piece of art can never have.*

Then Sam was talking about their vulnerability by sitting here. A hit team was probably on the way. They were in the kitchen so Daisy was able to slip out the front door undetected. She walked up the street so she couldn't be seen from the kitchen. Daisy didn't know about "ish-oo-WAH" or Mary Magdalene. All she knew was that she was her daddy's little girl. She knew magic, ritual and the power of unrelenting hatred caused by the deepest pain. She believed in the petrified piece of a serial killer's brain that she held in her pocket. She knew where Gadfan would be. She knew how to get there. She knew what she was going to do. She knew how to banish Gadfan from our world or kill him either way once and for all.

CHAPTER 36

Within two hours, Sam was standing in front of the just completed painting; the inks and paints still wet. He traced the outline of the pattern Rainbeaux had drawn. Working out the path through the maze with his finger. "Amazing, you didn't see the pattern but you drew it."

Rainbeaux stood by silently and studied Sam analyze her painting.

Mary was studying the painting with Sam when Brenner came in. "I did some checking for Chessman and myself. Our identities are erased. That means no passports, birth records, driver's license, no employment, school or credit records. It is as though we never existed."

"Perfect, so no credit cards, no access to money, no way to get around." Rainbeaux allowed some anger and frustration.

"I extrapolate that this was done to all of us. You'll be tracked if you try to use credit cards. The numbers are for other people now and they are listed as stolen," Brenner said.

Sam said, "He's taking some time and prepping to have us killed. Easier to get rid of people who don't exist. This way no one will miss us."

He suddenly looked pleased with the path he discovered on the labyrinth.

Rainbeaux said, "It sounds dire. But all this means is that for the time being," she made a motion with her hand, "we move underground." She looked at Mary, "Maybe catacombs. Then we hit 'em where it hurts."

Mary said, "I agree. We let them know we exist after all. I'll see what I can do to slow Gadfan down."

"Groovy," said Rainbeaux. "What if you do that in con-

269

cert with something the rest of us do? Any ideas?"

Sam stepped back and smiled, "I know exactly what to do. And Ms. Magdalene, slowing him down is all you have to do."

Mary addressed Rainbeaux, "I have a job for you. I suspect that Gadfan is facing a lot of pressure from the higher ups. He as a boss too. They always do."

"Right," said Rainbeaux, "there's this Tibetan Buddhist chant, beyond ... and beyond the beyond ... ever ever beyond. In other words follow the money."

"You got it. If I'm not mistaken, he wants to talk."

Rainbeaux's mood lightened to have something to do, "Then I'll go into the Spook Zone and do my Spook thing."

Mary said, "It is dangerous, but I think you are mostly relatively safe."

Rainbeaux smiled weakly, "Aw, there you go, building up my sense of lesser impending doom. Good on you."

Mary pulled her aside, "Seriously, don't engage Him in conversation."

"That goes without saying. On the other hand I want to give him a piece of mind."

Mary smiled as she said, "Get wise to yourself, Rainbeaux. That is exactly what you can't do."

Rainbeaux remembered her warning to Sam about detectives asking questions. "Right, I warned Sam about this. But he had started initiation by then."

"What do you think the purification was about?"

"I was going to ask about that later."

"That is what pain and abuse were all about, it drives out the best parts of us and makes room for Him." Mary struggled not to become lost within herself for a moment.

Rainbeaux asked, "You okay?"

"Yes, just had to ... You are in danger of taking on His karmic energy."

"How?"

"Let me explain it this way, Y'shua taught non-attachment for a reason. On an emotional level you are very attached to Gadfan. Don't argue with me, I can see it. It leads to this whole Bridal Chamber thing. There is a divine marriage and you become responsible for his Karma."

Rainbeaux wrinkled her nose, "I don't want to marry the bastard, I want to kick his ass."

Mary sighed. "Anything other than the walk behind me thing is a mistake."

"Thanks for the heads up. Anything else."

"Good luck," Mary smiled at her.

Rainbeaux mumbled, "Lesser impending doom ..."

Within minutes she entered the Psychotorium. She felt the seconds tick away as she entered her Spook Zone. The screen flashed with the same supernal light. Yet, something had changed.

Up on the screen: dig that crazy labyrinth. Dark colors. Twisty shapes of ghosts. Blind corners. Movement out of the corner of her eye. Long travel down and up. An altered sense of time; taking forever to get there; not remembering how long it takes. She hears smells and tastes colors. Just like the purification. Like she's in a haunted house as large as a train station but entering inter-dimensional doors. A panic that she shouldn't be going here. Then a reassuring presence. Sam appears, stark and white as a ghost, he guides her to the final door. He delivers her here after all. Just like the Red River Motel. She goes through the door –

She steps outside into a forest. Lights from houses shine through the trees. The weather is dark and rainy; misty and wintery. She wears a thin white floor length dress. She's barefoot as she enters a rock path that leads up to a large house. The house looks like something out of Wuthering Heights. She walks and walks up the winding garden path. Her feet barely touch the stones. She finally

271

stands before a weathered vine covered wooden door with oiled iron hinges; just like on her copy of the Nag Hammadi Library at home.

She enters and is suddenly transported to a brightly lit room. Comfortable furniture. A fire in the hearth against the cold outside.

Gadfan sits in front of her. A big comfortable chair with a glass of wine on the stand beside Him. She sees His face. His face in this world. His skin red with a smoke or steam rising off it, teeth sharp, hoofed feet in slippers, wearing nice dress slacks and a smoking jacket, "Whatdasay, Girlie?"

"A cheerier place than we have met before."

She waits a moment. Which also seems forever. Then, "Walk behind me, Gadfan."

He sits there, implacable. "You aren't Mary, She of the Stairway, you know."

"Damn. There went my last bit of hope."

"Don't get bummed out by how long you are here. It's all perception as you know. Plus, I have minions ..."

"There are always minions."

"... On the way to your place. You will die on your beloved couch staring up at the screen, looking into eternity."

"What a relief! Just when this was starting to get boring."

Gadfan drinks some wine and shrugs His shoulders. "Even now at the end ..."

"Spare me any regrets you have about killing me."

"I do. I have them. Tell me, here, at the end, what was it you really wanted? The most that is."

She knows she must remember something but the thing to remember slips away from her. "This isn't some bullshit judgment day is it?" The longer she keeps him talking, the more she learns. Wait, that's bad isn't it?

"What they didn't tell you about judgment day, is that

it is your judgment about what you got out of this. Not mine, not some eternal judge or lord over all men. Sorry, make that lord over women too."

"Do I get to go back and try again if I don't like what went down?"

Gadfan laughs. "No, 'fraid not. This is what you get."

For some reason, Rainbeaux takes this seriously. It strikes her, this really is judgment day. Should she really trust Gadfan with her judgment?

He nods. "I can read your mind. But you knew that, right?"

"What the hell. Alright, I wanted to marry Sam. Have a couple of kids. Gold Rolex. Mercedes convertible. Attain the Barbelo Aeon. You know, the usual."

"Barbelo, eh? The influence of Mary of the Stairway to Heaven is showing. Too bad. I had hoped you wanted something original." Gadfan looks at her with mock disappointment.

"Is it so bad to want a world released from fear? From pain?"

"How about a love released from fear and pain?"

When He says that, He surprises her. "Bless me, you are making sense."

He drinks more wine. His glass refills as if by magic. "I don't know what hurts more. That I am going to lose you or that you are surprised that I can carry an honest intimate conversation."

Rainbeaux feels stunned, "You regret losing me? Isn't this what you wanted when you built your system. Your city?"

"I built the City. But sometimes there are unexpected consequences. Yes, that includes my feelings for you."

Rainbeaux still shocked, "You won't get what you want." She stops. Something Mary said that must remember.

"Because?"

"Because you are the monster that built the city but it isn't your garden."

Gadfan surprises her again by appearing to think about that. "No," He says sadly. "It isn't. Never mine in a true sense. Say, when they make a movie of this, you don't think they'll get Walken to play me do you?"

"I imagine not. Since you are going to destroy everything anyway."

"I am. No Christopher Walken. Michael Cain is out of reach too. Damn."

"Is there any way out of this for us?"

"Us? No. You are all damned, kiddo. That's the way it goes."

She knows better but she pushes it anyway, "A way out for you too. It seems to me you are as trapped as the rest of us."

"How astute of you. But I don't want out. I like where I am."

"Where is that, Gadfan? A minor demigod so far down the chain of command you eat whatever the higher power shits down to you?"

The Blasphemer let out a whopping laugh. For a moment or so He can't stop. Then there are tears in his eyes. "You are so, so. Correct. Never doubt that I like you, Rainbeaux. You really have what they call Gnosis."

"Can the knowledge save me? What if I can save us both?"

He smiles wistfully, "I wish that were so. I wish you could. You don't want to do that."

"I'll bite. Why not?"

"To do that, to save me as you save yourself, you have to take on my Fate in the Big Nowhere. Think it through, the Karmic Fate of a demigod. Especially with the blood metaphorically and literally I have on my hands."

"What? Across centuries? Continents?"

"Now you insult me, Lady Spook. No, more than that. Much more. Try across worlds, across gulfs too big for you to cross even with all your powers. Dimensions. Time. Going back to when I was formed out of light."

She knows she is in danger but likes what she learns from Him. "Then what? Fell into darkness?" Rainbeaux feels she is getting somewhere even if Mary warned her not to go here. Now she remembers!

He shakes His head. "You have no idea for real darkness. Away from the Source. The True Source of everything."

"Tell me more."

"You know what your whole universe is? Your whole universe is built on the membrane on a bubble. A bubble among other bubbles in the foam on top of a wave. A wave that will crash down so far into the future you have no idea how to measure it. A wave among countless waves in the vast oceans of existence."

As that sinks in she feels a smallness, a sadness at her own insignificance. It overwhelms her to the point she can't breathe, react, think, reply. She struggles to regain her composure. She needs to be at the top of her game against Gadfan. She counters, "If I am this infinite smallness, how can I began to grasp what you describe? Yet I can. I am conscious of this vastness. How small am I when I can perceive this?"

She can tell He is impressed, "You can't, you know? You can't overmatch me. You don't distract me enough to let your friends do their worst. I know about all of you. Let me help you come back from the ocean of the ominverse. I am aware of everything you and your friends are about to do. I know Daisy is coming to me. Walking into a trap. So is Sam. Mary of the Stairway has more compiling to do before she is anything like a threat to me." Then Gadfan appears pained as though he is slammed by something big. "Wow, she knows what I just said. Ouch! That showed me. Still even with that, the best she could do is bring in some of her friends from way beyond to help her. She isn't there yet."

Rainbeaux chews on this. "You keep calling her Mary of the Stairway. What do you mean?"

"It means what it means. That Magdalene jazz wasn't a town she was from. She was from Bethany, a suburb of Jerusalem, anyway. The place where the lepers lived. No, her name 'Magdalene' refers to the quality of her spiritual life. She is an example on how to walk the Stairway to Heaven."

"Just like the Led Zeppelin song."

Gadfan touched his nose. "Still more than that. She represents the means to go to Heaven and see Il, the one with the juice."

"The Elohimist tradition."

Gadfan claps for her. "You know the tradition. Ah, the old time religion going back to Akkad and Sumer. You know of En Heduanna? Good, I see you do. Magdalene refers to a ladder or a tower. Like Jacob's Ladder or the Tower of Babel. Even the rocky path up Mount Horeb. Rising up to see the Big Himself. Make sense?"

Rainbeaux's smile is grim. "Yes, you just told me everything I need to know."

"Did I?" He looks her up and down. "You still have a question."

"Yes, I do. Here it is: why talk to me like this? I was warned not to talk to you. But this isn't going as badly as I anticipated. I mean, this isn't the way you initiated Sam into your bullshit cult."

The Blasphemer appears sad. "In case I fail."

"To do what? Destroy us? Why? Wait, we were supposed to find the initiates of the cult who weren't on board. But there is more. If Mary is real, then He was too.

And you were beaten. You were outta here. You got your power back. How?" She snaps her fingers when she realizes something. "Then someone must have called you ..." She stops talking and thinks, *Back from the Big Nowhere.*

"They did," He finishes for her. "I was called back by the rich and powerful. They need an advocate too."

"But you have free will ..." (don't you?)

"It is not my nature to go where I am not invited."

Something about His last statement awakens something within her. She slaps her forehead. She was warned and did it anyway. But she doesn't feel any different.

He laughs at her as he drinks more wine.

She gathers up her sense of lesser impending doom. "Get behind me, Gadfan. I reject you. To crowd you out, I fill myself ..." (with supernal light.)

Gadfan gives her a dismissive wave of his clawed hand, "Back, go back little rainbow. Go back down the slide."

Instantly Rainbeaux finds she stands on a bridge over a roaring water fall. She watches the water gush from somewhere underneath her feet one hundred feet down into a blue pool of very deep water. Then she realizes she is looking up at her hair and that it is hanging straight down. That is when she understands that she is upside down as though she stands on the bottom of a globe. Or the membrane of a bubble. There is a gate in front of her. Without being able to stop it, she watches her hand open the gate. She sees her foot lift over the edge of the bridge. Her foot dangles perilously in the space over the steep drop. She feels her body lean forward. The feeling of being upside down again. Without being able to stop it, she falls upward from the bridge for a long time before plunging into the cold swirling blue water above her head.

CHAPTER 37

Mary Magdalene sat slumped in the papa san chair. Her head snapped up. She looked around the living room. "Time is wonky," she said suddenly awake.

"All the time," Brenner said apparently very puzzled.

"No, something is happening up there. With her. And time is moving out of joint and at a different pace here and there. All around us."

Brenner got up, walked to the kitchen and put his coffee cup in the sink. "I wish I had your ability to discern. I don't feel any of that, that's for sure."

"You could learn it." She called to him.

Then from outside sounds of screeching tires, men yelling at each other. Brenner and Mary at the window in the living room in a flash. More men in black. They pulled their firearms and began a coordinated approach on the house.

Mary Mags said in a command voice, "Walk behind me."

Brenner jumped around behind her. "Exorcism," was all she said. Brenner moved to the window again. He saw the men standing back on the front lawn. "That's embarrassing. Looks like I'm just strong enough to keep them out."

Brenner asked, "My question is why sacrifice those men? Unless ..."

She left Brenner at the window and ran toward the back of the house. Brenner followed her. Sure enough, more men in black were at the back door. At her command, some collapsed while others stepped back. "I need time to build more strength."

Brenner asked, "Will they be able to get inside?"

There was more commotion outside. Peering out the window again they saw more men in black in a running gun fight with men and women wearing blue blazers that identified them as Federal Agents.

Before Mary could say anything, a stream of lead poured through the walls and window. Mary yelled out, "Walk behind me!" Then silence.

She and Brenner looked at each other. "I had to try."

"Something happened." This was followed by a careful knock at the door. Brenner opened the front to find Roswell Hane waiting there with five more special agents. All of them armed, smoke curling from the barrels of their weapons.

Hane said, "We are here to move you to a safer location."

Brenner observed, "There are no safe locations. On the other hand ... there is no other hand to that."

"It won't do us much good," said Mary. "Although I want to face Gadfan again."

Hane motioned with his head toward the lawn, "He sent some men over to pick you up."

Mary said, "Or off."

Hane nodded grimly, "Where's Rainbeaux?"

Brenner said, "Last we knew she was in the Psychotorium."

CHAPTER 38

She woke on her couch and gasped for breath. She realized she was alive. Dry. But not alone.

Hane stood beside her. "You okay?" he asked.

Quick as a wink she raised up and slapped him. "Where the hell have you been?"

Hane was shocked and hurt by her reaction, "Putting together a hostage rescue team."

Rainbeaux sat up. She rubbed her face. "You might be just in time too. If we can find them."

She put her shoes on while Hane stood up and smoothed his suit coat. "Them who?"

"Sam and Daisy." Rainbeaux stood up.

"Sam Chessman and Daisy Yancy slipped by us. Embarrassing. But we have Brenner and Marilyn LezElvis or whatever name she goes by nowadays."

Rainbeaux caught that Hane knew about Mary's transformation. She let it go. She exited the room before he could turn around. "What are we waiting for?"

Within minutes they were in an unmarked Federal car. Rainbeaux and Mary rode in back, with Hane in the front, while an agent drove them to the Federal Building on Sixth Street. Brenner was in another car behind them.

They passed within blocks of Daisy. She walked up the street clutching the sliver of Cade's brain in the small coffin box. She giggled knowing what she had in her hands, knowing that most other people didn't know what she carried. How freaked they would be if they did. But she was smarter than them. They would never know. Only she knew and it proved how smart she was. Anyway it wasn't people she had to worry about. She looked up into a sky that was an admixture of bright sunlight and dark clouds.

A dreamlike state suddenly came over her. Like nothing was real. She felt this before, many times.

Alert! She saw a car that gave her a hinky feeling. A large black sedan with two men dressed in black sitting in front.

She turned and walked up a different street. She walked half way down the block. Then another black sedan pulled up along side her. She didn't know if it was the same sedan. The men looked the same. Men in black with mirror shades on. Her face got red with anger. "How cliché!", she yelled through the window at the men.

She ran down to the corner. She faked a right then turned left. She walked down a street then headed down an alley. She looked behind her and saw the large black sedan park at the end of the alley as though to cut her off. She looked ahead. The way was clear. She didn't trust it.

So she headed through a door into a restaurant. It was an Indian joint and the place was busy and Daisy almost collided with wait staff carrying trays of dirty dishes into the kitchen. She looked around the tables. She saw them off to the side, two more men in black. They saw her too.

One of them stood as though to catch her before she made it to the door. But Daisy ran out the front door. She looked back. The place was half full with men in black.

There were men in black mixed with the crowd multiplying all around her. Three men in black held hands while they crossed the street; two of them smaller than the third. Another came out of a coffee house. Another looked out the window of the coffee house at her. He played guitar for the other men in black sitting inside.

She glanced around the street. Large black sedans started coming from every direction. A parade of these cars rolling down the avenue toward her.

Daisy started to run. She ran three blocks into more and more men in black with more black sedans all around her.

As she ran from them she tripped and fell down to the concrete sidewalk. No, no, no, something felt wrong. She was hurt and it was hard to get up. She realized how out of breath she was. She tried to push herself up but her arms gave out. She laid down and got ready for another shot at it.

Then before she could recover, one of the men in black rolled her over. He started going through her pockets. "Let me see what I can find."

Daisy panicked when she felt his hand reach into the pocket that held the small coffin box and the precious piece of Cade's brain. The one thing that kept Gadfan anchored to this world.

Rip had been thinking about what happened the night before at DA's office. He knew Sam was in trouble and he was worried. So he was out looking for him. He heard over the squad car's radio that there was some trouble downtown at Sixth and Congress.

When he got there he saw a commotion up the street. He ran up and flashed his badge. There were a group of people standing around a homeless man who was fighting with a young woman under him. She kept something tight in her fist. The bum laughed as he tried to take it from her.

He stopped laughing when Rip slapped a cuff on him. Then he wrenched the hand and the arm it belonged to behind the bum and grabbed the other arm. SNAP the other cuff was on.

"Hey man!" he yelled as Rip pulled him off Daisy. She looked up. "Men in black," was all she said.

Rip looked around. "No one here but a cop, that'd be me, and some civilians."

He recognized her, knew her from TV.

Daisy looked wild eyed. She struggled to get up and run.

"I think you better let me get you some help."

But Daisy found the strength to jump up and she fled. Rip pulled out his walkie. "She was here."

Daisy continued to run down the street. Everyone turned back into people. Mind tricks, she thought. He was playing mind tricks on her. She had played enough on herself that she knew how to reground herself. She stopped and as she reminded herself where she was. She took some deep breaths.

After she refocused, she ran up to a car stopped at a light. She beat on the window. The driver, a middle aged man, looked at her shocked. "You have to help me!"

He yelled back, "Get away you crazy bitch!"

"I'm Daisy Yellow Yancy. Please take me home."

The guy was shocked but he opened the door. "Why didn't you say so? I worked for your dad. Get in."

Rip got into an unmarked cruiser and followed them.

Earlier when Sam left Rainbeaux's house not sure if he would ever return. He wanted to go back but didn't believe that he should have the right. In fact, he knew he shouldn't go back. Now he just wanted to find his way out of the labyrinth. He didn't know how that would help but knew that it would. Maybe he could see how to kill Gadfan. Or take him in. That was a laugh. What to do with him in central booking? You couldn't exactly put him in general population and wait overnight for the judge could you?

There is an extra street in front of him. He walks down that street. He doesn't recognize it. Then another street he doesn't recognize. Yet he knows from the painting of the labyrinth where he is going.

Then he sees that he walks on a street that leads up into the air. *I transcend airy earth*, he thinks. Then he thinks *this isn't so bad*. He looks down from here into the maze beneath him. He looks up and sees another maze above. He looks around and sees several doorways. He tries to move around them but they keep coming up in front of him again and again. He finds he can't stop his hand from reaching out and opening one of the doors. He is in a theater. *NO*, he screams inside his head louder than he thought possible.

Gadfan stands in front of an audience. The people in the audience are in shadow from the house lights being dim and the stage lights shining into Sam's eyes. Sam knows that not all the people in the audience are alive. But they know anyway. They watch them anyway. And the living people. And those who weren't people. Never were human.

Gadfan holds his hands to stop applause though no one claps.

Sam rushes past him and out through a side entrance.

Gadfan yells joyously to the audience, "Exit, stage left!"

Sam back in his father's library. His father sits stern and angry. He slowly starts to raise from his leather chair. Sam remembers what this means. He wants out of there. He runs around the library. The Old Man cuts him off from the door. Sam knows, somehow, to climb out a window.

Sam in his room. Mother holds him in her lap. She whispers that what happened is his fault. Sam pushes away from her. He opens the closet door.

Sam now climbs from darkness into another library. He stands inside the Austin History Center of the Public Library in Austin Texas. Angelique is there. She smiles at him. He smiles back, surprised at how he feels about her now. He still finds he loves her. She winks at him. He leans over to kiss her. The flesh drips away from her face. Sam stops a centimeter from the skull face of his first love. He jerks backs as she laughs at him. They are in the Galleria Mall in Houston Texas. He holds a flower out to her. She pushes him away. She says that what happened is his fault. Sorrowful and bewildered Sam ...

... Runs into the room with the Fong Torres family. They sit around a glowing TV covered in their blood. But they are distracted from dying by the clownish antics of politicians on a news show. As the politicians yell and scream, the Fong Torres Family laugh and bubbles of blood come out of their mouths.

Sam opens the door to Fong Torres's home office. He enters the cafe with Aziz again. Sam wants to cry at the second chance.

"Aziz! I'm so sorry. All I wanted to do was help you. Believe me, man."

Aziz says solemnly, "Come with me." As they walk out the front door of the cafe ...

... Sam stumbles into the warehouse. He looks for Aziz but doesn't see him. "I'm up here."

Sam looks up. Aziz is on scaffolding above his head. "I'm coming up!"

"No, Detective Chessman, don't. You won't make it!"

Sam, determined, starts the long climb.

CHAPTER 39

Rainbeaux felt kind of numb as she sat next to Mary in the back seat of the car. Hane sat in the front passenger's seat, his attention focused on his cell phone. She knew that Brenner was in another car that was behind theirs.

Then she was aware that Mary asked, "You said that you learned everything you need to know. What was it that learned?"

Rainbeaux saw Hane put his cell away. She knew he listened intently to them.

Rainbeaux didn't look at her, "I don't know what I meant by that. I couldn't tell you now."

"But you remember what you learned?"

"Yes, but I don't know how it will help. It's like a dream. It makes sense until you wake up. I mean he told me about your name, the meaning of it, that he has beings above and below him. We knew that already."

"What else did you notice?" asked Mary.

"I don't ..."

Mary was insistent. "Yes, you do," she said this evenly and slowly.

Rainbeaux thought for a moment. "He seems to live out there at the same time he exists here."

"And?" Mary smiled ever so slightly.

"He exists on multiple levels. But then I guess we all do. Say, when He is finally exorcised will He withdraw out there?"

"Your question gives you your answer."

"Then maybe we don't want Him out there. Is there a way to trap Him in one place? All his composite parts together?"

"You are very wise in your ...."

She felt the car slam into something, they were jerked to a halt.

Hane looked from his cell to the scene in the street in front of the Federal Building. "Well, that's out," he said.

She saw that the Federal Building was surrounded by every sort of Federal law enforcement officer. "I can see that I slowed Him down not at all."

She felt reassuring warmth as Mary reached over and held her hand.

"We can't stop here," Hane said to the driver.

"I have to, Sir," the driver said. "Orders."

Hane pulled his service weapon. He pushed the barrel hard into the driver's ear. "I have some new orders for you."

The driver turned down Colorado and away from the Federal Building. "Where would you like to get out?"

"By the river," said Rainbeaux.

The driver said, "They're going to find you anyway."

Hane pushed the driver's head with his service weapon again, "Just drive."

They were let out by Town Lake and the walking/jogging trail. Hane gave the driver instructions to drive down to Barton Creek and turn North up MOPAC.

Rainbeaux said, "That will buy us thirty seconds."

Hane said, "We'll make it a good thirty seconds. Suggestions?"

She said, "Here I thought you always had a plan?"

"RV's watch us, remember?"

She remembered. "Remain unpredictable. Alright, I say we head West."

"Why?" he asked.

"No reason."

"Perfect," he replied.

Mary looked at the car with Brenner. "We were followed. I'll get Sebastian."

Rainbeaux said, "Do that, then skedaddle. We'll meet up later."

Mary ran to the car behind them.

"Somehow," Rainbeaux added. She looked up and Hane followed her gaze. She saw a man walking on clouds.

"What's that?"

She said simply, "Sam."

"What?"

"He's above us."

"Is he dead?"

"No," she said. "He's watching us."

Then she took her cell phone and turned it on. Then she ran up to a car at a stop light traveling east. She slipped the cell in the bumper of the car.

"Thirty more seconds," said Hane as she walked back to him.

"In the spirit of unpredictability, let's split up."

She heard Hane say as she ran, "In fact, I'll let them find me and help you get more time."

"Don't know yet what I'll do with it. But thanks."

She saw the sedan with Hane turn in the road back toward several cars coming at them with blinking lights. Rainbeaux looked around and didn't know where she would go. Then she remembered watching a movie about some guy on the lamb.

She went down to the river, took off her shoes and slipped into the water. This was a mistake, the water was fifty-five degrees Fahrenheit. Plus, she knew the danger of dipping her head under the water of the Colorado. The water was untreated and it was possible to become ill if she drank it or it got in her ears. Which meant that she couldn't hide in the river. Suddenly this was a bad idea.

She made herself feel that very strongly. More than that, she made her emotions bottom out completely. As her mood dropped a deathly depression descended on her. A hopelessness that made her want to slip under that water forever. To die in the river.

She hid as best she could. She watched as an assembled team of US Marshals, FBI agents and APD were at the very point on the river bank. They reported back that she wasn't there. They couldn't find anything of her except for a sweater that was floating in the water. The Dive Team was called out. They would sweep the river until they found her body.

She had to act fast. There was a homeless guy a hundred or so meters from her. She had an idea.

A few minutes later Rip came and stood by a bus bench and watched. He was right beside her. Her heart was pounding. She hoped he didn't notice the rather disheveled homeless man dripping water on the bench. She got up and shambled away and hoped all he saw was an old homeless man. When she looked over her shoulder Rip didn't even look at her.

Until another homeless man, almost naked stopped her. "Hey, dude, how am I supposed to buy new threads if they won't let me in the store."

She looked over her shoulder to see if Rip saw her now. "All they want is money," Rainbeaux said through her soggy disguise. She tossed him a wet twenty which she didn't have to give away. "Thanks for the beard."

The other homeless man rubbed the stubble on his face. "Quick shave. Close one too."

CHAPTER 40

Rip turned and looked at them. He saw a common street scene of two homeless guys sharing money. As she tried to make progress down the street she was afraid that she looked familiar. He wouldn't have a reason to stop her though.

So Rip returned to the river down the street from the courthouse. When he got there, he saw Marilyn LezElvis. He didn't recognize the man with her.

He took a chance and walked up them. "Can I help you?" Both of them stopped and looked at him with fear. "I'm a friend of Sam's. Let me give you lift."

Brenner started to say something, but Mary cut him off. "It's okay, he's with us."

They followed him to his squad car. Inside the squad car they introduced themselves. Only Mary still called herself Marilyn in front of Rip. He said to her, "You look younger."

"I started watching what I eat," she said.

The traffic moved slow. So Rip had time to turn in his seat to talk to them, "I've been worried about Sam. He's changed and I don't know what to do about it."

Brenner asked, "When did you notice a change?"

"After he found the body at the Yancy place. It wasn't all at once. More like a spiral." Rip made a dipping motion with his hands. "Did you see anything?"

Brenner said, "I met Sam after he discovered the corpse. Two corpses. The other at the Red River Motel."

Rip looked at Mary, "Speaking of that, I have to ask."

Mary looked put out with Rip, but Brenner thought that might be show. "You know that scene in the detective story when the crusty old PI says everyone is a suspect ...?

Rip grinned at her, "I gotcha. What can we do for Sam now? Is all ..." (this for him?)

Just then two blue suited Feds walked up to the window of the sedan. One of the them knocked loudly on Rip's window interrupting him. "We need to take these suspects with us."

Mary looked around for a place to run. But the sedan was suddenly surrounded.

Rip lowered his window. "I have custody of these folks. They aren't the people you are looking for."

Mary closed her eyes and went deep inside. The personnel surrounding them on the outside pointed their weapons at the police sedan.

The officer next to Rip's window said, "Open your doors slowly and exit the vehicle."

Those guns looked big through the window.

Rip said to Mary and Brenner, "I thought the Force had an effect on the weak minded."

Mary said, "Working on it."

Rip stalled for time when he said to the Federal officers, "I have to follow my SOP. Let me take them to Central Processing. We can do the hand over there."

The Feds outside the car weren't having any part of it. Almost as one being, they aimed their weapons at Rip's squad car. "Move!" was all the Fed by the window said. To the other agents he yelled, "On three. One!"

Rip touched the lift on his power window control. "Two!"

The window worked its way up far too slowly. "Well," he said, "I guess we get out of the car."

"Three!"

CHAPTER 41

She knew her disguise would do for a few hours unless someone took too much notice of her. She walked like a girl after all. That beard of real human hair wouldn't stay on too long. Not to mention she couldn't wait to get out of these clothes. It was hot and wearing these filthy clothes over hers was making her sweat. She would need water and soon.

Right now her hope was in the strong emotion she created by the river for the benefit the RV who was watching her. That strong emotion was like a beacon that would distract the RV and the Feds for a few hours. She used the time to think. She wanted to hook up with who ever was left of their little group. Sam and Roswell were out. Unless Roswell talked his way out of his situation. She couldn't put it past him to do that. Then he could help her. Sebastian maybe.

But the one she was really wanting to reach was Mary. How could she find Mary? Where would Mary go?

Then she had an idea. She jumped onto one the University of Texas shuttle buses. She rode toward Mary's neighborhood. The bus didn't go all the way. It was a twenty minute walk to Mary's place.

It was getting dark when she arrived. The lights were off. It didn't appear that anyone was home. She decided that was for the best. She went around back, used her otherwise useless credit card to jiggle the lock on the back door. It worked and she slipped inside the sixties style Bachelorette pad.

She crept around the house. There was no one else there. She went to the utility room and peeled the homeless man's clothes off. These she washed separately from her own clothes. While her clothes washed she went in the bathroom to clean herself. The shower felt good; then she allowed time to soak in the bathtub. Then she went to the kitchen and got a good long drink of water. She folded the homeless man's clothes to return to him. Someday, somehow. When her clothes were dry she dressed again.

Back in the living room she stretched out on the couch. Refreshed and relaxed she felt safe. She couldn't help slipping into a peaceful sleep.

Then she knows she is asleep. How odd, she thinks, that I can sleep like this with everything that has happened and with all that is going on. She is aware that Mary stands in the room with her. Mary stands there like a ghost and watches her for a long time. How unlike Mary she thinks. She tries to wake up but Mary's hand rests lightly on her forehead. Rainbeaux submits and lies there peacefully.

Next thing she knows she walks down the street. A church on the street to her left. The parking lot is full of cars. She didn't know there was a service today; a week day. She hears piano music very beautifully played. The sound attracts her. She walks in. Inside someone gives her a program. She drops it on the floor. She sits in the middle of the sanctuary. The sound from the piano washes over her. It vibrates in her. And it goes on and on as she loses herself in the music. She knows that soon Mary will come. They will work out a plan. Stop the hurt. Stop the suffering. She opens her eyes.

She sees a woman in a white wedding dress. The woman's face is covered in a veil. There is something familiar about the woman. She walks right by Rainbeaux. Now Rainbeaux looks up at the front of the sanctuary. There are flowers arranged around the alter. A minister who holds his Bible in his left hand stands at the altar. Above the alter is a banner that reads **My Filthy Marriage**. A stench fills Rainbeaux's nose. The groom enters

at the back. As she turns to watch him walk down the aisle
...

... She is alone in a dark room. It is as though she waits for something. She still feels the sound of the beautiful piano music within her.

Then after a time she thinks she hears Mary Magdalene say, "Come with me and I will show you a mystery."

Rainbeaux leaves her secrets behind. She offers her hand to Mary. They hold hands as Mary leads her along. Maybe this isn't Mary but she holds hands with someone, as they walk to Another Place. There is some comfort in that. Rainbeaux didn't realize how much she needed it, that comfort. She thinks this Place is like nothing else in the Spook Zone. She had never worked out if the Zone was a mental state of hers or a cross dimensional place, or rather an imaginal place, to which she travels. If there are cross dimensional or imaginal "places", this is it. As she gets there, she notices Mary Magdalene isn't standing beside her.

"Where are you, Mary?" She looks around. "I'm alone."

She isn't. Someone else is there waiting for her.

CHAPTER 42

"**I**'m standing right here!" he shouts.

Gadfan stands impossibly tall and thin in a crisp white suit leaning against a crooked utility pole. Before him is a fetid stagnant pool of filthy water. Garbage and pollution float in the cesspool.

Around them dizzily foaming about them like a stage are cyclopean slum houses built for the ragged beings who live there, dirty gray dingy concrete with broken windows, covered with graffiti made up of arcane magical symbols and images of obscene sex. The darkening sky above them is filled with blue- black clouds the color of a bruise and smoke that smells like rotting flowers and sour milk; the smell of a decaying human corpse. Add to that the sharp acrid smell caused by burning flesh. The smell of rotting trash, stinking garbage, urine and shit along with burning flesh fill her nostrils. Rainbeaux gags.

Then she startles to discover she is aware of Presence all around them. Sentient beings, some human or were at some point, smaller meaner beings and vast intelligences that control titanic tidal forces that create and shape all creation watch them. From the tiny bubble that make up this universe to the billions of other bubbles to the waves that crest and form bubbles in their foam and beyond. Ever, ever beyond.

Gadfan reads her mind. "Yep, we have an audience. Time for your story."

"Story?" she asks bewildered.

He replies, "It's show time."

"Show time?" She looks around the gigantic ageless slum more than a little confused. "Mary Mags was right here."

So much of her plan is dependent on Mary. She notices that His words are slurred and there is a whine in His voice. She has to listen to figure what He is saying.

"She can't come up here yet and she'd know that. I don't know what car wash you kids worked at, and I own a fucking car wash. But thessss is you alone."

Rainbeaux lost her patience for him, "Cut the noise. Why isn't she here?"

"The principals of ascent and descent and coming and going." Then He broke into a stream of gibberish. Or at least He was saying something she couldn't understand.

"You aren't still on that whole truth telling thing are you? Cuz, that's just plain unnervin'."

"I say whatever I need to get what I want. And what I want is the story you have to tell."

Rainbeaux smiles. Of course, now Gadfan's statement about story makes sense; this was in every detective story ever written. "So it's time for the big reveal. Okay, I'll play. If I'm correct, you let me and my friends go, we get our identities back."

He shakes his head. "Sorry sweet knees, it doesn't work like that round these parts. But tell you what, you tell a good story, I'll do right by you."

"I don't like this deal."

The Blasphemer makes a grand gesture with his arms and hands, "But I'm smilin' like a salamander."

And he is.

Rainbeaux glances around. She wants to walk around the pool to him. But she sees that she is barefoot and the area around the pool is full of broken glass and little piles of greasy shit. She sees that the pool and the ground around it stretch out into eternity and if possible beyond. There is a sound of wind and the rumble of earth that vibrate constantly.

She is aware again of an audience. She sees their dim

outlines sitting in the windows of the dilapidated houses and apartments that surround them. Sitting on chairs and benches, something like cigarettes dangle from their mouths; half finished drinks or cups of coffee in their hands.

This freaks her a little bit. It brings to mind her vision of the dark city with its labyrinths and all the creatures, and Sam too, who inhabit it. Then the stench fills her nose again at the next inhale of breath. It is all too much to take in all at once. She tries to ground herself but it doesn't work. *Duh, I'm not standing on the ground*, she thinks. Then she thinks that this isn't glass or shit either. She twirls around and tries to smile like a salamander herself.

"Fact, you were brought to our world by arcane witch-craft using a mummified piece of a killer's brain."

She stops and watches him. He continues smilin' like that salamander.

"Fact, you run a cult of assassins." Salamander Smile keeps grinning.

"Fact, I have met you out here in the Imaginal Plane. Three times. The first time scared me so badly I quit the DoD. Then earlier today. Twice. And now. Three times."

Gadfan yawns and says, "I have things to do, Darlin'. You coming to a point anytime soon?"

"It was Mary Magdalene, Daisy and Aziz who kept leaving Sam and I clues. They rebelled against you. Now I wonder, why are you so concerned?"

It slowly dawned on her. She needs to make Him mad again. Mad enough to kick her out of here. And she needs to stop talking to Him. This is a mistake. But for her, at this time, it looks like there is no other way.

"Because you have a huge ego? Maybe. You have a world to run. You aren't the minion of the Demonic World Ruler. That is who you are; the Prince of the Air, the Ruler of the World. The Harsh Boss."

She walks across a small bit of ground, around the jagged glass and feces. "And why do you need that serial killer's brain to anchor you to our world? You aren't strong enough to come down anytime you want?"

He is calm but watchful, "It's your story. Write it and live your myth."

"Mary Magdalene is back on earth to complete the transformation of our world. Y'shua started the work ..."

Gadfan spreads his arms expansively, "If you really believed, you would have asked your god to help you. I know for a fact you haven't done anything of the kind. And the same can be said for your sorry excuse of a human race. Now you know why I'm so happy each and every day. I have no worries, no worries at all, Remote Viewer Le Blanc."

Rainbeaux looks around at the factories spouting smoke. She intuits something about Gadfan. He feeds the factories.

"You are by nature a predator. That is why you do what you do."

But something else too. If we are complex, then he is complex. How to access that other part of Him? Rainbeaux remembers what she said to Mary Magdalene to help her remember her identity. It was worth a shot.

"Get wise to yourself, Salamander Smiler. You have lots of people to worry about. That's why you had the assassins work for you."

Then Rainbeaux remembers her conversation with Virginia Van Horn. And what she and Sam talked about after. It hit her like a ton of bricks. Again.

She said, "As the World Ruler you are the one behind everything. You are behind the Conspiracy to disenfranchise millions of Americans. You are the one who keeps people the world over in poverty. You turn them into second class citizens. You brought slavery, real people owning other people slavery back into America. When people turn to use racism to stop racism, you are behind that. When manipulators use the faith of honest people to deceive them, you are behind that too."

Here the Blasphemer shrugs his shoulders. "You got me, except I don't make folks do those things. They do them to themselves. I am the agency, you might say, by which it happens."

"So, you what, capitalize on people fucking up?"

Gadfan smiles again, "What can I say? Sin happens."

Then she tries to use what she learned from her encounter with Him earlier. "Let's go back to how you were defeated by Y'shua. That means that you were banished. And the piece of the killer's brain brought you back. But not by some poor kids fooling around with hokey magic out of a bad fantasy novel. It was ..."

"Yeah, the wealthy and the powerful. You won't make me angry enough to kick you out of here like I did before. Now I have you where I want you."

Rainbeaux desperately thought of what Mary Magdalene might say. She takes a stab at it, "Get wise to yourself, we can always turn the awful things people do into something positive. Zen happens too, Blasphemer."

He motions to someone she can't see. Two heinous Beings appear. They resemble human pictures of Baphomet; a horned goat's head on top of a fur covered human body with large furry Playboy sized breasts and enormous cocks swinging between their legs. Their cloven hooves clop on the dusty earth or slosh through the nasty water.

He sneers, "I'm going to kill all your little friends and I'll make you beg me to kill you so you don't have to watch."

Rainbeaux continues to use what she learned when she talked to him in the library. "Get wise to yourself, Salamander Smile. Are you aware you have a long Shadow?"

Gadfan grows angry. He stops smiling and takes on a frightening countenance. "No," he says darkly.

Rainbeaux continues, "That's my point, You do. It is a Positive Shadow. Goodness that is unrealized within you. There is a part of you that is ... reverent. Assigns value. It's undeveloped but it's there. I think you actually respect me."

His eyes begin to glow. Gadfan shutters and blinks. But the glow won't go away. "You can stop now," he growls.

Rainbeaux says, "Sorry, liking this too much. Yes, there are things you don't know. Even about yourself. What happens when you learn, Gadfan?"

He doesn't answer.

"Or shall I call you something else now? Belial? Yaldoboath? Azazel? Old Scratch? The trusty standby - Satan?"

He stands and appears to consider something. "No, not Belial. That name simply means worthless person. Or shitty guy in the vernacular. Azazel was a rocky cliff outside of Jerusalem. The ritual of throwing the goat over was cruel but symbolized the separation of the people from the power of a local desert deity. So they could worship ... the Other Side." Now when he smiles, it is a slight wistful smile. "It is true. I do learn."

Rainbeaux says, "Get wise to yourself, your consciousness is expanding." She laughs, "That's rich. The god's mind is expanding."

The Beings flanking Gadfan laugh too. He shoots them a hateful look and they stifle their laughter.

Then she presses forward, "Can you believe that there are levels to this? And that you are on a lower level?"

Gadfan smashes his fist down on a table that appears just in time for that purpose. "NO! There is no other god but me."

"But there is, Mighty One. You refuse to see Her above you. Your Heavenly Mother, Hagia Sophia."

Rainbeaux glad she spends time studying the Nag Hammadi texts.

Gadfan becomes furious. "This is intolerable! I am finished with you."

As the two Demons take a step toward them, Rainbeaux realizes the kind of trouble she is in. She boldly moves closer to him. "There is nothing you can do to me that I can't handle. All you can do is make life difficult for me. But not impossible. I have lived and survived on the street since I was a girl. I can do it again."

Gadfan rises to his full height. He is giant now, with his head far above her. The two Beings take their place at his side. "I can do more than make life difficult. I can make it impossible. At least for now."

"Now?" Something about that intrigues her. "You told me I only get one life. You lied about that."

"It doesn't matter." His voice booms as he commands the two evil angels, "Finish her before she says anything else."

They start to move toward her. She backs away. "Say you gonna go Jake the Explainer and tell me what kind of Demons you have here?"

"No."

"Thanks for nothing." Then something else occurs to her. Something so obvious she knew it all along. "What if I know? Since I live on different levels too? That I don't travel to the Imaginal Place so much as move into different parts of my larger Self?"

So far she kept ahead of the two Baphomets.

Gadfan sneered, "That's it, you two are doddering. Move fast."

Instantly the two Bapomets are on each side of her. Rainbeaux dives out from under them. She is hampered by the fact that she can't move as fast as they can. The fallen angels reach out for her. She looks across the wide yard and focuses on a building far away. Instantly she is there. The Bapomets shake their horned heads. Then Rainbeaux feels the icy grip of cold fear. Something in the building behind her causes her to scream. She looks at the other buildings. She knows there are things in each of them that scare her.

"Hey Gadfan, how come I don't know my way around Hell?"

He doesn't respond to her. He yells something intelligible at the two minions.

"So I don't know my way around Hell. Must mean that part of me isn't here." Then to herself, "Good on me."

She zaps herself around the courtyard just ahead of the Bapomets. Suddenly Gadfan reaches out and catches her.

"Snatched out of thin air. And the air is so very thin here Desk Analyst Rainbeaux."

He takes her by her hair inside a concrete building with rusty metal doors.

Inside are large furnaces hooked to pipes that wind out to skylights. The furnaces chug out the nasty fetid smoke that burns her nose.

"Impressive, isn't it?"

He turns her around by twisting her hair. The place was huge. She doesn't say anything.

He strides up a metal catwalk. He waves his hand. A creaking metal door opens to the blast furnace. The heat is already unbearable for her. It feels like it will burn her to death in seconds.

"You know what this is for?"

She closes her eyes. An icy fear gripes her by her entrails and squeezes.

"Here I burn human souls to power the satanic mills of

Hell."

Rainbeaux knows a tear starts to run down her face but is vaporized before it goes very far.

Then a phrase from *Thunder: Perfect Mind* comes to her:

I am the lamp of the creation of souls

A statement of identity against the crush of trespassing society. But also a promise. She clings to that promise as Gadfan lifts her up. He swings her back and forth to throw her into the furnace.

Against all hope, she has a chance. She times the rhythm of the swing. As he rocks her back, she makes a knife hand and strikes his fingers.

Against all logic, it works! Her hair slides out of his grasp. She is throw away from the furnace. She lands on what passes for a hard concrete floor. They look at each other.

As he steps toward her, she looks for the door out of there. She sees an exit and runs for it ...

CHAPTER 43

Mary and Brenner exit the police sedan with Rip. They are surrounded by blank faced people dressed as Federal agents. "Not looking good," said Brenner.

Mary was worried, "No it's not. They're armed to the teeth. Even the teeth. If you want to be technical about it."

The leader of the group stepped forward. He was dressed in a blue suit with an FBI windbreaker on. He held a Remington shotgun on them. "Hands in the air."

Mary and Brenner put their hands up.

"You too, bozo," the agent directed this to Rip. He put his hands up too.

Next thing their hands and arms were roughly wrenched behind them. The cuffs were slapped on nice and tight. They were marched in double time not toward the courthouse but to an area by Lady Bird Lake with lots of shade tree cover.

"Huh oh," said Rip.

Mary said, "I'm not liking this either."

"SHUT UP!" yelled the agent.

As they were moved into position under the cover of the trees, Mary closed her eyes. Their cuffs fell off. She said, "Don't move your hands. Yet."

The lead agent also closed his eyes, listening to something. "We are to use one weapon. Put it in the uniform's hands after the deed."

"What deed?" Mary asked.

"The deed of ..." the agent hesitated.

"Murder. How does it happen?" she was walking on a thin edge here by asking.

"In the back, like you are trying to escape. Then he is shot."

"But," Mary pressed on, "how do you keep covering everything up? Not even he can help you unless you give some plausible reason."

"Escape, then he shoots you, then we shoot."

"But why? Notice how this doesn't make sense."

Brenner leaned over to her, "It does if you are ..."

"Paranoid," she finished for him. To the agents she proclaimed, "This makes no sense unless you are a lunatic. Notice the trance logic they use to possess you. Now I speak to each of you and to those who hold you. Depart from these people you who live in the airy earth."

Immediately the agents shake their heads, blink their eyes.

"That's it," Mary continued, "wake up."

To Brenner and Rip she said, "That worked. Now let's get Director Hane."

Rip led the way back to his squad car. When they got there a few minutes later, it was surrounded by police and more state and Federal agents. Rip turned around, "What do I do?"

Mary said, "Keep moving."

As they walked up to the car the officers closed around it. Helicopters flew overhead. "More cops," said Rip.

"Harder than cockroaches to get rid of too," Mary replied. Just then back in the Imaginal World...

CHAPTER 44

Rainbeaux is back where she started from. Gadfan behind her. She smiles that she at least makes this far.

Gadfan starts to say something when ...

A mid-size American car drives into the scene. The middle aged driver pushes Daisy out of the car. She stumbles out looking frightened. The driver climbs out and says, "Look who I found."

The driver morphs into a Baphomet look-alike and takes his place beside Gadfan.

Daisy holds the box with the bit of Cade's brain. She looks up at him in his great height, like a mouse staring up at a cat. She smiles a sad sweet smile. She holds the box and says in a command voice not heard from her before, "I command you to come down to me."

And it is so. He shrinks to his human height.

Rainbeaux is as surprised that Gadfan obeyed Daisy. She flows back to them.

"I seek an audience with you." Daisy has his attention. "You are not so mighty, Gadfan. I hold here the power of your exorcism."

The Mighty One appears worried, even concerned. He says evenly, "How weak and insignificant you are. But go for it, I've been kicked out of better Satanic rituals than this."

Daisy persists, "I use this connection you have to our world, to end your rule, Gadfan Blasphemer." She points the box toward Gadfan. "I command you to depart the realm of Earth and never return."

Gadfan stands shaking. His face distorts into a heinous grimace. He appears ready to explode.

Daisy smiles more broadly now, happy with what she

can do.

Only then Gadfan laughs in a deep and expansive baritone. Each of the women feel it reverberate through them.

Rainbeaux can tell Daisy is mystified by Gadfad's resistance to her power. She says by way of explanation, "We are in his plain of existence."

"Oh," Daisy gulped. "I guess we should go back."

"Shut up!" Gadfan's scream sounds like peels of thunder. It scatters the dark clouds overhead which are quickly replaced with more.

Rainbeaux says quickly, "Yes, use that to command him back to earth. Mary Magdalene won't let him hurt us there."

Daisy yells in frustration, "Get us out of here!"

Gadfan screams! The words are inarticulate. There is something as frightening in that scream as the smell of decaying human flesh.

Daisy commands once more, "Take us back. Take us back so I can rid myself of you once and for all. I hate you! I HATE YOU!"

Rainbeaux sees him distort again but nothing changes except he is angrier than before. Rainbeaux gently places her hands on the box over Daisy's. "We use the power of this totem to realize the hidden part of you. Your Positive Shadow. The part of you that leads you back to the Light from whence you came. Return to your Source oh Gadfan. Become the Divinity you claim to be."

Gadfan's frightening countenance changes. He regains his composure. He shrinks to human size again. He looks at them with a surprised half smile. He starts to talk then the words don't come. He wants to say something but can't articulate what he wants to say.

Finally, "Indeed. What you say is correct."

Then he considers something. He thinks and thinks. Something about him changes. As though a new thought occurs to him. A life changing observation. He rises to his full height again. "Alright, Rainbeaux Le Blanc and Daisy Yellow Yancy, since you have reveled something of myself to me ..."

Off to the side a door slams open like a blunt force trauma. Now Sam stumbles out of one of the buildings. He appears sick and disoriented. He looks up at Gadfan with hatred in his eyes. "Gadfan!" He takes in the scene and struggles to understand it. All he can see is that Gadfan threatens Rainbeaux.

Gadfan holds up his hand and continues, "I was about to ..."

Sam yells out, "Halt! I am an officer of the law."

Daisy and Rainbeaux move toward him swiftly. Though he appears close it takes them a ridiculously long time to cover the distance between them.

Sam holds up his badge. Gadfan waves his hand and the badge flies out of Sam's hand. Sam reacts by saying, "I order you to cease and desist. I order you to return with us."

Gadfan starts to shake. Sam continues, "I am taking you in."

Something about this alarms Rainbeaux. "Sam, no. You don't know what you are saying."

Then Daisy is beside Sam. He grabs the small coffin box from Daisy, "Come with me. I'm taking you in now!"

Quick as a wink, Gadfan's body disintegrates into a pile of decaying flesh as he leaves the essence of dead cult members bodies behind. The whole scene around them shakes. The buildings start to lose brick. Water sloshes out of the filthy sewer pond. A huge dark cloud, in the middle of which is a hideous distorted face, swirls around them. Then the cloud with the insanity inducing face pours into Sam's mouth in a lightning tinged vortex. This goes on for what may seem like hours. Then all is still.

Sam's face takes on a green tint. "I think I swallowed something."

Rainbeaux hears Mary's sweet voice only there are no words. Grim finality. There is nothing to say now.

Rainbeaux knows they have to run to get out of there before Gadfan's Domain falls on them. She reacts without thinking and grabs Sam's hand. She and Daisy clasp hands while they run.

What followed was a dreamy half asleep period of time. They soon left Gadfan's Domain. They wandered back through unimagined countries and vast spaces of disorganized time and eventually ...

They woke in Rainbeaux's house.

At first she was happy to be home. Until the awful memory of what just happened hit her like a sledge hammer. Rainbeaux had thought it was over with Sam. She thought that she was mourning the loss of that relationship. But now things were clearer. Things were worse. Now he really was lost. Now, with that Beast inside him, it was over and couldn't be bought back. How could there be anything between them if he contained something so monstrous?

She was in her room again. Then she went downstairs. Brenner was in the living room. So was Daisy who sat and rocked and stared at the wall. Mary was busy in the kitchen.

Sam was no where to be seen.

Brenner said that their existence was restored. He laughed at that statement. They had their ID's and money back. Their education records. All of it. Daisy still didn't say anything.

When she finished what she was doing in the kitchen, Mary Magdalene went around and tried to support everyone. Rainbeaux was put out at first. Nothing could be the way it was. What was she doing? After Mary spoke to her she felt some comfort from that. Then upon reflection she knew that while Mary couldn't undo what had been done, it was still better that she was around. Paradoxically this allowed her to feel her unending grief. Rainbeaux sobbed and sobbed. All joy gone. Every romantic dream dead. How could there ever be light or sunshine again?

CHAPTER 45

A few days later, Rainbeaux stood on a hill and watched Mary Magdalene gather the first members of her circle around her. There was an older woman who looked like she wandered in from the street, a young adolescent girl with bright red hair, a brown skinned man wearing dread locks with a barrel chest who laughed a lot, an older man in a suit and tie with thick mane of wavy silver hair. There were some spaces in the circle. Rainbeaux thought about who else could be part of it. She wondered if there was a place there for her.

At that moment Mary looked up at her. Then they sat and Mary Mags began to instruct them. She couldn't hear what Mary said but enjoyed sitting there, feeling the presence.

After some time Rainbeaux slipped away. She walked down to the path around Town Lake. She strolled along and looked at the water. Something had changed. While she was feeling grief, there was new hope in the newly elected president. People seemed looser, less dependent on the past. On what had been deceptively called "traditional values". There seemed to be more honesty. A new sense of hope. A desire for change that makes sense.

A couple of days later Roswell Hane called her. He said the noose had been taken from around his neck. He told her among certain moneyed people there had been an alarming number of suicides that were discretely hushed up. To avoid panic with stock holders of course. The economy was in enough trouble without this news getting out. She asked about Daisy. He reported that she has a huge trust fund that was converted to bonds before the newest round of economic trouble began.

She hadn't heard much from Sam. She called Brenner who quickly told her that he was holed up in his room. Sam refused to talk to anyone.

What Brenner didn't tell Rainbeaux is that he went to see Sam every day. He was worried about him. Sam looked like hell. He didn't take care of himself unless someone insisted he bathe. He was losing weight so they took him food and saw to it that Sam had anything else he needed. Most days it was good Tex Mex from one of the fine restaurants in town and a six pack of Shiner Bock. Sometimes it was Old Speckled Hen, the ale Rainbeaux loved. Sam was grateful for the food and beer.

What Sam didn't tell Brenner is that Gadfan was trying to claw his way out twenty-four seven. That he was being shredded by an all powerful supernatural being from the inside out.

That first day they talked for a little while. Sam said he still had his job at the DA's office. His mother had called. It looked like he and his Father and family were going to reconcile. Sam would even get his trust fund back. They didn't talk about anything else. Later Sam said that Rip would come and look in on him too. Brenner was pleased about that. And after Brenner and Rip kept in touch with each other and how they found Sam that day.

After a few weeks, Sam was more talkative than usual. He was sick all the time. Vomiting blood and unable to keep anything down. He looked worse, pasty white and thin as a rail. He was no longer the strapping handsome young man Brenner met just weeks before. He was a small reedy shell now. He looked like he needed to be on hospice care. Brenner wouldn't say that.

That day, for the first time in a long time, Sam asked about Rainbeaux. What he didn't say, was that he longed to look into her mysterious blue/green eyes again.

Brenner said, "She's fine. Or as fine as any of us can be."

"Does she miss me?" Sam asked.

If only Sam could see her now, he would know she had been down at the classic auto restoration shop. They had just finished work on that beautiful candy apple red '69 Firebird convertible. She looked it over and made sure, or as sure as she could be, that they had done the work. She could see the twin four barrel Holly crabs sitting on the Eldeblock manifold. She could see the twisting exhaust pipes snake back to the firewall and disappear under the chassis. It appeared that all the work was done.

The shop foreman offered to put a power steering pump in after all.

She smiled, finished paying for it right then and there. As she drove it home she was more troubled by the empty seat beside her than with how hard it was to steer. And it was a bitch to steer. She ignored that and tried to be brave and imagine all the cool new guys she could drive around. But when she got inside her garage, she just sat in the car.

Meanwhile Brenner looked Sam in the eye, "I don't know. You'll have to call her."

Sam didn't say anything for a few minutes. Brenner said, "Things will work out for the best for you two."

And if only Sam could see her now. He would see her cry sitting in the seat of her new car, missing the one man she really wanted beside her.

"I know," said Sam through numbing grief. "That girl's got style."

The imprisoned Gadfan stopped his clawing and laughed from deep within Sam. His laughter peeled like a bell ringing through eternity.

THE END
Of *TRANCE LOGIC*
But Rainbeaux and friends will return in
THE BOUNDARY SHIFTER

Thank you for reading.
Please review this book. Reviews help others find New Pulp Press and inspire us to keep providing these marvelous tales.

If you would like to be put on our email list to receive updates on new releases, contests, and promotions, please go to NewPulpPress.com and sign up.

About the Author

Rich Billingsley is a writer of weird fiction. He lives in Austin, Texas, USA.

NewPulpPress.com
or AbsolutelyAmazingEbooks.com

www.ingramcontent.com/pod-product-compliance
Lightning Source LLC
Chambersburg PA
CBHW070831280626
47161CB00015B/435